EVERYONE

Raves for the blockbuster MA

#1 *New York Times* Bestseller
Publishers Weekly Bestseller
An ALA Quick Pick for Young Adults
An ALA/*VOYA* "Teens' Top Ten" Pick
A *VOYA* Review Editor's Choice
A New York Public Library "Books for the Teen Age" Selection

"**Flying, fighting evil and friends forever** — it's a formula for one of the tricks James Patterson does best — landing on the best-seller lists." —*Cleveland Plain Dealer*

"**Readers are in for another exciting wild ride** of fights (bloody) and flights (in the sky) as Max and her flock struggle to stay alive . . . **leaving readers breathless for the follow-up to this action-packed page-turner.**" —*Kirkus Reviews*

"Smart-mouthed, sympathetic characters and copious butt-kicking make this fast read **pure escapist pleasure.**" —*The Horn Book Guide*

"Not surprisingly, most **adult readers** addicted to Patterson's Alex Cross and Women's Murder Club books **couldn't resist.**" —*Rocky Mountain News*

"Patterson's **super-fast pace** keeps the action moving and the suspense tense." —*Newark Star-Ledger*

"This **eagerly awaited sequel** to *MAXIMUM RIDE: THE ANGEL EXPERIMENT* . . . does not disappoint. They end up in one 'gnarly sitch' after another in this breathless adventure, which is full of action, swooping flights and fierce fights — **a sure bet for the movies, along the lines of the *X-Men*.**"

—*KLIATT*

"Max's sarcastic first-person voice and her interactions with her ragtag adopted family keep the narrative percolating . . . **Exhilarating.**" —*San Francisco Chronicle*

"**Heart-stopping** . . . The six unforgettable kids are back for more adventure." —*Costco Connection*

"Written for a young adult audience but recommended here for a wide audience of adults as well is the second book in the MAXIMUM RIDE series . . . Fans of *THE ANGEL EXPERIMENT* will love this second book, but newcomers will also find it highly accessible and impossible to put down. **It's a shame to limit its audience to advanced teen readers — so don't: pick up a copy and fly.**" —*California Bookwatch*

"**Fans of the first book will be delighted** with this continuation of the story . . . The book leaves the fate of the flock wide open."

—*Booklist*

"**A gripping sequel** to *MAXIMUM RIDE: THE ANGEL EXPERIMENT.*" —*Sweet 16* magazine

"As with the first book, the action is **fast-paced** and keeps the reader engaged." —*VOYA [Voice of Youth Advocates]*

"**James Patterson dishes up what readers want to read.**"

—*RT Bookclub*

"This is an exciting science fiction thriller for teens. It is similar to James Patterson's adult novels in that there is **lots of action and suspense**. A good summer read for teens who like fast-paced plots." —*Central Wisconsin Sunday*

★★★★★ "An **action-packed, thrilling**, and truly amazing book! It's great for sci-fi lovers, and pretty much anyone!"
—BookReporter.com

"**James Patterson again delivers an engaging, action-packed adventure** for this close-knit group of kids who've survived horrors together and have come through them with flying colors."
—Bookloons.com

"***MAXIMUM RIDE: SCHOOL'S OUT—FOREVER* will entertain readers** . . . The premise is creative and will cause readers to use their imaginations." —About.com

"Talented and accomplished author James Patterson has scored again in this action-packed sequel filled with **adventure, mystery and lots of sidesplitting hilarity**. And it doesn't stop here — the saga continues with a third book in the series due out next year. **So hold on tight for an exciting journey into the imagination, and into the clouds!**" —TeenReads.com

"James Patterson has written a book in which the pages are turned almost as fast as the eye can read as the reader tries to figure out what is coming next . . . ***MAXIMUM RIDE: SCHOOL'S OUT—FOREVER* is a fast-paced and thrilling novel . . . [It] will capture readers everywhere.**"
—Flamingnet.com

"This second book in the series is . . . **full of adventure, heart-stopping adrenaline, and edge-of-your-seat action**. Kudos to Mr. Patterson for another winner in the MAXIMUM RIDE series."

—TeensReadToo.com

"The second Angels thriller is **an exhilarating thriller** starring three teens and three preadolescents sticking together while eluding Erasers, FBI suits, school, and a clone. The story line is driven by the magnificent six [and] . . . once again James Patterson soars with his latest suspense-filled science fiction thriller."

—ReviewCentre.com

"I am a young 'middle-aged' woman who doesn't even like science fiction, but standing in the children's section of a local bookstore while waiting for my daughter to choose a book, I picked up *MAXIMUM RIDE: THE ANGEL EXPERIMENT* and got sucked in from the first page. I ended up buying the book and couldn't wait for the second in the series, ***MAXIMUM RIDE: SCHOOL'S OUT—FOREVER***, to be published. Again, once I started reading, **I couldn't put the book down**. I passed on both MAXIMUM RIDE stories to my 12-year-old nephew. So, **although these books are written for the middle school age group — it even has appeal for those of us who are 'kids at heart.'"**

—Reviewer, ScienceDaily.com

"I got ***MAXIMUM RIDE*** in the mail the same day *Star Wars III* came out on DVD . . . Should I watch *Star Wars III* or jump into this advance reader's copy of ***MAXIMUM RIDE***? The decision was killing me, **but I chose *MAXIMUM RIDE*.** Hey, I could always watch *Star Wars III* another time . . . **You need to read this novel."**

—Dot

"***MAXIMUM RIDE: SCHOOL'S OUT—FOREVER* grabs readers straight from the start** and reels them in with new excitements on every page. Adventure, fighting, backstabbing, and love abound throughout the book."

—Rebecca, teen reviewer for *VOYA*

"***MAXIMUM RIDE: SCHOOL'S OUT—FOREVER*** is a page-turner if I have ever read one. **I actually stayed up the entire night just to see how this one ends!** The continuation of *MAXIMUM RIDE: THE ANGEL EXPERIMENT* not only measures up to the already high standards set by James Patterson, but exceeds them with flying colors. The story of Max and her 'flock' of genetically engineered 'Avian Americans' starts off big and just keeps going . . . **From one twist to the next, Patterson keeps you guessing."**

— Abdul

"Want an action-packed novel that any teen would enjoy? *MAXIMUM RIDE: SCHOOL'S OUT—FOREVER* is the book for you . . . The exposition of this story is well-written and full of intrigue . . . After all of this, I can't wait for part 3! **I didn't put this book down from the moment I picked it up."**

—Missy

"***MAXIMUM RIDE: SCHOOL'S OUT—FOREVER*** is a thrilling read! It's very fast-paced, suspenseful, and yet funny . . . **It kept me glued to the very last page, wanting more.** Patterson kept the excitement coming . . . All I can say is: **I hope there are many more rides to come!"**

— Kendall

SCHOOL'S OUT—FOREVER

JAMES PATTERSON

NEW YORK BOSTON

Hachette Book Group USA
1271 Avenue of the Americas, New York, NY 10020
Visit our Web site at www.hachettebookgroupusa.com

First Mass Market Edition: April 2007
First published in hardcover by Little, Brown and Company in May 2006

Cover design by Gail Doobinin
Cover image of figure © David Perry/Getty Images, sky © Pete Turner/Getty Images, road © Rob Matheson/Corbis
Maximum Ride logo design by Jon Valk

Library of Congress Cataloging-in-Publication Data
Patterson, James.
School's out — forever / by James Patterson. — 1st ed.
p.cm. — (Maximum Ride; #2)
Summary: After a short stay with an FBI agent who gives them a chance to attend school and live a normal life, the six genetically altered, winged youths head toward Florida and Max's ultimate destiny — to save the world, whether she wants to or not.
HC ISBN: 0-316-15559-4
MM ISBN-10: 0-446-61889-6
MM ISBN-13: 978-0-446-61889-2
[1. Genetic engineering — Fiction. 2. Adventure and adventurers — Fiction. 3. Schools — Fiction. 4. Science Fiction.] I. Title. II. Series: Patterson, James. Maximum Ride; #2

10 9 8 7 6 5 4 3 2 1

Q-BF

Printed in the United States of America

For everybody out there
who spreads the joy of reading

To the reader:

The idea for Maximum Ride comes from earlier books of mine called *When the Wind Blows* and *The Lake House*, which also feature a character named Max who escapes from a quite despicable School. Most of the similarities end there. Max and the other kids in Maximum Ride are not the same Max and kids featured in those two books. Nor do Frannie and Kit play any part in Maximum Ride. I hope you enjoy the ride anyway.

PART 1

NO PARENTS, NO SCHOOL, NO RULES

1

Sweeping, swooping, soaring, air-current thrill rides — there's nothing better. For miles around, we were the only things in the infinite, wide-open, clear blue sky. You want an adrenaline rush? Try tucking your wings in, dive-bombing for about a mile straight down, then *whoosh!* Wings out, grab an air current like a pit bull, and hang on for the ride of your life. God, *nothing* is better, more fun, more exciting.

Okay, we were mutant freaks, we were on the lam, but man, flying — well, there's a reason people always dream about it.

"Oh, my gosh!" the Gasman said excitedly. He pointed. "A UFO!"

I silently counted to ten. There was nothing where the Gasman had pointed. As usual. "That was funny the first fifty times, Gazzy," I said. "It's getting old."

He cackled, several wingspans away from me. There's nothing like an eight-year-old's sense of humor.

"Max? How long till we get to DC?" asked Nudge,

pulling up closer to me. She looked tired — we'd had one long, ugly day. Well, *another* long, ugly day in a whole series of long, ugly days. If I ever actually had a good, easy day, I'd probably freak out.

"Another hour? Hour and a half?" I guessed.

Nudge didn't say anything. I cast a quick glance at the rest of my flock. Fang, Iggy, and I were holding steady, but we had mucho de stamina. I mean, the younger set also had stamina, especially compared to dinky little non-mutant humans. But even they gave out eventually.

Here's the deal — for anybody new on this trip. There are six of us: Angel, who's six; Gasman, age eight; Iggy, who's fourteen, and blind; Nudge, eleven; Fang and me (Max), we're fourteen too. We escaped from the lab where we were raised, were given wings and other assorted powers. They want us back — badly. But we're not going back. Ever.

I shifted Total to my other arm, glad he didn't weigh more than twenty pounds. He roused slightly, then draped himself across my arm and went back to sleep, the wind whistling through his black fur. Did I want a dog? No. Did I need a dog? Also no. We were six kids running for our lives, not knowing where our next meal was coming from. Could we afford to feed a dog? Wait for it — *no.*

"You okay?" Fang cruised up alongside me. His wings were dark and almost silent, like Fang himself.

"In what way?" I asked. I mean, there was the headache issue, the chip issue, the *Voice-in-my-head-constantly* issue, my healing bullet wound. . . . "Can you be more specific?"

"Killing Ari."

My breath froze in my throat. Only Fang could cut

right to the heart of the matter like that. Only Fang knew me that well, and went that far.

When we'd been escaping from the Institute, in New York, Erasers and whitecoats had shown up, of course. *God forbid* we should make a clean getaway. Erasers, if you don't know already, are wolflike creatures who have been chasing us constantly since we escaped from the lab, or School as we call it. One of the Erasers had been Ari. We'd fought, as we'd fought before, and then suddenly, with no warning, I was sitting on his chest, staring at his lifeless eyes, his broken neck bent at an awkward angle.

That was twenty-four hours ago.

"It was you or him," Fang said calmly. "I'm glad you picked you."

I let out a deep breath. Erasers simpled everything up: They had no qualms about killing, so you had to lose your squeamishness about it too. But Ari had been different. I'd recognized him, remembered him as a little kid back at the School. I knew him.

Plus, there was that last, awful bellow from Ari's father, Jeb, echoing after me again and again as I flew through the tunnels:

"You killed your own brother!"

2

Of course, Jeb was a lying, cheating manipulator, so he might have just been yanking my chain. But his anguish after he'd discovered his dead son had sounded real.

And even though I loathed and despised Jeb, I still felt as though I had an anvil on my chest.

You had to do it, Max. You're still working toward the greater good. And nothing can interfere with that. Nothing can interfere with your mission to save the world.

I took another deep breath through clenched jaws. *Geez, Voice. Next you'll be telling me that to make an omelet, I have to break a few eggs.*

I sighed. Yes, I have a Voice inside my head, I mean, another one besides my own. I'm pretty sure that if you look up the word *nuts* in the dictionary, you'll find my picture. Just another fun feature of my mutant-bird-kid-freak package.

"Do you want me to take him?" Angel asked, gesturing toward the dog in my arms.

"No, that's okay," I said. Total weighed almost half of

what Angel weighed — I didn't know how she'd carried him as far as she had. "I know," I said, brightening. "Fang will take him."

I gave my wings an extra beat and surged up over Fang, our wings sweeping in rhythm. "Here," I said, lowering Total. "Have a dog." Vaguely Scottie-ish in size and looks, Total wiggled a bit, then quickly settled into Fang's arms. He gave Fang a little lick, and I had to bite the inside of my cheek to keep from snickering at Fang's expression.

I sped up a bit, flying out in front of the flock, feeling an excitement overshadowing my fatigue and the dark weight of what had happened. We were headed to new territory — and we might even find our parents this time. We had escaped the Erasers and the whitecoats — our former "keepers" — again. We were all together and no one was badly wounded. For this brief moment, I felt free and strong, as if I was starting fresh, all over again. We *would* find our parents — I could feel it.

I was feeling . . . I paused, trying to name this sensation.

I felt kind of optimistic. Despite everything.

Optimism is overrated, Max, said the Voice. *It's better to face reality head-on.*

I wondered if the Voice could see me rolling my eyes, from the inside.

3

It had gotten dark hours ago. He should have heard by now. The fearsome Eraser paced around the small clearing, and then suddenly the static in his ear made him wince. He pressed the earpiece of his receiver and listened.

What he heard made him smile, despite feeling like crap, despite having a rage so fierce it felt as if it were going to burn him up from the inside out.

One of his men saw the expression on his face and motioned the others to be quiet. He nodded, said "Got it" into his mouthpiece, and tapped off his transmitter.

He looked over at his troop. "We got our coordinates," he said. He tried to resist rubbing his hands together in glee but couldn't. "They're headed south-southwest and passed Philadelphia thirty minutes ago. The Director was right — they're going to Washington DC."

"How solid is this info?" one of his Erasers asked.

"From the horse's mouth," he said, starting to check

his equipment. He rolled his shoulders, grimacing, then popped a pain pill.

"Which horse?" asked another Eraser, standing up and fastening a night-vision monocle over one eye.

"Let's just say it's insider information," the leader of the Erasers said, hearing the joy in his own voice. He felt his heart speed up with anticipation, his fingers itching to close around a skinny bird-kid neck. Then he started to *morph,* watching his hands.

The frail human skin was soon covered with tough fur; ragged claws erupted from his fingertips. Morphing had hurt at first — his lupine DNA wasn't seamlessly grafted into his stem cells, like the other Erasers'. So there were some kinks to be worked out, a rough, painful transition period he'd had to go through.

But he wasn't complaining. It would all be worth it the moment he got his claws on Max and choked the life right out of her. He imagined the look of surprise on her face, how she would struggle. Then he'd watch the light slowly fade out of her beautiful brown eyes. She wouldn't think she was so hot then. Wouldn't look down on him or, worse, *ignore* him. Just because he wasn't a mutant freak like them, he'd been nothing to her. All she cared about was the flock this and the flock that. That was all his father, Jeb, cared about too.

Once Max was dead, that would all change.

And he, Ari, would be the number-one son. *He'd come back from the dead for it.*

4

By dusk we'd crossed over a chunk of Pennsylvania, and a thin spit of ocean twined below us, between New Jersey and Delaware. "Look at this, kids, we're learning geography!" Fang called out with mock excitement. Since we'd never been to school, most of what we'd learned was from television or the Internet. And, these days, from the little know-it-all Voice in my head.

Soon we'd be over Washington DC. Which was pretty much where my plan stopped. For tonight, all I was worried about was food and a place to sleep. Tomorrow I would have time to study the info we'd gotten from the Institute. I'd been so thrilled when we'd hacked into the Institute's computers. Pages of information about our actual parents had scrolled across the screen. I'd managed to print out a bunch of it before we'd been interrupted.

Who knew — by this time tomorrow we might be on someone's doorstep, about to come face-to-face with the parents who had lost us so long ago. It sent shivers down my spine.

I was tired. We were all tired. So when I did an automatic 360 and saw a weird dark cloud heading toward us, my groan was deep and sincere.

"Fang! What's that? Behind us, at ten o'clock."

He frowned, checking it out. "Too fast for a storm cloud. Too small, too quiet for choppers. Not birds — too lumpy." He looked at me. "I give up. What is it?"

"Trouble," I said grimly. "Angel! Get out of the way. Guys, heads up! We've got company!"

We swung around to face *whatever* was coming. Fast!

"Flying monkeys?" The Gasman called out a guess. "Like *The Wizard of Oz*?"

It dawned on me then. "No," I said tersely. "Worse. *Flying Erasers.*"

5

Yep. Flying Erasers. These Erasers had wings, which was a new and revolting development on the Eraser front. Half-wolf, half-human, and now half-avian? That couldn't be a happy mix. And they were headed our way at about eighty miles an hour.

"Erasers, version 6.5," Fang said.

Split up, Max. Think 3-D, said my Voice.

"Split up!" I ordered. "Nudge! Gazzy! Nine o'clock! Angel, up top. Move it! Iggy and Fang, flank me from below! Fang, ditch the dog!"

"Nooo, Fang!" screeched Angel.

The Erasers slowed as we fanned out, their huge, heavy-looking wings backbeating the air. It was almost pitch-black now, with no moon and no city lights below. I was still able to see their teeth, their pointed fangs, their smiles of excitement. *They were on a hunt — it was party time!*

Here we go, I thought, feeling adrenaline speeding up my heart. I launched myself at the biggest one, swinging my feet under me to smash against his chest. He rolled back but righted himself and came at me again, claws slashing the air.

I bobbed, feeling his paws whip right past my face. I turned sharply just in time to have a hard, hairy fist crash into my head.

I dropped ten feet quickly, then surged back up on the offensive.

In my peripheral vision, I saw Fang clap both hands hard against an Eraser's furry ears. The Eraser screamed, holding his head, and started to lose altitude. Fang had Total *in his backpack.* He rolled out of harm's way, and I took his place, catching another Eraser in the mouth with a hard side kick.

I grabbed one of his arms, twisting it violently in back of him. It was harder in the air, but then I heard a loud *pop.*

The Eraser screamed and dropped, careening downward until he caught himself and flew clumsily away, one arm dangling.

Above me an Eraser lashed out at Nudge, but she dodged out of the way.

Max? Size isn't everything, said the Voice.

6

I got it! The Erasers were bigger and heavier, their wings almost twice as long as ours. But in the air, those were liabilities.

Panting, I ducked as an Eraser swung a black-booted foot at my side, catching me in the ribs but not too hard.

I zipped in and dealt out some powerful punches of my own, knocking his head sideways, then I flitted out of reach.

Compared to the Erasers, we were nimble little stinging wasps, and they were clunky, slow, awkward flying cows.

Two Erasers ganged up on me, but I shot straight up like an arrow, just in time for them to smash into each other.

I laughed as I saw Gazzy roll completely over like a fighter plane, smacking an Eraser in the jaw on the turn. The Eraser swung a hard punch, landing it on Gazzy's thigh, and Gazzy winced, then launched a side kick at the Eraser's hand, which snapped back.

How many of them were there? I couldn't tell — everything was happening at once. Ten?

Nudge, my Voice said, and then I heard Nudge cry out.

An Eraser had her tight in his arms, his fangs moving toward her neck. His teeth were just starting to scrape her skin when I dropped on him from above. I wrapped one arm around his neck and yanked hard, hearing him gag and choke. Grabbing my wrist with my other hand, I yanked harder until he let Nudge drop away from him.

"Scat!" I told her, and, coughing, she swooped away from the fight. My Eraser was still struggling but starting to weaken. "You better get your guys out of here," I snarled into his ear. "We're kicking your hairy butts."

"You're gonna fall now," I heard Angel say in a normal voice. I swung my head to see her gravely watching an Eraser who looked confused, paralyzed. Angel shifted her gaze to the dark water below. Fear entered the Eraser's eyes, and his wings folded. He dropped like a rock.

"You're getting scary, you know that?" I said to Angel, not really kidding. I mean, making an Eraser drop right out of the sky *just by telling him to* — jeez.

And Iggy, said the Voice. I veered off to help Iggy, who was in tight hand-to-hand with an Eraser.

"Ig!" I called, as he grabbed the Eraser's shirt.

"Max, *get out of here!*" Iggy yelled, and released the shirt, letting himself fall quickly out of reach.

I had time to think *Uh-oh,* and then the small explosive Iggy had stuck down the Eraser's shirt detonated, leaving an ugly gaping hole in his chest. Shrieking, the Eraser plummeted heavily downward.

And how did Iggy manage to stash his seemingly endless supply of explosives on his person without my even having a clue? Got me.

"You . . . are . . . a . . . fridge . . . with wings," Fang

ground out, punching an Eraser hard with every word. "We're . . . freaking . . . ballet . . . dancers."

Take a deep breath, Max, said my Voice, and I obeyed without question.

At that moment, I felt a blow to my back, between my wings, that knocked the wind out of me. I rolled, belly-up, using the oxygen I'd just gotten, trying to suck in more air.

Whirling, I snapped both feet out in a hard kick into the Eraser's face, then froze in shock. *Ari!*

He wheeled backward and I floundered away, wheezing and hoping I wouldn't pass out. *Ari! But he was dead — I'd killed him. Hadn't I?*

Ari lunged at Fang, just as I yelled "*Fang!*" Ari managed to take a swipe at Fang's side, shredding his jacket.

Drawing back, gasping, I took stock of the situation. The few remaining Erasers were falling back, retreating. Below, I saw a white splash as an Eraser hit the ocean. That had to hurt.

Now it was just Ari against us. He looked around, then fell back as well, closer to his squad.

The six of us slowly regrouped as Ari began to fly clumsily away, his enormous wings working hard to keep his heavy body aloft. His squad surrounded him, a bunch of huge, hairy crows gone wrong.

"We'll be back!" he snarled.

It was really Ari's voice.

"Boy, you just can't kill people like you used to," said Fang.

7

We hovered in place for several minutes, waiting to see if there would be a second attack. For the moment, we seemed in the clear, and I took the time to catalogue our injuries. Fang was flying awkwardly, his arm pressed against his side.

"I'm fine," he said curtly, noticing me watching him.

"Angel? Gazzy? Nudge? Report," I said.

"Leg hurts, but I'm okay," said the Gasman.

"I'm fine," said Angel. "And so are Total and Celeste." Celeste was the small angel-dressed stuffed bear Angel had — well, let's say — been given at a toy store in New York.

"I'm okay," said Nudge, but she sounded whipped.

"My nose," said Iggy, pressing it hard to stop the bleeding. "But no biggie."

"Okay, then," I said. "We're almost to DC, and it should be easy to get lost in another big city. We good to go?"

Everyone nodded, and we swung in a tight, graceful arc to return to our flight path.

"So . . . what was with the flying Erasers?" Iggy said a few minutes later.

"I'm guessing a new prototype," I said. "But, man, they're failures. They were having a hard time flying and fighting at the same time."

"Like they'd just learned to fly, you know?" said Nudge. "I mean, compared to hawks, we look clumsy. But compared to those Erasers, we're, like, poetry in motion."

I smiled at Nudge's description, silently checking out my own aches and pains.

"They were bad fliers," Angel chimed in. "And in their minds, they weren't all *Kill the mutants,* like they usually are. They were like, *Remember to flap!*"

I laughed at her imitation of a deep, growly Eraser voice. "Did you pick up on anything else, Angel?" I asked.

"You mean besides dead Ari showing up?" Gazzy said, sounding bummed.

"Yeah," I said. Just then I caught a warm updraft and coasted for a minute, enjoying a feeling of pure bliss.

"Well, none of them really felt familiar," said Angel, thinking.

Having a six-year-old mind reader came in handy. Sometimes I wished Angel's mind reads were a little more specific, or that they'd come when we wanted. Then maybe she'd be able to warn us that an Eraser was about to drop in and say hi. But sometimes she just gave me the willies. Angel was starting to control people with her mind — not just Erasers — and I wasn't sure when she was crossing the line into, say, *witchcraft,* for instance.

A while later, I realized that Fang wasn't beside me and I looked around to see him below, maybe twenty feet back. He'd been silent, not unusual for him, but now I could see that his flying was ragged and off-balance. His face seemed paler, and his lips were pressed tightly together.

I dropped back and swooped down next to him.

"What's going on?" I said in my no-nonsense tone. It had never worked on him before, but a girl had to keep trying.

"Nothing," he said, but that one word was tight and strained. Which meant he was lying through his teeth.

"Fang —," I began, and then saw that the arm pressed against his side was dark and wet. Blood. "Your arm!"

" 'S not my arm," he muttered. Then his eyes fluttered shut and he started to lose altitude fast.

Really fast.

8

"Iggy!" I yelled, as cold panic ripped right through me. *Not Fang. Please let Fang be okay.* "Over here!"

Then Iggy and I flew beneath Fang, supporting him. I felt Fang's dead weight on me, saw his closed eyes, and suddenly I felt as if I couldn't breathe.

"Let's land, see what's wrong!" I told Iggy, and he nodded.

We flew hard toward the narrow, rocky shore edging the black ocean. Iggy and I landed awkwardly, Fang limp between us. The younger kids scurried over to help us carry him to a flattish, sandier place.

Stop the bleeding, said the Voice.

"What's the matter with him?" Nudge asked, dropping to her knees next to Fang.

Checking him out, I saw that Fang's shirt and jacket were soaked with blood, the dark fabric gleaming wetly. I tried to keep my face calm.

"Let's just see what we're dealing with here," I said steadily, and quickly unbuttoned Fang's shirt.

Now I saw that the shirt was shredded, and beneath it, so was Fang. Ari had managed to do this . . . obscenity.

Nudge drew in a quick gasp when she saw the damage, and I looked up. "Nudge, you and Gazzy and Angel rip up a shirt or something. Make strips for bandages."

Nudge just stared at Fang.

"Nudge!" I said more firmly, and she snapped out of it.

"Uh, yeah. Come on, guys. I have an extra shirt here . . . an' I got a knife. . . ."

The three younger kids moved away while Iggy's sensitive hands brushed Fang's skin like butterflies.

"This feels real bad. *Real* bad," Iggy said in low voice. "How much blood has he lost?"

"A lot," I said grimly. Even his jeans were soaked with it.

"Jus' a scratch," Fang said fuzzily, his eyelids fluttering.

"Shhh!" I hissed at him. "You should have told us you were hurt!"

Stop the bleeding, the Voice said again.

"How?" I cried in frustration.

"How what?" Iggy asked, and I shook my head impatiently.

Put pressure on it, said the Voice. *Press the cloth over it and lean on the wounds with both hands. Elevate his feet, Max.*

"Iggy," I said, "lift Fang's feet. Guys, you got those strips ready?"

The Gasman handed me a bunch, and I quickly folded them into a pad. Placing it over the gaping slices in Fang's stomach was like putting my finger in a dike to stop a flood, but it was all I had, so I did it. I pressed both my hands over the pad, trying to keep a steady pressure on it.

Under Fang's side, the sand was turning dark with his blood.

"Someone's coming," said Angel.

Erasers? I looked up to see a man jogging along the shore. It was almost dawn, and seagulls were starting to wheel and cry above the water.

The man slowed to a walk when he saw us. He seemed ordinary, but looks could be deceiving, and usually were.

"Kids, you okay?" he called. "What are you doing out here so early?" He frowned when he saw Fang, then looked scared when he figured out what all the dark wet stuff was.

Before I could say anything, he'd whipped out his cell phone and called 911.

9

I looked down at Fang, then glanced over at Iggy's tight face. In a second I realized we had to suck it up — Fang was hurt bad. We needed outside help. Everything in me wanted to grab Fang, get the flock, and tear out of here, away from strangers and doctors and hospitals. But if I did that, Fang would die.

"Max?" The Gasman sounded scared. In the distance, the obnoxious wail of an ambulance siren was drawing closer.

"Nudge?" I said, speaking fast. "Take Gazzy and Angel and find a place to hide. We'll go to the hospital. You stay around here, and I'll come back when I can. Quick, before the EMT guys get here."

"No," said the Gasman, his eyes on Fang.

I stared at him. "What did you say?"

"No," he repeated, a mulish look coming over his face. "We're not leaving you and Fang and Iggy."

"Ex*cuse* me?" I said, steel in my voice. Fang's blood had soaked the cloth and was seeping between my fingers. "I'm telling you to get out of here." I made myself sound cold as ice.

"No," Gazzy said again. "I don't care what happens — you're not leaving us again."

"That's right," said Nudge, crossing her arms over her skinny chest.

Angel nodded next to her. Even Total, sitting on the sand by Angel's feet, seemed to bob his head in agreement.

My mouth opened, but nothing came out. I was stunned — they'd never disobeyed a direct order.

I wanted to start shrieking at them, but it was already too late: Two paramedics were running across the sand, holding a body board. The flashing lights of the ambulance made intermittent rosy stripes across all our faces.

"Goveryou," I said tightly, using a secret language that went back to when we were kept in a lab. It was used in cases of extreme emergency when we didn't want anyone to understand us. "Allay. Todo ustedes. Egway."

"No," said the Gasman, his lower lip starting to tremble. "Neckerchu."

"What's happened here?" One of the paramedics dropped down next to Fang, already taking out his stethoscope.

"Accident," I said, still glaring at Gazzy, Nudge, and Angel.

Reluctantly I removed my hands from the soaked pad. Fang's face was white and still.

"Accident?" repeated the paramedic, staring at the injury. "With what, a rabid bear?"

"Kind of," I said tensely. The other paramedic shone a

small flashlight into Fang's eyes, and I realized Fang was truly unconscious. My sense of fear and danger escalated: Not only were we about to enter a hospital, which would freak us all out, but it might end up being for nothing.

Because Fang could die anyway.

10

The ambulance felt like a jail cell on wheels.

The antiseptic smell inside made my stomach knot with nightmare memories of the School. In the back of the ambulance, I held Fang's cold hand, which now had a saline drip taped into it. I couldn't say anything to the flock, not in front of the EMT, and I was too upset, scared, and mad to come up with anything coherent anyway.

Is Fang okay? I silently asked my Voice. Not that the Voice had ever once answered a direct freaking question. It didn't break the pattern now.

"Uh-oh — he's fibrillating," one paramedic said urgently.

He pointed to the portable EKG machine, which was going *thump-thump-thump* very fast. "Get the paddles."

"No!" I said loudly, startling everyone. The paramedic held the shock paddles, looking surprised. "That's *always* how his heart is. It *always* beats really fast. That's *normal* for him."

I don't know if the paramedic would have used the

paddles anyway, but just then we roared into the hospital emergency bay and all was chaos.

Orderlies ran out with a gurney, the EMT guys started rattling off Fang's stats to a nurse. And then Fang was wheeled out of sight, down a hall and through some doors.

I started to follow, but a nurse stopped me.

"Let the doctors see him first," she said, flipping a page on her clipboard. "You can give me some information. Now, what's his name? Is he your boyfriend?"

"His name is . . . Nick," I lied nervously. "Nick, um, Ride. He's my brother."

The nurse looked at me, my blond hair and fair skin, and I could tell she was mentally comparing me with Fang — who had black hair, dark eyes, olive skin.

"He's all of our brother's," said Nudge ungrammatically.

The nurse looked at Nudge, who was black, and at the rest of us, none of whom really matched, except Angel and Gazzy, the only true siblings among us.

"We were adopted," I said. "Our parents are . . . missionaries." Excellent! I mentally patted myself on the back. Brilliant! Missionaries! "They're away on a . . . short mission. I'm in charge."

A doctor in green jammies hurried up to us. "Miss?" he said, looking at me, glancing at all of us. "Could you come with me, right now?"

"Think he noticed the wings yet?" I heard Iggy barely murmur.

I tapped Iggy twice on the back of his hand. It meant, *You're in charge till I get back.* He nodded, and I followed the doctor down the hall, feeling like I was on death row.

11

Walking quickly, the doctor looked at me in that zoo-exhibit way I've become familiar with. My heart sank.

All of my worst fears were coming true. I could already see the mesh of a big dog crate closing in around me. Those freaking Erasers! I hated them! They always showed up, and when they did, they destroyed everything.

You have to respect your enemy, Max, said the Voice. *Never, ever underestimate them. The second you do, they'll squash you. Be smart about them. Respect their abilities, even if they don't respect yours.*

I swallowed hard. *Whatever.*

We pushed through heavy double doors and were in a small, tiled, very scary room. Fang was on a gurney.

He had a tube going down his throat and more tubes attached to his arms. I pressed my hand to my mouth. I'm not squeamish, but cracked, painful memories of the experiments done on us at the School were seeping into my brain, and I wished that my Voice would keep talking, say something really annoying to distract me.

Another doctor and a nurse were standing by Fang. They had cut his shirt and jacket off. The horrible jagged claw wounds in his side were still bleeding.

Now that he had me here, the doctor didn't seem to know what to say.

"Will — will he be okay?" I asked, feeling as if I were choking. Life without Fang was unimaginable.

"We don't know," said one of the doctors, looking very concerned.

The woman doctor gestured to Fang. "How well do you know him?"

"He's my brother."

"Are you — *like* him?" she asked.

"Yes." I set my jaw and kept my eyes on Fang. I felt my muscles tighten, a new, unwelcome flood of adrenaline icing its way through my veins. *Okay, first I would slam this little trolley against the nurse's legs. . . .*

"So you can help us," the first doctor said, sounding relieved. " 'Cause we're not recognizing this stuff. What about his heartbeat?"

I looked at the EKG. The blips were fast and erratic.

"It should be smoother," I said. "And faster." I snapped my fingers a bunch of times to demonstrate.

"Can I . . . ?" the doctor asked, motioning his stethoscope toward me. I nodded warily.

He listened to my heart, a look of total amazement on his face.

Then he moved his stethoscope over my stomach, in several places. "Why can I hear *air* moving down here?" he asked.

"We have air sacs," I explained quietly, feeling as if my throat were closing. My hands tightened into fists by my sides. "We have lungs, but we also have smaller air sacs. And — our stomachs are different. Our bones. Our blood." Gee, pretty much everything.

"And you have . . . *wings?*" the second doctor asked in a low voice. I nodded.

"You're a human-avian hybrid," the first doctor said.

"That's one name for it," I said tightly. As opposed to, say, mutant freak. "I prefer Avian American."

I glanced at the nurse, who looked scared and like she'd rather be anywhere but here. I *so* related.

The female doctor became all business. "We're giving him saline, to counter the shock, but he needs blood."

"You can't give him hu— regular blood," I said. All the scientific knowledge I'd gleaned over the years from reports and experiments started coming to the surface. "Our red blood cells have nuclei." Like birds'.

The doctor nodded. "Get ready to give him a donation," she instructed me briskly.

12

Twenty minutes later, I was two pints lighter and dizzy as a dodo bird from it. I shouldn't have given that much blood, but Fang needed even more, and it was the best I could do. Now he was in surgery.

I made my way down the hall to the waiting room, which was crowded — but not with bird kids.

Quickly I walked the perimeter, in case they were under chairs or something. *No flock.*

My head swiveled as I checked one hall and then another. I was already weak and kind of nauseated, and the fear of losing my flock made me feel like hurling was seconds away.

"They're down here." A short, dark-haired nurse was speaking to me. I locked my gaze on her.

She handed me a small plastic bottle of apple juice and a muffin. "Eat this," she told me. "It'll help with the dizziness. Your . . . siblings are in room seven." She pointed down the hall.

"Thanks," I muttered, not knowing yet if I meant it.

Room 7 had a solid door, and I opened it without knocking. Four pairs of worried bird-kid eyes looked up at me. Relief — however temporary — made my knees weak.

"You must be Max," said a voice.

My stomach seized up. *Oh, no,* I thought, taking in the guy's dark gray suit, the short, regulation hair, the almost invisible earpiece of his comm system. *Eraser?* It was getting harder to tell with each new batch. This guy lacked a feral gleam in his eyes — but I wasn't going to let down my guard.

"Please, sit down," said another voice.

13

There were three of them, two men and a woman, looking very governmenty, sitting around a fake-wood conference table.

Iggy, Nudge, Gazzy, and Angel were also sitting there, with plastic cafeteria trays of food in front of them. I realized that none of them had touched their food, despite the fact that they must be starving, and I was so proud of their caution that tears almost started in my eyes.

"Who are you?" I asked. Amazingly, my voice was calm and even. Points to me.

"We're from the Federal Bureau of Investigation," one man said, reaching out to hand me his business card. It had a little federal seal and everything. Not that that meant squat. "And we're on your side. We just became aware that you were having some trouble here, and we came to see if we could help."

He sounded so *sincere.*

"How nice of you!" I said, sinking into a chair before I fainted. "But aren't most people in a hospital, uh, *having some trouble?* I doubt the FBI comes calling on *them.* So what do you want with us?"

I saw one agent stifle a grin, and their eyes all met for a second.

The first man, Dean Mickelson according to his card, smiled ruefully. "We know you've been through a lot, Max. And we're sorry that . . . Nick got hurt. You're in a bad spot here, and we can help."

I was really tired and needed to think. My flock was watching me, and I could smell their hot breakfasts from where I sat. "Angel," I said, "give Total some of your food and see if he keels over. If he doesn't, you all can go ahead and eat."

As if he knew his name, Total leaped up onto a chair next to Angel and wagged his tail. Angel hesitated — she didn't want to take a chance.

"Look," said the female agent. She stood up and took a bite of Angel's scrambled eggs.

The other two agents followed her lead, sampling the three other trays. Just then there was a tap on the door, and a younger agent handed in a fifth tray, for me. An agent took a bite off my plate, then set the tray on the table. "Okay?" he asked.

We watched the agents with interest, waiting to see if they would suddenly clutch their throats and fall gasping to the floor.

They didn't.

"Okay, dig in, guys," I said, and the flock fell on their food like, um, Erasers.

Gazzy was done first — he'd practically inhaled his. "Can I have maybe two more trays?" he asked.

Startled, Dean nodded and went to give the order.

"So, how are you here to help us?" I said between bites. "How did you know we were here?"

"We'll answer all your questions," said the other guy. "But we need you to answer some questions too. We thought it might be easier if we went one-on-one — less distracting. If you're done eating, we can move into here."

He opened a door behind him leading into a larger conference room. Several more agents were milling around, and they stopped talking to look at us.

"You're not separating us," I said.

"No, just separate tables," said the woman. "All in the same room, see?"

I groaned inwardly. When was the last time we had slept? Was it only two days ago we were escaping through the sewer tunnels in New York? Now Fang was under the knife, we were surrounded by God knows who these people really were, and I didn't see a way out of it. Not without leaving Fang behind. Which I wouldn't do.

Sighing, I pushed away my empty tray and nodded to the others.

Let the questioning begin.

14

"And what's your name, sweetie?"

"Ariel," said Angel.

"Okay, Ariel. Have you ever heard of anyone named Jeb Batchelder?"

The agent held up a photograph, and Angel looked at it. Jeb's familiar face looked back at her, and it hurt her heart.

"No," she said.

"Um, okay . . . can you tell me what your relationship is to Max?"

"She's my sister. You know, because of the missionaries. Our parents."

"Okay, I see. And where did you get your dog?"

"I found him in the park." Angel fidgeted and looked over at Max. She thought, *Okay, enough questions. You can go.*

The agent sitting across from her paused and looked blankly at the notes she was writing.

"Uh — I guess that's enough questions," the agent said, looking confused. "You can go."

"Thanks," said Angel, slipping out of her chair. She snapped her fingers for Total, and he trotted after her.

"And how do you spell that?" the agent asked.

"Captain, like the captain of a ship," the Gasman explained. "And then Terror, you know, T-E-R-O-R."

"Your name is Captain Terror."

"That's right," the Gasman said, shifting in his chair. He glanced at Max, who was speaking very quietly to her agent. "Are you really FBI?"

The agent smiled briefly. "Yes. How old are you?"

"Eight. How old are you?"

The agent looked startled. "Uh . . . um, you're kind of tall for an eight-year-old, aren't you?"

"Uh-huh. We're all tall. And skinny. And we eat a lot. When we can get it."

"Yes, I see. Tell me . . . Captain, have you ever seen anything like this?" The agent held up a blurry black-and-white photo of an Eraser, half-morphed.

"Gosh, no," said the Gasman, opening his blue eyes wide. "What *is* that?"

The agent seemed at a loss for words.

"And you're blind?"

"Uh-huh," Iggy said, trying to sound bored.

"Were you born that way?"

"No."

"How did you become blind, uh, Jeff, is it?"

"Yeah, Jeff. Well, I looked directly at the sun, you know, the way they always tell you not to. If only I had listened."

* * *

"And then I had, like, three cheeseburgers, and they were awesome, you know? And those fried pie things? Those apple pies? They're really great. Have you ever tried them?" Nudge looked hopefully at the woman sitting across from her.

"Uh, I don't think so. Can you spell your name for me, sweetie?"

"Uh-huh. It's K-R-Y-S-T-A-L. I like my name. It's pretty. What's your name?"

"Sarah. Sarah McCauley."

"Well, that's an okay name too. Do you wish it was something different? Like, sometimes I wish my name was kind of fancier, you know? Like — Cleopatra. Or Marie-Sophie-Therese. Did you know that the queen of England has, like, six names? Her name is Elizabeth Alexandra Mary. Her last name is Windsor. But she's so famous she just signs her name 'Elizabeth R,' and everyone knows who it is. I'd like to be that famous someday. I would just sign 'Krystal.' "

The agent was silent for a moment, then she seemed to recover herself. "Have you ever heard of a place called the School?" she asked. "We think it's in California. Have you ever been to California?"

Nudge looked thoughtfully at the ceiling. "California? Like, surfers and movie stars and earthquakes? No. I'd like to go. Is it pretty?" Her large brown eyes looked innocently at the agent.

"You can call me Agent Mickelson," he told me with a smile. "What about you? Is Max short for something? Maxine?"

"No, Dean. It's just Max."

He blinked once, then referred back to his notes. "I see. Now, Max, I think we both know your parents aren't missionaries."

I opened my eyes wide. "No? Well, for God's sake, don't tell them. They'd be crushed. Thinking they're doing the Lord's work and all."

Dean looked at me, I dunno, as if a hamster had just snarled at him. He tried another tack. "Max, we're looking for a man named Jeb Batchelder. Do you have any knowledge of his whereabouts?" The agent held up a picture of Jeb, and my heart constricted. For a second I was torn: give that lying, betraying jerk up to the FBI, which would be fun, or keep my mouth shut about anything important, which would be smart.

I shook my head regretfully. "Never seen him."

"Have you ever been to Colorado?"

I frowned. "Is that one of those square ones, in the middle?"

I saw Dean take a deep breath.

Quickly I glanced around. Angel was on the floor by the door, eating my muffin, sharing it with Total. Iggy's and Nudge's agents were conferring, whispering behind some papers, and Iggy and Nudge lounged in their chairs. Nudge was looking around curiously. I hoped she was memorizing escape routes. The Gasman got up, cheerfully said "Bye" to his agent, and went over to Angel.

"Max, we want to help you," Dean said quietly. "But you've got to help us too. Fair is fair."

I stared at him. That was the funniest thing I'd heard in days.

"You're kidding, right? *Please* tell me you have a stronger motive for me than 'fair is fair.' Life isn't *fair,*

Dean." My voice strengthened, and I leaned forward, closer to the agent's impassive face. "Nothing is fair, *ever.* That's the stupidest thing I've ever heard. I need to help you because *fair is fair?* Try, 'I need you to help me so I won't rip out your spine and beat you with it.' I *might* respond to that. *Maybe.*"

Dean's jaw clenched, and two pink splotches appeared on his cheeks. I got the feeling that he was more mad at himself than at me.

"Max," he began, his voice tense, but was interrupted.

"Thank you, Dean," said a woman's voice. "I'll take over from here."

15

Dean straightened up and smoothed his expression. The new woman gave him a friendly smile and waited.

She was blond — I couldn't tell how old. She had the sort of professional polish and attitude of a major-network news anchor. She was pretty, actually.

Dean gathered up his files, nodded at me, then went to confer with another agent. The new woman sat down across from me.

"They're all kind of full of hot air," she whispered behind her hand.

I was startled into a grin.

She reached her hand across the table for me to shake. "My name is Anne Walker," she said. "And yes, I'm one of Them. I'm the one they call in when everything goes kablooey."

"Have things gone kablooey?" I asked politely.

She gave a short laugh. "Uh, *yeah,*" she said in a "duh" tone of voice. "When we get a call from a hospital saying they've got at least two and possibly six previously unknown recombinant DNA life-forms and one of them is gravely injured, then, yes, I think we can safely say that things have gone kablooey with a capital 'kuh.' "

"Oh," I said. "Gee, we sound so important."

One side of her mouth twitched. "Uh-huh. Why the surprise? Hasn't anyone ever told you you were important?"

Jeb. The one word shocked my senses, and I went into total shutdown so I wouldn't start bawling like the goofy recombinant life-form that I am. Jeb had made me feel important, once upon a time. He'd made me feel smart, strong, capable, special, important . . . you name it. Lately, though, he mostly made me feel blinding rage and a stomach-clenching sense of betrayal.

"Look," I said coolly, "we're in a tough spot here. I know it and you know it. One of my fl— brothers is hurt, and we need help. Just tell me what I have to do so we can get that help, and then we'll be on our merry way."

I shot a quick glance at the flock. They were sitting together, eating bagels and watching me. Gazzy cheerfully held up a bagel to show he was saving one for me.

Anne's sympathetic look set my teeth on edge. She leaned over the table so she wouldn't be overheard. "Max, I'm not gonna tell you a bunch of crap," she said, surprising me again. "Like the crap you're giving us about your parents being missionaries. We both know that isn't true. And we both know that the FBI isn't in the business of just helping people out because they're so wonderful and special. This is the deal: We've heard about you. Rumors have been filtering into the intelligence community for years about a hidden lab producing viable recombinant life-forms.

"But it's never been verified, and people have always dismissed it as urban-legend stuff. Needless to say, the very possibility that it could be true — well, we've got people assigned to finding out and cataloguing info, hearsay, or suspicion about you. You and your family."

Wait till she found out about the Erasers.

Anne took a breath and sat back, keeping her eyes on me. "So you see, we consider you important. We'd like to know everything about you. But *more* important, if the stories are true, then our entire country's safety could be at stake — if your so-called family were to get into the wrong hands. You don't know your own power."

She let that sink in for a moment, then smiled ruefully. "How about we make a trade? You give us a chance to learn about you — in nonpainful, noninvasive ways — and we'll give Nick the best medical care available and the rest of you a safe place to stay. You can rest up, eat, Nick can get better, and then you can decide what to do from there."

I felt like a starving mouse staring at a huge hunk of cheese.

Set right in the middle of an enormous, Max-sized trap.

I put a look of polite disinterest on my face. "And I believe that this is all straight up because . . ."

"It would be great if I could offer you guarantees, Max," said Anne. "But I can't — not anything that you would believe. I mean, come on." She shrugged. "A written contract? My word of honor? A really sincere promise from the head of the FBI?"

We both laughed. Those wacky agents.

"It's just — you don't have a lot of choices here, Max. Not right now. I'm sorry."

I stared at the tabletop and thought. The horrible thing was, she was right. With Fang in such bad shape, she had us over a barrel. The best thing I could do was accept her offer of shelter and care for Fang, bide my time, and work out an escape later. Silently I swore a whole lot. Then I looked up.

"Well, say I accepted. Where's this safe place you're dangling in front of me?"

She looked at me. If she was surprised that I was going along with it, she didn't show it.

"My house," she said.

16

Fang came out of surgery almost two hours later. I was waiting outside the OR, wound tighter than a rubber ball.

The doctor I'd talked to came out, still in his green scrubs. I wanted to grab the front of his shirt, throw him against a wall, get some answers. But I'm trying to outgrow that kind of thing.

"Ah, yes, Max, is it?"

"Yeah. Max it is." I waited tensely. If the unthinkable had happened, I'd snag the kids and make a run for it.

"Your brother Nick — it was a little dicey for a while. We gave him several units of blood substitute, and it brought his blood pressure up to a safe range."

My hands were clenching and unclenching. It was all I could do to stand there and focus on the words.

"He didn't go into cardiac arrest," the doctor said. "We were able to patch up his side, stop all the hemorrhaging. A main artery had been hit, and one of his . . . air sacs."

"So what's he like now?" I forced my breathing to

calm, tried to shut down my fight-or-flight response. Which in my case is, you know, *literal.*

"He's holding steady," the doctor said, looking tired and amazed. "If nothing goes wrong, he should be okay. He needs to take it easy for maybe three weeks."

Which meant probably about six days, given our incredibly fast healing and regenerative strengths.

But jeez. Six days was a long time.

"Can I see him?"

"Not till he comes out of recovery," the doctor said. "Maybe another forty minutes. Now, I'm hoping you can fill me in on some physiological stuff. I noticed —"

"Thank you, Doctor," said Anne Walker, coming up behind me.

"I mean, I wanted to know —," the doctor began, looking at me.

"I'm sorry," said Anne. "These kids are tired and need to rest. One of my colleagues can answer any questions you might have."

"Excuse me, but your colleagues don't know jack about us," I reminded Anne through clenched teeth.

The doctor looked irritated, but he nodded and went back down the hall.

Anne smiled at me. "We're trying to keep your existence somewhat quiet," she said. "Until we're certain you're safe. But that's great news about Nick."

We walked to the waiting area. The flock jumped up when they saw me. I smiled and gave them a thumbs-up. Nudge whooped and slapped high fives with Gazzy, and Angel ran over to hug me hard. I swung her up and held her tight.

"He's gonna be fine," I confirmed.

"Can we see him?" Iggy asked.

"Ig, I hate to break this to you, but you're blind," I said, my relief making me tease him. "However, in a little while you can go listen to him breathe and *maybe* talk to him."

Iggy gave me a combination smile-scowl, which he's extraordinarily good at.

"Hi, everyone," said Anne. I'd forgotten she was right behind me. "Max may have told you about me — I'm Anne Walker, from the FBI. Has Max filled you in on the agreement we made?"

She was smart: If I hadn't already told them about it, she'd just confirmed that it was a done deal.

"Yes," said Angel, looking at her. "We're going to stay at your house for a teensy little while."

"That's right," said Anne, smiling back.

"Us and Total," Angel said to make sure.

"Total?"

"My dog." Angel pointed under her chair, where Total was curled up, head poised neatly on his paws.

"How did you get a dog in here?" Anne asked, amazed.

I didn't want to delve into that too much. "Yes! So, well, as soon as F— Nick is somewhat mobile, we'll go to Anne's house, rest up, get Nick up to a hundred percent. Cool?"

The others nodded with varying levels of enthusiasm.

"Fnick?" Iggy muttered, smirking.

I ignored him.

"Actually, Nick won't be mobile for at least a week," Anne said. "So we can all head to my place today, and he can come out when he's ready."

I saw Gazzy blink and Nudge frown.

"No," I said to Anne. "That wasn't what I agreed to. We're not leaving Nick here alone."

"He'll have doctors and nurses and two agents at his door. Round the clock," Anne promised.

I crossed my arms over my chest. "No. Two of your agents would be a snack for an Eraser."

Anne ignored my joke. Not surprisingly, since she probably didn't have a clue what I was talking about.

"It will be more comfortable for you at my house," Anne said. "Much better for you."

"But not much better for Nick," I said.

"But — Nick can't be moved," Anne said. "Were you planning to just hang out in his room?"

17

"The girls can have the bed," Gazzy said. "Iggy and I can sleep on the floor."

"Excuse me, sexist piglet?" I said, raising my eyebrows. "How about the two smallest people share the bed 'cause they'll *fit.* That would be you and Angel."

"Yeah," said Nudge, with narrowed eyes. "Like, I'm too much of a cream puff to sleep on the floor?"

Gazzy got his stubborn face on, so I walked across the room before he could start arguing. Fang's hospital room was a double, but the other bed was empty. The two smaller kids would sleep in it, and the rest of us would make do.

"Of course, the prince gets his own bed all to himself," I said to Fang.

"That's right," Fang said hazily. "The prince has a gaping side wound."

He still looked like death, extremely pale and groggy. He couldn't eat, so he had an IV drip. Iggy had given him another pint of bird-kid blood, and that had helped.

"Well, they sewed you up," I said. "You're pretty gape-free at this point."

"When do I get out of here?"

"They say a week."

"So, like, tomorrow?" he said.

"That's what I'm thinking."

"So, Fnick, can I change the channel?" Iggy asked. "There's a game on."

"Make yourself at home, *Figgy,*" Fang said.

We crashed early and hard, given what we'd been through in the last twenty-four hours. By nine o'clock I was listening to the flock sleeping all around me. The agent guys had come up with some, like, yoga mats for us, and they weren't bad. Especially if you've logged time on rocky cave floors and concrete ledges in subway tunnels.

Now it was quiet, and I was trying to shut my brain down. *Voice? Any last-minute remarks you want to get off your chest before I crash?*

You chose to stay with Fang.

No duh, I replied silently. What Gazzy had said, back on the beach . . . the little twerp was right. I shouldn't split us up again, even when it seemed safer to do it. We did best when we were all together. The whole family together.

Family is extremely important, said the Voice. *Didn't you tell me that once?*

Yep, I thought. *That's why we're going to find our parents as soon as we get out of here.*

I took a deep breath, trying to relax. I was completely exhausted, but my brain was racing. Every time I closed my eyes, all sorts of images flashed through my mind —

like buildings exploding, a mushroom cloud, ducks caught in oil slicks, mountains of trash, nuclear power plants. Waking nightmares.

So I sat up, eyes open, but it wasn't much better. I had started feeling bad earlier but hadn't told anyone. I had a headache, not a grenade-type headache, where my brain felt like it was being splattered against the inside of my skull, but just a regular headache. Fortunately the grenade-type headaches were much fewer and farther between than they had been. My theory was that they were my brain getting used to sharing office space with my rude and uninvited guest: my Voice. At any rate, I was incredibly glad they were on leave of absence lately.

This wasn't like that. I was hot; my skin was burning. I felt like adrenaline was pouring into my system, making me so jumpy I couldn't stand it.

Were the Erasers tracking the chip in my arm that I'd seen in that X-ray at Dr. Martinez's office so many days ago? How did they keep finding us? The eternal question.

I glanced at Total, sleeping on the bed with Angel and Gazzy. He was on his back, paws in the air. Was he chipped? Were they tracking him now?

Ugh. I felt so hot and twitchy and sick. I wanted to lie down in snow, eat snow, rub it over my skin. I fantasized about throwing open the window and taking off into the cool night air. I imagined flying back to Dr. Martinez and her daughter, Ella, the only human friends I'd known. Dr. Martinez would know what to do. My heart was pounding so fast it felt like a staccato drumroll in my chest.

I stood up and picked my way quietly over sleeping bodies to the small sink in one wall. I turned on the cold water and let it run over my hands. Leaning down, I splashed my face again and again. It felt good, and I wished I could stand under an icy shower. *Please don't let me get sick,* I prayed. *I can't get sick. I can't get Fang sick.*

I don't know how long I hung over the sink, letting water trickle over my neck. Finally I thought maybe I could try to sleep again, and I straightened up to dry my face.

And almost screamed.

I whirled around, but the room was quiet. I whipped back to stare in the mirror again, and it was still there: the Eraser.

I blinked rapidly. What the *h* was going on? The Eraser in the mirror blinked rapidly too.

The Eraser was me.

18

In an instant, cold sweat coated my forehead and the back of my neck.

I swallowed, and the Eraser Max in the mirror swallowed.

I opened my mouth and saw the long, sharp canines. But when I touched them with my finger, they felt small, smooth, normal. I touched my face and felt smooth skin, though the mirror showed me totally morphed.

I remembered how ill I had felt, hot and heart-poundy. Oh, God. What was this all about? Had I just discovered a new "skill," like Angel reading minds, Gazzy able to imitate any voice, Iggy identifying people by feeling their fingerprints? *Had I just developed the skill of turning into an Eraser, our worst enemy?*

I felt sick with revulsion and dread. I glanced guiltily around to make sure no one could see me like this. I didn't even know what they would see if they woke up. I *felt* normal. I *looked* like an Eraser. Kind of a cuter, blonder, Pekingesey Eraser.

Respect and honor your enemies, said my Voice. *Always. Know your friends well; know your enemies even better.*

Oh, please, I begged silently. *Please let this be just a horrible lesson and not reality. I promise, promise, promise to know my enemies better. Just let me lose the muzzle.*

Your greatest strength is your greatest weakness, Max.

I stared at the mirror. Huh?

Your hatred of Erasers gives you the power to fight to the death. But that hatred also blinds you to the big picture: the big picture of them, of you, of everything in your life.

Um. Let me think about that and get back to you. Okay?

Ow. I winced and pressed my fingers to my temples, trying to rub the pain away. I touched my face one last time to make sure it really was smooth, and then I went and looked at Fang.

He was still breathing, sleeping. He looked better. Not so embalmed. He was going to be all right. I sighed, trying to release my pain and fear, then I curled up on my mat next to Nudge. I closed my eyes but didn't really have any hope of sleeping.

I lay quietly in the darkness. The only thing that made me feel better was listening to the even, regular, calm breathing of my sleeping flock.

19

"I don't understand it," said the doctor, gazing at Fang's wound.

Yeah, well, I thought, *that's the whimsy of recombinant DNA.*

The doc had come in to change the bandages this morning and found that Fang's gashes were almost healed, just thin pink lines of scar tissue.

"Guess I'm good to go," said Fang, trying to sit up. He was alert, himself, and happiness filled my heart. I'd been so scared — what would I do without Fang?

"Wait!" Anne Walker said, holding up her hand. "You're nowhere near ready to move or leave. Please, Nick, just lie still and rest."

Fang regarded her calmly, and I smirked to myself. If Anne thought *I* was uncooperative, wait till she dealt with a recovered Fang.

"Nick, now that you're feeling a bit better, maybe you can convince your brothers and sisters to leave with me," Anne said. "I've offered for all of you to come stay at my house, to rest and regroup." She gave a slight smile. "Max refused to leave without you. But I'm sure you can see that it's pointless for them to stay here and be uncomfortable. And you'd be joining us in a week or so."

Fang just looked at her, waiting.

I leaned against the wall and crossed my arms.

"So, how do you feel about it, Nick?"

Actually, I'd already briefed him, early this morning. Since we were up at six. Since, at six, the nurse had been overcome with an overwhelming compulsion to take Fang's temperature *right then.*

Fang met my eyes, and I let one side of my mouth droop.

"Whatever Max says," he said evenly. "She's in charge."

I grinned. I'll never get tired of hearing that.

Anne turned to look at me.

"I can't leave Nick," I said, sounding regretful.

"If you all stay, maybe I could examine —," the doctor began, and Anne turned to him as if she'd forgotten he was there.

"Thank you, Doctor," she said. "I appreciate all your help."

It was a dismissal, and the doctor didn't look happy. But he left.

"We heal really quickly," I told Anne. Last night Fang had still looked bad. And I had too, I thought, remembering the horrible Eraser reflection. But this morning I looked like me, and Fang looked much more like himself again.

Fang sat up. "What do I have to do to get some food in this joint?"

"You still have an IV," Anne said. "The doctors don't want you eating solid . . ." Her voice trailed off as Fang's eyes narrowed.

"We saved a tray for you," I said. An orderly had brought us breakfast, and we'd saved some of everything for Fang.

Anne looked as though she wanted to say something but held it back. A good move on her part, I must say.

I gave the tray to Fang, and he dug into the food with quick precision.

"I need to get out of here," he said between bites. "The hospital smells alone are making me crawl the walls."

I knew what he meant. We all had the same reaction: Anything antiseptic-smelling, hospitally, science labby, brought back years' worth of bad memories.

I looked at Anne. "I think F— Nick is ready to come with us."

She looked at me, clearly thinking things through.

"Okay," she said finally, and I kept the surprise off my face. "Let me go clear up the paperwork. It'll take about an hour and a half to drive to my home. I live in northern Virginia. Okay?"

"Yeah," I said.

Anne left, and I looked around at the flock. "I don't know what's coming, guys, but keep your eyes open and heads up." I glanced at Fang. "You sure you can move?"

He shrugged, looking tired again, and pushed away the food tray. "Sure." He lay back down and shut his eyes.

"After all, Fnick is Superman," said Iggy.

"Shut up, Jeff," I said, but I was smiling. I lifted Iggy's fingers to my face so that he knew.

20

"Gol, Virginia is shore purty," I said to the Gasman, and he grinned.

But it really was. There were many hills of the "gently rolling" type, miles of trees that had been dipped in fiery, autumny paint, and swelling waves of green pastures, some even dotted with actual horses. It was gorgeous here.

Anne's huge Suburban held us all, and Fang got to recline most of the way. I kept an eye on him, noting the way his jaw tightened when we hit bumps, but he didn't complain.

Another fly in the ointment: I was having the same waves of heat and racing heart I'd had last night. My breath came in little pants, and I was so jumpy it felt as if bugs were crawling all over me.

Total had been sitting on my lap, looking out the window, and now he glanced at me with his shiny black eyes. Deliberately he got up and picked his way over Fang's lap and onto Angel's, as if to say, If you're going to be that hot, forget it.

"Oh, gosh, look at that," Nudge said, pointing out her window. "That horse is totally white. Like an angel horse. And what are those rolled-up straw things?"

"Bales of hay," said Anne from the front seat. "They roll them like that instead of making haystacks."

"It's so pretty here," Nudge went on, practically bouncing in her seat next to Anne. "I like these hills. What's the kind of tree with pointy leaves and all the colors?"

"Maples," Anne said. "They usually have the most color."

"What's your house like?" Nudge asked. "Is it all white with big columns? Like Tara? Did you see that movie?"

"*Gone with the Wind,*" Anne said. "No, I'm afraid my house isn't anything like Tara. It's an old farmhouse. But I do have fifty acres of land around it. Plenty of room for you guys to run around. We're almost there."

Twenty minutes later, Anne pulled into a driveway and clicked an electronic gadget. A pair of wrought-iron gates swung open, and she pulled through.

The gates closed behind us, which made my sensors go on precautionary alert.

It took almost a whole minute to get to her house. The driveway was made of crushed shells and wound through beautiful trees arching overhead. Red and yellow leaves fluttered gently down onto the car.

"Well, here we are," she said, pulling around a corner. "I hope you like it."

We stared out the car windows. Anne's house looked like a painting. It had rounded river rocks on the bottom part, and clapboards above, and a big screened porch that covered almost the whole front. Large shrubs circled the yard, and some of them still had faded hydrangea blooms.

"There's a pond out back," Anne said, pulling into a parking space in front of the house. "It's so shallow that it might still be warm enough to swim in, in the afternoons. Here, everyone pile out."

We poured out of the car, glad to be in a wide-open space again.

"The air smells different here," said Nudge, wrinkling her nose. "It smells great."

The house stood on the top of a low hill. Sloping away from us were wide lawns and an orchard. The trees were actually covered with apples. Birds twittered and sang. I couldn't hear traffic, or smell road tar, or hear any other person.

Anne opened the front door. "Well, don't just stand there," she said with a laugh. "Come see your rooms."

I nodded, and Angel and Nudge started toward the house, followed by Gazzy.

Iggy was standing next to me. "What does it look like?" he asked in a low voice.

"It looks like paradise, Jeff," said Fang.

21

The rough bark of the tree was cutting into his legs, but Ari paid no attention.

After the pain of having huge wings retrofitted onto his shoulders, this was child's play. He grinned at that thought. Technically, anything he did was child's play: He was only seven years old. Eight next April. Not that it mattered. He wouldn't get presents or a cake. His dad probably wouldn't even remember.

He put the binoculars to his eyes again, clenching his jaw. He saw the mutant bird freaks get out of the car. He'd already been over the grounds, looked in the windows of the house. Those kids were in a for a cushy stay. At least for a while.

It wasn't fair. There wasn't even a word for how unfair it was. Ari's hand clutched a small branch so tightly that the branch snapped, sending a long, thin sliver under his skin.

He looked at it, waiting for the pain signals to make their sluggish way to his brain. Bright red blood welled around the splinter. Ari pinched the splinter out and threw it away before his brain even recognized that he'd been hurt.

Here he was, in a tree, his team camped nearby, stuck watching the mutant freaks through binoculars.

He should be on the ground, tapping Max on the shoulder, seeing her whirl, then smashing his fist right into her face.

But no. Instead, she was sashaying inside the fancy house, thinking she was perfect, better than anyone, better than him.

The one fun thing of the last forty-eight hours had been Max's expression when she'd seen he was alive. She'd been shocked. Shocked and horrified, Ari remembered proudly. *He wanted her to look like that every time she saw him.*

So, fine. *Get some R&R, Maximum,* Ari thought acidly. *Your time is coming. And I'll be there waiting for you. I'll always be there.*

The hatred coiled in his gut, twisting his insides, and he felt himself morphing, his facial bones elongating, his shoulders hunching.

He watched as the coarse hair covered his arms, lightning fast, and ragged claws erupted from his fingertips. He wanted to rake these claws down Max's face, that perfect face. . . .

Anguish welled up and choked him, turning his world black, and without thinking, he sank his fangs into his own arm. Clenching his jaw hard, he waited for the physical pain. Finally, gasping, he sat back, his mouth red with blood, his arm coldly numb with pain. Ah. That was better.

PART 2

PARADISE OR PRISON?

22

Guess how many bedrooms Anne's little country shack had. Seven. One for her, one for each bird kid. Guess how many bathrooms it had. Five. Five bathrooms all in one house.

"Max!" The Gasman pounded on my bedroom door.

I opened it, my hair still wet from my long, incredibly hot shower.

"Can I go outside?" he asked.

"Gee, I had forgotten the natural color of your skin," I told him. "I was convinced you were kind of dirt colored."

He grinned at me. "Call it camouflage. Can I go outside?"

"Yeah, let's all go together, give Iggy some landmarks."

"What is that, like, a plane hangar?" Nudge asked.

A grove of trees had hidden the big red building from

the house, but now that we were doing recon, we were finding all kinds of things.

"It's a barn," said Fang.

I was keeping an eye on him. As soon as he started to look tired, I was going to send him back to the house.

"A barn with animals?" asked Angel excitedly.

Just then, Total started barking, as if he'd picked up something's scent.

"Yep, guess so," I said, scooping Total up in my arms. "Listen, you," I told him. "No more with the barking. You're going to spook somebody."

Total looked offended but stayed quiet as long as I held him.

"That first one is Sugar," said Anne, coming up behind us. She'd given us free rein of the place after she'd shown us our rooms and stuff.

We stood in the open barn doorway and watched Sugar, a pale gray horse who was looking back at us with interest.

"He's beautiful," Nudge whispered.

"He's big," said the Gasman.

"Big and sweet," said Anne, opening a box and taking out a carrot. She handed it to Nudge and nodded at the horse. "Go on. He likes carrots. Hold it flat in your hand."

Cautiously Nudge stepped forward, holding out the carrot. This is a kid who could break a man's ribs with a well-placed kick, but she was almost trembling as she approached the horse.

Sugar very delicately lipped up the carrot, then crunched it with satisfaction.

Nudge turned to me, her face glowing, and my heart caught in my throat. It was like we were inner-city kids getting a week on the farm as part of a social service program. We were surrounded by beautiful scenery and fresh air, there were animals, and —

"You guys have another half hour," Anne said, turning to go back to the house. "Dinner's at six."

And, I was going to say, *plenty of food.* It was amazing.

Where was the catch? 'Cause I *knew* one was coming.

23

"Oh, *yeah!*" said the Gasman, looking at the pond. "I am so there!"

Anne's pond was about as big as a football stadium, with a small, rocky shore edged by cattails and daylilies.

I stared at it suspiciously, waiting for the Pond Ness Monster to rise out of its depths. Okay, call me hopelessly paranoid, but this whole place was starting to seem creepily idyllic. Like, my bedroom was charming. *Charming!* What did I know about charming? I'd never called anything charming before in my life.

And now here I was, eyes narrowed at a picture-perfect pond. Was this some new freakish test?

"We don't have time right now, Gazzy," I said, clamping down on my rising fears. "But maybe we can go swimming tomorrow."

"It's just so beautiful here," Nudge said, gazing at the untrustable rolling hills, the dark, secret-concealing orchard, the pond (see above rant re pond), the small, *liter-*

ally babbling brook that ran into the pond. "Like the Garden of Eden."

"Yeah, and *that* turned out so well," I muttered under my breath.

"Look, there are more animals over there," said Angel, pointing.

No doubt tidy, Martha Stewart, heirloom pedigree animals enclosed in chintz pens.

"Okay, we can swing by 'em on the way back to the house. I don't know about you guys, but I'm starving." I glanced over at Fang, who was starting to look a little pale. Tonight after dinner I would try to get him to take it easy in one of the too-comfortable recliners by the horribly cozy fireplace.

"Sheep!" Angel cried, catching sight of some fluffy brown wool.

"Anne is quite the animal lover," Fang said to me as we followed Angel. "Horses, sheep, goats. Chickens. Pigs."

"Yeah," I said. "I wonder who's for dinner?"

He flashed one of his rare smiles at me, and it was like the sun coming out. I felt my cheeks get hot and strode on ahead.

"Pigs, look," said the Gasman excitedly. "Come here, Ig." Gazzy guided Iggy's hand down, and Iggy scratched a small brown pig behind its ears, sending it into ecstatic squeals.

"Pigs are so lucky," said the Gasman, as images of bacon danced in my head. "No one cares if *they're* dirty or live in a pigsty."

"That's because they're *pigs,*" I pointed out. Just then, Total leaped out of my arms, scratching me.

"Hey!" I said, and then saw a large black-and-white shepherdy-looking dog bounding up. Total braced his front legs and barked loudly, and the other dog barked back.

"Total!" I called, clapping my hands. "Stop it! It's his yard. Angel!"

Angel was already trotting over, and she grabbed Total's collar.

"Since when does he have a collar?" I asked.

"Okay, Total, calm down," Angel said, stroking his head. Total stopped barking, then shook his head in disgust and said, "Putz."

I blinked in surprise and opened my mouth — and then saw Gazzy loping up, hands in his pockets, whistling. I absolutely refused to give Gazzy the satisfaction of freaking out over his latest voice-throwing trick and didn't say a thing.

"Come on, guys," I said. "Let's go chow."

24

“Okay, let’s see what we have here,” I muttered. The six of us were in “my” room. The notes we’d gotten from the Institute in New York were spread out on my bed. When we’d found the files in the computer and printed them out, some of the information had been readable. Now those pages were gone, leaving us with lines of numerical code. What had happened to the readable pages? Dunno. Was it another test?

So basically, we were looking at reams of numbers. Every once in a while a real word leaped out at us. Some of the real words were *us,* our names. Somewhere in these pages was info about our parents.

“How about we each take two pages and comb through them,” I suggested. “Figure out what we can. See if anything about the numbers looks familiar or has a pattern.”

“Sounds like a plan,” said Iggy. “Except for me.”

“I’ll read you out some numbers,” said Fang.

Iggy nodded, and I passed out the sheets. Fang started reading softly to Iggy, who concentrated hard, nodding every so often.

I took my two sheets and sat at the desk. For the next hour, we tried every basic code-breaking technique we knew. We looked for patterns, hexagons — and came up with nada, nothing.

Another hour later, I dropped my head into my hands. "This is impossible," I said, ready to scream in frustration. "This is probably a computerized code. If it is, we'll never break it."

"But isn't everything a test?" the Gasman asked, his small face tired. It was almost ten. I had to get these guys into bed. "Didn't Jeb tell you that everything is a test, back at the School, when we were rescuing Angel? So that would mean we're supposed to be able to break this somehow."

"I thought of that," I said. "That's what's so irritating. I've tried everything that would occur to me. So I guess I'm flunking this test."

A tap on my door interrupted us. The door opened a bit, and Anne poked her head around it.

"Hey, guys," she said with a smile. "Sleepy yet? Krystal? Want to get ready for bed?"

"Yep," said Nudge. "I'm beat."

Gazzy looked at me, and I nodded at him.

"Yeah," he told Anne. "We were just about to crash."

"Good," she said easily. "Anyone need anything? Before you crash?"

"No, we're fine," said Angel, following Anne out. They walked down the hall, and I heard Anne say, "Ariel, how about letting Total out one last time?"

"Okay," said Angel.

I stood in my room, feeling a little bad, feeling as if someone else was taking care of my flock.

25

Welcome to another day at Camp Agent!

To start, a hearty breakfast that Iggy and I made. That's because on our first morning here, we had discovered that single-woman Anne Walker considered a protein bar and an orange-flavored sports drink to be an acceptable breakfast.

Which, if we were Dumpster diving or stealing from a 7-Eleven, would be great. But since we were in a seven-freaking-bedroom country château with a Sub-Zero fridge and Viking range at our disposal, it didn't cut it.

So it was massive infusions of scrambled eggs, bacon, toast, etc., for everyone.

Next, quaint housekeeping issues. Anne made each of us responsible for keeping our bedchambers tidy and worthy of a photo shoot. And here's what really ticked me off: The flock actually did it.

Had I asked them a thousand times to keep their rooms straight at home, when we had a home? Yes. Had they done it? No. However, they were all over the bed-making and shoe-lining-up situation here, for a *stranger.* Little buggers.

Then, rousing exercise in the country-fresh air. Flying, sparring, playing, swimming, horseback riding.

Lunch. Anne got the fine art of making sandwiches down to a science.

Post-lunch rest, play, etc. Anne occasionally took us aside one by one and interviewed us, had us show her what we could do. She loved to watch us fly — made us feel like marvels, swooping around in the sky.

She would watch us for hours, with binoculars, and the look of wonder and delight on her face could be seen from two thousand feet away.

Dinner. Anne really tried. But this was a woman whose main source of nutritional comfort came in single-serve microwavable packages. After the first day, she'd gone shopping and brought home fifteen bags of groceries and a cookbook. With mixed results.

But you know what? The food was hot and someone was fixing it for us, which made it fabulous in my book.

After that first day, I tried to start getting the flock ready for bed before Anne could do it. It bothered me, her doing it. Taking over my role. I was still the leader. Soon Anne and her comfy house would be just a memory. Just like Jeb. Just like Dr. Martinez and Ella. Just like everything in our temporary lives.

One night after we'd been there almost two weeks, I was lying in bed listening to my favorite, *favorite* singer, Liam Rooney. *Liam, Liam, you are my inspiration.* The younger kids were already asleep. There was an almost silent tap on my door.

"Yeah?"

Fang came in.

"What's up?"

"Look." He put some of the coded sheets from the Institute on my lap, then hauled a big spiral-bound book onto the bed. He opened it up across my knees.

"I was looking at this stuff, going nuts, you know? And suddenly it looked like map coordinates."

I drew in a breath. As soon as he said that, I could see the possibility.

"This is a book of detailed street maps of Washington DC," he said. "I got it out of Anne's car. Look — each page is numbered, each map is numbered, each grid of each map is numbered. And look at this clump of stuff here, by Gazzy's name. Twenty-seven, eight, G nine.

"So I go to page twenty-seven, and it's a section of town, see?"

"Yeah," I breathed.

"This section has twelve smaller maps. I go to map eight." He turned pages. "Which is a blowup of one section. Then I go to column G and trace it down to row nine." His finger slowly moved down the map. "And it's a pretty specific little chunk of streets."

I looked at him. "Oh, my God," I said. "Did you try any others?"

He nodded. "This one by Nudge's name. Same thing — I actually end up with a real place."

"You are so brilliant," I said, and he shrugged, looking almost embarrassed, except that Fang never gets embarrassed. "But I thought Nudge was pretty sure she'd found her parents in Arizona," I added.

He shrugged again. "I don't know. The woman we saw

was black, but it wasn't like Nudge was a photocopy of her. You think this is worth checking out?"

"Absolutely," I said, swinging my legs out of bed. "Everyone else asleep?"

"Yeah. Including the Annemeister."

"Okay. Gimme a minute to get some jeans on."

26

"Hmm," I said.

Fang propped the map book on a fire hydrant and braced it with one knee. He took out the page of code, and I held the penlight so he could see. He double-checked the coordinates, showing them to me. I looked at the street signs at each end of the block.

"No, you're right," I said. "This is it. If those are map coordinates, then this is where we should be."

We looked at the building across from us. It was not a cute house with a picket fence, suitable for bringing a baby home to, a baby that would later be turned into a mutant bird kid by mad scientists. No, *it was a pizza parlor.*

On this block were a car wash, a bank, the pizza joint, and a dry cleaner. On the opposite side of the street was a park. No houses, no apartment buildings, no place where someone could have lived.

"Well, crap," said Fang.

"I concur with that assessment," I said, crossing the

street. "Maybe there was an apartment building here and it got torn down."

We stood in front of the darkened store and peered inside. Hanging on the wall was a black-and-white photo of a bunch of people standing in front of a new, shiny version of the store. "Here since 1954," the caption under the picture said.

"So much for that theory," said Fang.

"Do you want to swear this time or do you want me to?" I asked.

"You can," said Fang, stuffing the page back into his pocket.

"Well, *crap,*" I said. "Okay. Let's try the next one. Maybe we'll get lucky."

And we did get lucky — in that the next address was actually a house.

Unfortunately, it was an abandoned apartment house in the middle of a hellhole block inhabited by some of the more scum-sucking members of society — many of whom were conducting "business" right now, at two in the morning.

"Let's check it out anyway," I said, drawing farther back into the shadows.

We had landed on the tarry roof of the building next door. Half an hour of waiting and watching had shown us that at least two guys, and maybe more, seemed to be squatting in this bombed-out wreck of a building.

Twenty minutes after the second guy left and didn't come back, I stood up. "Ready?"

"Ready," said Fang, and we jumped across to the other roof.

27

"Least favorite place," I whispered to Fang. "Sewer tunnels of New York? Or abandoned home of squatting crackheads?"

Fang thought about it, moving silently across the room, staying out of the squares of moonlight coming through the gaping windows.

"I'd have to go with sewer tunnels of New York," he whispered back.

We started on the second floor and moved down, opening doors, looking up fireplaces, tapping walls for hidden compartments.

Two hours later, I rubbed my forehead with a filthy hand. "We got nothing. This stinks."

"Yeah." Fang breathed out. "Well, get this last closet and we'll split."

I nodded and opened the hallway coat closet. It was empty, its walls nothing but broken plaster, showing the bare laths within.

I was about to close the door when a thin strip of white

caught my eye. I shone the penlight on it, frowning, then reached down to pick at it. Something was wedged in back of a lath.

"What?" Fang asked quietly.

"Nothing, I'm sure," I whispered back. "But I'll just get it. . . ."

I pried it out with my fingernails, and it turned out to be a square of paper, about four inches across. I turned it over, and my breath caught.

It was a photograph.

Fang leaned over my shoulder while I focused the light on the photo. It was a picture of a woman holding a baby in her arms. The baby was plump, blond, blue-eyed . . . the spitting image of the baby Gasman — cowlick and everything.

28

"Holy moly," I breathed. Just then we heard heavy footsteps coming up to the front door.

"They're back," Fang whispered. "Upstairs!"

We whirled and ran up the steps. But the moonlight streaming through the windows cast our shadows down the stairs.

I heard the front door shut, and then a voice bellowed, "Hey!"

Heavy, uncoordinated footsteps pounded up behind us, and it sounded like someone swung a baseball bat against a wall. We heard a heavy *thunk* and then the sound of breaking plaster.

"That's your head!" one guy shouted. "We're gonna bust you up!"

At the top of the stairs, I darted to the right, the way we had come in. I was past several rooms when I realized Fang wasn't with me. I skidded to a halt and spotted him at the other end of the hallway.

I motioned to Fang, but just as he started toward me,

the two crackhead squatters lurched into the hall between us.

One of them slapped the bat against his open palm with chilling smacking sounds. The other held a broken bottle.

"So," one growled. "You think you can pop our crib?"

Pop their crib? Come again?

They stopped for a moment, then their smiles grew wider. Grosser.

"It's a chick, man!" one exclaimed.

The bottle-holding slug pulled a wicked-looking knife out of his belt. He held it up so it caught the moonlight.

Fang? You go ahead and make your move. Any time now, I thought tensely. *Where are you, Fang?*

"We don't care whose chick you are," one said. "For the next hour, you're gonna be *our* chick." The guys were totally scuzzy, grinning horribly, showing holes where teeth should be.

"Excuse me?" I said acidly. "Can we say sexist?"

They didn't have time.

"Boys, God doesn't like you," Fang intoned behind them.

Whaaaaat? I thought, dumbfounded.

"Wha!" they said, whirling.

At that moment, Fang snapped out his huge wings and shone the penlight under his chin so it raked his cheekbones and eyes. My mouth dropped open: He looked like the angel of death.

His dark wings filled the hallway almost to the ceiling, and he moved them up and down. "God doesn't like bad people," he said, using a really weird, deep voice.

"What the hell," one of the squatters muttered shallowly, his mouth slack, his eyes bugging out of his head. "I'm trippin'."

"I see it too," whispered the other one. "We're both trippin'."

I whipped my own wings open — impressive as all get-out. Fun, anyway.

"This was a test," I said, using my best spooky voice. "And guess what? You both failed."

The bums stopped dead, looks of horror and amazement on their faces.

Then Fang growled, *"Rowr!"* He stepped forward, sweeping his wings up and down: the avenging demon. I almost cracked up.

"Rowr!" I said myself, shaking my wings out.

"Ahhh!" the guys yelled, backpedaling fast. Unfortunately, they were standing at the top of the staircase. They fell awkwardly, trying to grab each other, and rolled down two flights like lumpy bags of potatoes, shrieking the whole way.

Fang and I slapped each other a quick high five — and we were out of there, jack.

And then my Voice was in my head. *So glad you're having fun, Maximum. While the world burns.*

29

I'll say this for the world, and civilization: The whole hot-shower thing totally worked for me.

Reluctantly, I turned off the water and got out, then wrapped myself in my own personal towel, Dove fresh. On the other hand, civilization had its own quirky demands: remembering to brush your hair, wearing different clothes every day — details I wasn't used to.

But I was dealing.

"Max?" Iggy knocked on the door. "Can I come in? I just have to brush my teeth."

"No — I'm in a towel," I called back.

"I'm *blind,*" he said impatiently.

"No! You're kidding! Are you sure?" I grabbed my comb and rubbed a hole in the fogged-up mirror — then stifled a shriek. Eraser Max was back.

"Very funny," said Iggy. "Well, don't take forever. Primping's not going to do much for you, anyway."

I still hadn't taken a breath by the time I heard his footsteps reach the end of the hall.

Swallowing hard, I reached up with trembling fingers and touched my cheek. It was smooth skin. The mirror showed a hairy paw with ragged claws, caressing my muzzle.

"How is this happening?" I whispered, terrified.

Eraser Max smiled at me. "But we're not so different," it said. "Everything is connected. I'm part of you. You're part of me. We can help each other."

"You're not part of me," I whispered. "I could never be like you."

"Max, Max," Eraser Max said soothingly. "You already are."

I whirled away from the mirror and burst out of the bathroom. Quickly I went to my room and shut the door, before anyone could see me.

I sat on my bed, shaking, and kept touching my face over and over to make sure I was still me. "Am I really, finally going crazy?" I murmured.

30

A little tap on my door made me jump, every muscle bunched with fear. It had to be Iggy. “I’m out of the bathroom,” I called, hearing my voice shake a little.

“Yeah,” Fang said. “I can tell, ’cause your voice is coming from in there.”

“What do you want?”

“Can I come in?”

“No!”

So of course the door opened. Fang leaned in the doorway. He saw how I looked, pale and big-eyed and freaked. Compulsively I touched my face, looked down at my hands. Still covered with plain skin.

One of his dark eyebrows rose, and he came in and closed the door. “What’s going on?” he asked.

“I don’t know,” I whispered. “Something’s wrong with me, but I don’t know what.”

Fang waited for a moment, then sat next to me on the bed and put his arm gently across my shoulders. I was all huddled up, damp in my towel, feeling miserable and more scared than I'd been in — days.

"You'll be okay," he said.

"How do *you* know?"

"Because I know everything, as I keep reminding you."

I was too miserable to smile.

"Look," he said. "Whatever this is, we'll deal with it. We always have before."

I swallowed. I was dying to tell him about Eraser Max but was too afraid and ashamed.

"Fang — if I'm changing, if I'm turning into something . . . bad — will you deal with it?"

He was silent, his eyes on me.

I took a deep breath. "If I turn into an Eraser," I said more strongly, "will you deal with it? To protect the others?"

Our eyes met for a long time. He knew what I was asking him. If I turned into an Eraser, it would be his job to kill me.

He looked down at his feet, then up at me. "Yes. I'll do what has to be done."

I breathed out in relief. "Thank you," I said quietly.

Fang stood up and squeezed my shoulder. "You'll be okay," he said again. He leaned down and quickly kissed my forehead. "I promise."

Then he was gone, and I was more confused than ever.

31

"Bombs away!" the Gasman yelled, right over my head.

I looked up, startled, and saw Gazzy flying low over the pond. He tucked his wings in, curled into a ball, and dropped, cackling maniacally. I winced as he crashed into the water, sending up a huge craterlike wave.

Soon his blond head surfaced, a smile splitting his face. "Did you see that?" he crowed. "That was so awesome! I'm going to do it again!"

"Okay," I said, grinning. "Don't hurt yourself."

"And don't hurt *me!*" Nudge yelled, as Gazzy clambered out of the water. "Watch where you drop! You almost landed on me!"

"Sorry," Gazzy said.

I was glad that he and Nudge weren't letting their disappointment get to them too much. Fang and I had told them about our fruitless search for our parents in the city. It had been one more false lead.

I typed in another command and shielded the screen so I could read it. Yes, this was the ticket, going wi-fi out by the private pond. I'd pulled over an Adirondack chair and borrowed Anne's laptop, and I had lemonade close at hand. It was a tough life, but someone had to live it.

The search results popped up on the screen. I scanned them and frowned.

Ten kids had gone missing in the DC area in the last four months. Had whitecoats taken them, as fodder for their experiments? I could only imagine what the families were going through. What had happened when we had gone missing? Our parents had cared, hadn't they? They'd missed us, right?

Hmm. That was a thought. I typed in a new Google search.

Angel's head popped out of the water. "Max!" She'd been under about ten minutes. Even though I knew about her ability to breathe under water, it still took all my self-control not to leap in after her when I didn't see her come up for a while.

"Yeah, sweetie?"

"What's the best way to catch a fish?"

I thought. "Well, I guess it depends on the kind of fish," I began.

"No, what's the best way to catch a fish?" Angel asked again.

Oh. "I don't know?" I said warily.

"Have someone throw it to you!" Angel laughed, I groaned, and, next to me, Total chuckled.

"Good one," he said, and I rolled my eyes, looking around for the voice-throwing Gasman.

Uh, but Gazzy was fifty feet in the air, dive-bombing the pond again.

Total trotted off, sniffing for rabbits, and I looked at Angel.

"Angel?"

"Yeah?" She looked up, all blue-eyed innocence.

I felt stupid, but . . . "Can Total, um, talk?"

"Uh-huh," Angel said casually, squeezing water out of her hair.

I stared at her. "He *talks*. Total talks, and you didn't tell me?"

"Well . . ." Angel looked for him, saw he was pretty far away, and lowered her voice. "Don't tell him I said this, but he's actually not that interesting."

I was nonplussed. My mouth was hanging open, and I shut it before I started catching flies. I turned to see the small dog trotting among the cattails and daylilies.

"Total?" I called. He looked up alertly, then ran over to me, small pink tongue hanging out.

"Total?" I said when he was close. "Can you talk?"

He flopped down on the grass, panting slightly. "Yeah. So?"

Jeezum. I mean, mutant weirdos are nothing new to me, you know? But a talking dog?

"Why didn't you mention this before?" I asked him.

"It's not like I lied about it," said Total, reaching up with a hind leg to scratch behind one ear. "Between you and me, I'm still trying to get used to the whole flying-kid thing."

32

That night I was lying awake in “my” bed, watching the moonlight create shadows on “my” walls, so I heard the door open almost silently.

“Max?” Angel’s whisper barely disturbed the air.

I sat up. “Yeah, sweetie?”

“I can’t sleep. Can I go fly around?” she asked.

I glanced at the clock. Almost midnight. The house was quiet and still. Except for the soft footsteps padding down the hall.

The Gasman put his head around my door.

“Max? I can’t sleep.”

“Okay, put your clothes on. Let’s go take advantage of the wide-open spaces.”

In the end we all went, including Total.

“I love flying!” he said, leaping into Iggy’s arms. “Just don’t drop me.”

It was glorious. Out here in the country, there were few lights, no planes, and, so far, no Erasers.

The air was crisp and cool, near forty degrees, and felt

like liquid oxygen in our lungs. I swooped in huge arcs, catching wind currents, coasting, feeling almost weightless. It was times like this that I felt the most calm, the most normal. As if I were just a normal part of the world and I actually fit into it.

You do fit into it, Max, said the Voice. *You're part of everything, and everything is part of you. Everything should flow together. The more you resist, the more pain you'll feel. The more you go with the flow, the more whole you'll be.*

I frowned. Was that a bumper sticker?

Don't resist the flow, Max, said the Voice. *Become one with the flow.*

Well, since I didn't have a single freaking clue about what *that* meant, I decided to go with the airflow right now and enjoy myself.

"Look, bats!" said Nudge.

33

As soon as I looked, I saw them, hundreds, if not thousands, of fluttering bats. They swept jerkily among the trees, odd little black quotation marks against the deep purple night sky. We'd flown with hawks before, but not bats.

"Hey, they're mammals, like we are," I said. Were they more like us than birds? Well, not the whole eating-insects thing.

"My ears hurt," Total complained.

"It's their echolocation," I heard Iggy explain. "It's way cool. Now be quiet, I'm trying to concentrate."

Total huffed and settled down.

Nudge, Angel, and I swung into a circle, each keeping one wing tip touching the others', and flew around like feathered spokes on a wheel.

Then Gazzy came up and whapped Nudge on the back with one wing. "You're it!" he cried, and darted away.

Fang was up high, doing steep circling moves, banking, practicing the techniques he'd learned from the hawks out west. It was hard to see him — except when he passed in front of the moon.

Then all at once I felt the all-too-familiar rush of heat flooding me, washing my face with fire. I began breathing fast, the adrenaline jump-starting my heart. Quickly I put my hand up to my face, hoping I didn't look like an Eraser now, in front of the others.

The next thing I knew, I was streaking into the sky like a rocket, my hair streaming in back of me, wind stinging my eyes. I was going incredibly fast, and I could hardly feel my wings moving. *Oh, my God, what is this?* I thought, seeing the earth blur beneath me.

The flock and I could keep up a steady pace of eighty miles an hour with no effort, and could sprint at a hundred and twenty. Dive-bombing, we'd hit speeds of a hundred and eighty.

I was going way faster than that now, straight out, by myself.

It so totally *rocked.*

A giddy joy rose up in me, but my laugh was snatched away, left far behind me as I shot into the night. Eventually I came back to myself, felt myself slowing.

I wasn't even breathing hard. Laughing again, I turned and headed back toward Anne's house. I figured I'd gone about . . . *thirty miles.*

The flock was where I'd left them. I saw them long before they saw me.

I slowed and coasted up to them. Five faces turned toward me, looking stunned. Six, if you count Total.

The Gasman was the first to speak. "You have warp drive," he said faintly.

"I want to ride with *you,*" Total said, trying to escape Iggy's hold.

I laughed and held my arms out, and he leaped into them. In his excitement, he licked my neck, which I could have lived without, but whatever.

"What was that, Max?" Angel asked, wide-eyed.

"I think I just developed a new skill," I said, grinning big.

34

Take! *Crack.* That! *Crack.* Max! *Crack.*

So Max could fly at the speed of light, eh? Snarling, Ari leaped forward again, smashing the bo across his opponent's back. The heavy wooden stick, taller than he and as thick around as his wrist, made a dull, sickening thud.

The Eraser dropped to the mat and lay there, groaning thinly.

"Next!" Ari growled.

Another member of his team morphed and sprang into the circle with him, his own bo at the ready. Ari went into attack mode, the blows of the heavy staff sending shock waves up his arms.

He had clocked Max at more than two hundred miles an hour. He'd also seen the delight on her face, seen her hair whipping around her head like a halo.

Jeb just kept giving the flock more gifts. And what had he given Ari? Unnatural, painful, heavy wings. He'd thought he wanted to fly, to be more like the flock. But having wings grafted onto an Eraser's body wasn't even close to what the flock had. Gall rose in Ari's throat, burning him, and with a roar, he smashed his bo down on the other Eraser's head.

He would do that to Max, he thought. She was fourteen, and he was only seven, but he was three times as big as she was. He had huge muscles and a wolf's power — a wolf's nature too.

Jeb had said it was necessary. Jeb had said to trust him. And look where that had gotten him. He had huge painful wings. And Max was still laughing at him. Well, those days were over.

Soon he would be the golden boy, and Max would be a distant memory of an experiment gone bad.

It had been approved by the higher-ups.

It was a done deal.

"Next victim!"

35

The first two addresses in Washington hadn't panned out, but Fang's map code was still the only thing we'd been able to come up with. And we *had* found that photo of the Gasman at the second address. At least, I was pretty sure it was Gazzy. So maybe it hadn't been a complete waste.

At any rate, we had two more addresses to check out. No information about me or my possible parents had turned up yet. I tried not to mind.

"Wait, Total!" I said, as I pulled on my new jacket. It had big hidden slits for my wings, and I wondered where Anne had gotten it. Bird Kids "R" Us? Total kept trying to leap into my arms, determined not to be left behind.

"Total? Maybe it would be better if you stayed home," I said, zipping up. "You know, maybe guard the house or something."

Total stood still and looked at me. "That is so condescending," he said.

Angel went and put her arms around him. "She just meant because, you know, you're so fierce and stuff, and have great hearing and those big teeth," she said soothingly.

Inwardly I rolled my eyes. "Yeah — not just because you're a dog or anything."

Total sat down, looking just as stubborn as Gazzy did sometimes. "I want to go with."

Fang smirked at me over Total's head. I breathed out heavily.

"Fine," I said tightly, and Total leaped into my arms and licked my cheek. I was gonna have to talk to him about that.

Five minutes later we were airborne and headed to DC.

"So, Angel?" I said, looking over at her. She was gliding through the night sky, her eight-foot white wings looking like a dove's. "Have you picked up anything from Anne, about anything? Anything off?"

"Not really." Angel thought. "From what I can tell, she does work for the FBI. She does care about us and wants us to be happy. She thinks the boys are slobs."

"I'm *blind,*" Iggy said irritably. "How am I supposed to make everything all tidy?"

"Yeah, because you're so handicapped," I said sarcastically. "Like — you can't build bombs or cook or win at Monopoly. You can't tell us all apart by the feel of our skin or feathers."

Gazzy giggled next to Iggy, and Iggy frowned.

I turned back to Angel. "Anything else?"

"There is something she isn't telling us," Angel said slowly. "But I don't know what it is. It's not even clear in her mind. Just something that's going to happen."

All my senses went on alert. "Like what? Is she going to turn us over to the whitecoats?"

"I'm not sure she even knows what whitecoats are," said Angel. "I don't know that it's something bad. It could be, like — she's going to take us to the circus or something."

"Wouldn't that be redundant?" Fang muttered.

"Hmm. Well," I said. "I know how easy it's been to relax there, guys. But let's try to keep on guard, okay?"

"Okay," Angel said.

"I'm chilly," said Total.

My eyes narrowed.

Angel smiled at me.

"You're wearing a fur coat," I pointed out.

"It's chilly up here."

I gritted my teeth, unzipped my coat, zipped Total into it, and tried to ignore how the boys were snickering. Total's little head peeped out at the neck of my jacket.

"Much better," he said happily.

"Yo — first address is down there," said Fang, pointing. "Showtime."

36

"Maybe her dad was a barber?" Nudge said.

I looked over at Fang. This was the address that had been closest to his name, the address where his mom had supposedly lived. We thought she'd been a single mom, a teenager, and that she'd given Fang up for adoption. But like the first two addresses, this was a bust — a barbershop in the shadow of an office building.

Fang shrugged, looking unconcerned. But I knew him, and the stiff set of his jaw.

"I'm sorry," I said softly. For just a moment, he met my gaze, and I saw his emotion. Then his eyes went flat again.

"No big. Didn't think it would add up to anything anyway," he said. "It's probably more wasting of our time, but should we check out this last one?"

"Yes," said Iggy. It was the address next to his name.

"Okay, let's go," said Fang, and he took off, not turning to see if we were following.

"He's really upset," Angel whispered to me, as Nudge and Gazzy leaped into the air.

"I know, sweetie," I whispered back.

"I don't care where I came from," Angel said earnestly, looking into my eyes. "Wherever I came from, I don't want to go back. Not if you can't come too."

I kissed her forehead. "We'll deal with that if and when it happens," I said. "But right now, let's catch up to everyone else."

"Hang on," said Total, trotting over to a fire hydrant. "Potty break."

37

"Are there apartments on top of the stores?" Iggy asked, his feelings written all over his face.

"No." I heaved a sigh. Iggy's coded address had turned out to be an Asian food store in a little strip mall.

"What's across the street?" Iggy asked.

"A used-car lot," I said. "I'm sorry, Ig."

"It's my fault, guys," said Fang. "I thought I'd cracked the code, but obviously I was totally off my gourd."

"Well, if you were wrong," Nudge said, "then we don't have to be disappointed, right? It just means we still don't know."

"Yeah, that's right, Nudge," I said, thankful that she was taking it so well.

"This sucks!" Iggy shouted suddenly, his voice echoing off the glass storefronts. He punched a telephone pole in front of him, hitting it accurately. He winced, and I saw the scraped skin and bloody knuckles.

"I'm sorry, Ig —," I began.

"I don't care if you're sorry!" Iggy shouted at me.

"Everyone's sorry! That doesn't matter! What matters is that we find where we belong!" He walked angrily away from us, his boots kicking up stones in the parking lot. "I mean, I just can't take this anymore!" he yelled, waving his arms and heading back to us. "I need some answers! We can't just keep on wandering from place to place, always on the run, always hunted. . . ." His voice broke, and we all looked at him in shock. Iggy hardly ever cried.

I went over and tried to put my arms around him, but he pushed me away.

"We *all* want answers, Iggy," I said. "We all feel lost sometimes. It's just — we have to stick together. We won't stop looking for your parents, I swear."

"It's different for you," Iggy said, his voice quieter but bitter. "You don't know what it's like. Yeah, I make jokes, I'm the blind kid — but don't you see? Every time we move on, I'm lost all over again. You guys — it's so much easier for you. Even your lost isn't as bad as *my* lost, you know?"

I'd never heard Iggy admit to feeling scared or vulnerable.

"We're your eyes, Iggy," said the Gasman, sounding small and anxious. "You don't need to see when you've got us."

"Yeah, but I won't always *have* you!" Iggy said, his voice rising till he was shouting again. "What happens if you get killed? Of course I need to see, you idiot! I *remember* seeing! I know what it's like! I don't have it anymore, and I won't ever have it again. And someday I'm going to lose you, lose all of you — and when that happens, I'll lose . . . myself."

His face was contorted with rage, and he swept one

hand down and picked up a chunk of asphalt. Whirling, he threw it hard against a storefront, where it shattered a big plate-glass window. Immediately alarms went off.

"Uh-oh," Iggy muttered.

"Let's split," Fang said. Angel, the Gasman, and Nudge took off. Total jumped up into my arms, and I zipped him into my jacket.

"No," said Iggy, and I skidded to a halt.

"What? Come on, Iggy," I said. "The alarm's going off."

"I know. I'm not *deaf* too," Iggy said bitterly. "I don't care. Let them find me, take me now. It doesn't matter. Nothing matters."

And, to my horror, he sat down on the curb. I heard police car sirens wailing toward us.

"Iggy, let's *go,* get *up,*" Fang said.

"Give me one good reason," Iggy said, dropping his head into his hands.

I tossed Total to Fang, and the dog yipped, startled, as Fang grabbed him. "You guys go," I ordered.

Fang took off, but the flock stayed nearby, hovering. The police sirens were getting closer.

I leaned down. "Listen, Iggy," I said tensely. "I'm sorry about tonight. I know how disappointed you are. We're all disappointed. And I'm sorry you're blind. I remember when you weren't, and I can't even imagine what it's like to lose that. I'm sorry we're mutant bird kids, I'm sorry we don't have parents, I'm sorry we have Erasers and people trying to kill us all the time.

"But if you think I'm going to let you give up on us now, you've got another think coming. Yes, you're a blind mutant freak, but you're *my* blind mutant freak, and you're coming with me, *now,* you're coming with *us* right *now,* or I swear I will kick your skinny white ass from here to the middle of next week."

Iggy raised his head. Flashes of light told me the cops were almost on top of us.

"Iggy, I *need* you," I said urgently. "I *love* you. I need *all* of you, all five of you, to feel whole myself. Now get up, before I kill you."

Iggy stood. "Well, when you put it that way . . ."

I grabbed his hand and we ran around to the back of the mall, then took off fast, racing toward the shadows at the edge of the parking lot. We stayed high, looking down to see two squad cars zoom into the lot.

We turned and headed toward Anne's house, and I made sure the tips of my wing feathers brushed against Iggy's on every downstroke.

"*We're* your family," I told him. "We'll always be your family."

"I know." He sniffled and rubbed his sleeve across his sightless eyes.

"Let's go *fast,*" Total said.

38

"What is *this?*" I said without thinking. "I mean — looks good. Smells good." I sat down at the table and held my plate out. "Is that broccoli? Yum."

Anne put a big spoonful of some casseroley-type stuff on my plate. I could identify peas and a possible carrot and something brownish that was probably of the meat persuasion.

I picked up my fork and put a smile on my face. "Thanks for making dinner, Anne," I said, taking a bite.

"Uh-huh," she said, giving me a wry look. "At least I made a lot of it. I'm learning."

"It's fine," I said with my mouth full. I waved my fork in the air. "'S great."

Fang passed Iggy his plate and tapped the table by his fork. Unerringly Iggy picked up his fork and started eating. I'd kept my eye on him since last night, but he'd been pretty okay today. At least, he hadn't blown anything up or set anything on fire, so that was good.

All of us cleaned our plates. Twice. We'd gone hungry too many times to be picky eaters.

Then, to add to the American domesticity of the scene, Anne brought out an apple pie.

"I *love* apple pie!" Nudge said excitedly.

"Do you have two of them?" Gazzy looked anxious, already mentally dividing it.

Anne brought over another one. "I told you, I'm learning."

Gazzy punched the air. "Yes!"

"I'd like to talk to you guys," Anne said, dishing up the pie. "Sort of a family meeting."

I kept my face blank, wondering whose family she thought she was talking about.

"You've all done beautifully here," she said, sitting back in her chair. "You've adjusted better than I thought possible. And I find I'm enjoying it more than I ever imagined."

I started to get a really bad feeling. *Please don't let her say something horrible,* like she wanted to adopt us or something. I had no idea what I would do if that happened.

"I think we're ready to take the next step," she went on, looking around the table at us.

Please no please no please no —

"So I've enrolled you in school."

Whaaat?

Fang burst out laughing. "Whoa, you had us going there for a minute," he said.

"I'm not kidding, Nick," Anne said quietly. "There's an excellent school nearby. It would be perfectly safe. You could meet other people your age, interact with them. And — let's face it: Your education has been spotty at best."

Or nonexistent at worst, I thought.

"School?" Nudge asked. "You mean, like, at a *school?*"

There was that word again.

"Going to a real school, with other people?" Angel looked concerned.

"Holy frijoles," Total muttered from under the table.

"You'll start on Monday," Anne said briskly, starting to gather empty plates. "I'll pick up your uniforms tomorrow."

Uniforms?

39

Without a word, I shoved my chair away from the table and stomped over to the back door. I yanked it open and jumped down the steps.

From there I did a running takeoff, snapping out my wings, feeling them push against the air filling my feathers. A couple of hard strokes and I was airborne, rising above the apple orchards, above the barn.

Once I was up high, I let the full range of my anger bloom. Taking a deep breath, I tried to remember how to fly really fast — and then, almost immediately, I was doing it, my wings seeming to move by themselves.

Let's see just how fast I can get out of here, I thought grimly, and poured on the speed.

Running away never helps, said the Voice in my head.

"Yeah, well, *flying* helps — a lot!"

Fang was waiting for me by an open window when I got back. He handed me a glass of water, and I sucked it down.

"Gone a long time," he said. "How far did you get? Botswana?"

I grinned wryly. "Just for a minute, before I had to turn around. They say hi."

"How fast do you think you go?"

"Over two hundred," I said. "Two twenty? Two forty?"

He nodded.

"Everything cool here?" I headed down the hall to my room, kicking off my shoes. The house was dark and quiet. My clock said one-thirty.

"Yeah. Wrangled Gazzy into the bath. Total fell in. Angel made Nudge change her mind about what book to read, and I came down on her."

I looked at him. "Sounds like you've got everything under control."

"I managed."

I sat on my bed, not knowing what to say.

Fang sat down next to me. "Did you want to just keep going out there?" he asked. "Keep going and not come back?"

I drew a shaky breath. "Yes," I whispered.

"Anne's never gonna take your place, Max," Fang said, his dark eyes on me.

I shrugged, not looking at him.

"Anne's just a — depot," he said. He seemed to be getting more, well, comfortable with me lately. "We can rest up, eat, hang out, while we plan our next move. The kids know that. Yeah, they like not having to run or sleep in subway tunnels. They like having the same bed every night. So do I. So do you. Anne's been nice to them, to us, and they like it. We don't get a lot of down days, where we can just chill. They're enjoying the heck out of this, Max. And if they weren't, it would mean they were so messed up they couldn't be saved, ever."

"I know," I whispered.

"But they know who's saved their bacon too many times to count. Who's fed them and clothed them and chased away the nightmares. Jeb may have gotten us out of our cages, but *you're* the one who's *kept* us out, Max."

PART 3

BACK TO SCHOOL (THE NORMAL KIND)

40

You know how some kids get excited about the first day of school and have an outfit all picked out and a new lunchbox and stuff? Well, they're bleeping idiots.

"Can we play hooky?" Iggy muttered as he scrambled eggs.

"Somehow I suspect they're picky about that," I said, dropping more bread into the toaster. "I bet they'd call Anne."

"I look like prep school Barbie," Nudge complained, as she entered the kitchen. She caught sight of me in my uniform and looked mollified. "Actually, *you* look like prep school Barbie. I'm just Barbie's *friend*."

I narrowed my eyes at her.

Our wings were retractable and pulled in pretty tightly to our backs, but you might say that we still looked kind of like a family of Olympic swimmers.

Angel arrived, and she looked cute in her plaid skirt and white blouse because she looks cute in anything. She put some eggs and bacon on a plate, then ripped up a piece of toast and set it on the table.

Total hopped up onto a stool and dug in, seeming almost doglike. "Woof!" he said, and chuckled to himself.

"Angel?" I said, bringing her a cup of coffee. I lowered my voice. "No funny business with the teachers, *comprende?*"

She glanced up innocently. "Gotcha," she said, taking a bite of bacon. I looked at her and waited. "I mean, unless I really have to," she added.

"Angel, please," I said, kneeling to her level. "Nothing that makes us stick out or look different, okay? Play by their rules." I stood up and addressed everyone. "That goes for all of us," I said quietly. "Try to blend, people. Don't give anyone ammo to use against us."

I got okays with various levels of enthusiasm.

"Goodness — you're all up," said Anne, coming into the kitchen.

She surveyed the production line of food, the flock packing it away. She smiled ruefully. "This beats frozen waffles. Thanks, Jeff. Oh, and Jeff — I meant to tell you. You and Nick will be in the same class. It'll help you get your bearings."

Iggy's face flushed.

"Can Total come?" Angel asked.

Anne came over and straightened Angel's collar. "Nope." She walked over to the cabinet and took down a mug.

"I'll be fine. Chase some ducks or something," Total whispered, and Angel patted his head.

"This uniform is so uncool," said Nudge.

"I know. Fortunately you'll be surrounded by a whole

bunch of other uncool uniforms," Anne said. She frowned. "Ariel, are you drinking coffee?"

"Uh-huh," said Angel, taking a big sip. "Get jump-started for first grade."

I felt Total's black eyes boring holes in me. Sighing, I got down a bowl and fixed him some coffee with milk and two sugars. He lapped it up happily.

Anne looked as if she was having some "pick your battles" thoughts and in the end decided to let it go.

"Okay," she said, putting her mug in the sink. "I'll bring the car around front. Wear jackets — it's chilly this morning."

41

The ride to school was short and silent — much as I imagine riding in a hearse would be.

When we pulled up to the building, I realized we'd seen it from the air. It looked like a great big private house, made of cream-colored stone. Ivy grew up one wall, and they'd let an OCD gardener have his way with the grounds. Extremely tidy.

Anne pulled into the drop-off line.

"Okay, kids," she said. "They're expecting you. All the paperwork is done." She looked back at us, sitting tensely in the rear seats. My stomach hurt from nerves, and I was pulling my wings in so tight that they ached.

"I know it seems scary," she went on gently. "But it'll really be okay. Please just give it a chance. And I'll have a treat waiting for you at home this afternoon. We clear on how you'll get home?"

I nodded, feeling as tight as a coiled spring. How about by way of Bermuda?

"It's about a ten-minute *walk,*" Anne confirmed. "And

here we are." She pulled up to the curb, and we piled out of the car. I took a deep breath, looking at the poor lemmings filing in through the big double doors.

"Here we go," lemming Max muttered, then I took Nudge's and Angel's hands as we walked into the school.

42

"Okay, they're here," Ari said into the mike clipped onto his collar. He refocused his Zeiss binoculars, but the hated mutants were already out of sight, inside the building.

He'd have to switch to the thermal sensor, one of his favorite toys. He pulled the headpiece on and slid the lenses over his eyes. Inside the school was a wash of red: warm human bodies streaming through the halls.

"There," he breathed, as six orangey yellow images emerged from the red river. He grinned. The bird kids ran hotter than humans, hotter than Erasers. They were easy to pick out.

"Wanna see?" Ari pulled off the headpiece and handed it to the person sitting next to him. She put it on, smoothing her hair under its straps.

"Cool," she said. "Did you check out those goofy uniforms? Jeez. I'm not gonna have to wear one, am I?"

"Maybe. How do the freaks seem to you?" Ari asked her, as she continued to watch them.

The girl shrugged, her hair brushing her shoulders. "They don't suspect a thing. Of course, this is just the beginning, really."

Ari grinned, revealing his canines. "The beginning of the *end,*" he said, and she grinned back. They slapped high fives, the sound like a rifle shot in the quiet woods.

"Yep. It's gonna be great," said Max II, and she popped a piece of gum into her mouth. "Now everything gets *doubly* interesting."

43

The distinct lack of an antiseptic smell was slightly encouraging, I decided. And the interior of this school looked nothing like the School, our former prison.

"Zephyr, is it?" A tweedy, teachery woman smiled uncertainly at us. She said her name was Ms. Cvelbar.

"Yeah?" said Gazzy. "That's me."

The teacher's smile grew. "Zephyr, you're with me," she said, holding out her hand. "Come along, dear."

I nodded briefly at Gazzy, and he went with the woman. He knew what to do: memorize escape routes, gauge how many people there were, how big they were, how well they'd be likely to fight. If he got the signal, he could burst through a window and be out of here in about four seconds flat.

"At least he's not Captain Terror anymore," I murmured to Fang.

"Yeah, *Zephyr*'s a big improvement," Fang said.

"Nick? And Jeff? I'm Mrs. Cheatham. Welcome to our

school. Come with me and I'll show you your classroom," another teacher chirped.

I tapped the back of Iggy's hand twice. Watching him and Fang go down the hall was really hard. Teachers came for Angel and Nudge, and then it was just me, fighting my overwhelming instinct to get out of there.

The teachers seemed okay. They hadn't really looked like possible Erasers — too old, not muscled enough. Erasers hardly ever made it past five, six years old, so when they weren't morphed, they looked like models in their early twenties.

"Max? I'm Ms. Segerdahl. You're in my class."

She looked fairly acceptable. Harmless? Whatever. Probably couldn't conceal many weapons under her skirt and sweater.

I managed a smile, and she smiled back. And our school day had begun.

44

"Now, does anyone remember this area's name?"

Angel raised her hand. She figured it was time to sound smart.

"Yes, Ariel?"

"It's the Yucatán. Part of Mexico."

"Very good. Do you know anything about the Yucatán?" Ms. Solowski asked.

"It has Cancún, a popular vacation spot," said Angel. "And Mayan ruins. And it's close to Belize. Its ports are some of the closest to America. So it's convenient for drug runners to siphon drugs up from South America, through the ports, and then on into Texas, Louisiana, and Florida."

Her teacher blinked. Her mouth opened and then closed again. "Ah, yes," she said faintly, stepping back to the world map hanging in front of the whiteboard. She cleared her throat. "Let's talk about the Mayan ruins."

* * *

"Tiffany."

"Tiffany?" The teacher looked confused. "I thought your name was Krystal."

"Uh-huh. Tiffany-Krystal." Nudge made a hyphen in the air with one finger.

"Okay, Tiffany-Krystal. In language arts we've been working on some cross-media spelling words." The teacher pointed to a list written on the whiteboard at the front of the class. "Those were last week's. This morning I'm going to give a pop quiz about this week's words, just to see where everyone is and where we need to focus."

"Well, all right," said Nudge agreeably. She waved a hand. "Bring it on. But just so you know, I can't spell worth crap."

"Do you know where the dictionary is?"

Fang looked at the girl who had spoken. "What?"

"Our reference materials are over here," the girl said, pointing. "When we have free study time, you can walk around and do homework. If you need to look up stuff, the computers and other references are over here."

"Oh. Okay. Thanks."

"No problem." The girl swallowed and stepped closer. She was shorter than Max and had long, dark red hair. Her eyes were bright green, and her nose had freckles.

"I'm Lissa," she said. "And you're Nick, right?"

What did she want? He looked at her. "Uh-huh," he said warily.

"I'm glad you're in our class."

"What? Why?"

She stepped still closer, and he could smell the lavender

scent of soap. Giving him a flirtatious smile, she said, "Why do you think?"

"Watch this! I'm gonna fly!"

The Gasman looked up with interest. Some spud from his class was balanced precariously on the top of the metal jungle gym, holding out his arms like wings.

I hope he's got more than arms, the Gasman thought. Well, maybe he *did* have wings. After all, maybe there were more kids like them out in the world. No way to tell. That was one of the mysteries to be solved.

"Yeah?" he said, shielding his eyes from the sun. "Let's see it."

The kid looked a bit taken aback, then set his jaw. He crouched down a bit and jumped off the top of the play structure.

He couldn't fly worth a nickel, hitting the ground almost instantly, landing in an awkward, crumpled heap. There was a stunned silence, and then he started wailing. "My arm!" he sobbed.

Immediately the playground supervisor hurried over, gathered up the kid, and rushed him toward the nurse's office. Gazzy went back to making a nice collection of hefty rocks. Weapons, if he needed them.

"What'd you do that for?" someone asked belligerently.

Gazzy looked up. "What?"

A larger kid was leaning over him angrily. "Listen, spaz, when some wingnut says he's gonna fly off of something, you tell 'im, 'Get the heck down from there!' You don't say, 'Let's see it!' What's the matter with you?"

The Gasman shrugged, but he was actually a little hurt inside. "I didn't know."

The kid stared at him. "What, you grow up under a rock?"

"No," said Gazzy, frowning. "I just didn't know."

The kid made a disgusted face and walked away. Gazzy heard him saying, "Yeah, he didn't know. 'Cause he's from the planet Dumbass."

Gazzy's eyes narrowed, and his hands formed into lethal little fists.

"Where did you get your hair done?" someone asked.

I turned to see a pale, skinny girl smiling at me. I pushed my lunch tray farther down the line. "Um, my bathroom?" Was she speaking in code? I had no clue what she meant. A recurring theme in my life.

She laughed and put a green apple on her tray. "No, I meant the blond streaks. They're awesome. Did you have it done in DC?"

Oh. My hair had blond streaks? Right. "I guess the sun did it," I said lamely.

"Lucky. Oh, look — banana pudding. I recommend it."

"Thanks." I took some, to be nice.

"My name's J.J.," she said, seeming completely comfortable with this social interaction. My palms were sweating. "It's short for Jennifer Joy. I mean, what were my parents *thinking?*"

I laughed, surprised that she would confide in me like that.

"Max is a cool name," J.J. said. "Sporty. Sophisticated."

"Yeah, that's me," I said, and she laughed some more, her eyes crinkling.

"Here's a couple spots," J.J. said, pointing to an empty lunch table. "Otherwise we'll have to sit next to Chari and her gang." She lowered her voice. "Don't mess with them."

I was halfway through lunch before I realized that J.J. and I had been talking for half an hour, and I apparently had not seemed so freakish that she'd run away screaming.

I had made a friend. My second one in fourteen years. I was on a roll.

45

"Capital of Paraguay?" the teacher asked.

Asunción. Inhabited principally by the Guarani. Explored by Europeans starting in 1518. Paraguay is a landlocked country in South America. Population, six million and change — I raised my hand. "Asunción?"

"Yes, that's right. Very good. Tonight I want you all to read about Paraguay in chapter eight of your world studies textbook. And now let's take out our science workbooks."

Feeling like a busy little student bee, I took out my science workbook. What further surprises would the Voice have for me? So far, it had been up on any number of subjects taught in the ninth grade. How handy. For once.

As I flipped past the bone structure of frogs, someone knocked on the classroom door. The teacher went over and had a whispered conversation, then turned to me. *What?*

"Max? They need you in the office for a moment." She gave me an encouraging smile, which somehow I didn't find all that encouraging.

Slowly I stood up and walked to the door. Was this it? Was it starting now? Was this person about to turn into an Eraser? My breath started to come faster, and my hands coiled at my sides.

Maybe not. Maybe there was something wrong with our paperwork. Something normal.

"In here." The assistant opened a door that led to a small anteroom. On two chairs in the little room were Iggy and the Gasman. Gazzy looked up at me and smiled nervously.

Oh, no. "Already?" I whispered to him, and he shrugged, wide-eyed.

"The headmaster will see you now," said the assistant, opening another door. "That's *right now.*"

46

The headmaster, William Pruitt, according to a gold plaque on his desk, did *not* look happy to see us. In fact, he looked like he was about to blow his top. The second I clapped eyes on him, I couldn't help it: I hated his guts. His face was red and flushed with anger. His lips were full and wet- looking, a gross dark pink. Sparse tufts of hair ringed his shiny bald head.

I had the sinking feeling that this schmuck's inside was going to match his heinous outside, and I went on full alert.

"You are Maxine Ride?" he said with a sneering British accent that made the hairs on the back of my neck rise.

"Just Max," I said, resisting the urge to cross my arms over my chest and scowl at him.

"These are your brothers Jeff and . . ." He consulted his notes. "Zephyr?"

"Yes."

"Your brothers have set off a stink bomb in the

second-floor boys' lavatory," said the headmaster. He sat back in his chair, lacing his beefy red fingers, and stared at me with cold, piggy black eyes.

I blinked, careful not to look at Iggy and Gazzy. "That's impossible," I said calmly. For one thing, they hadn't had enough time to acquire the materials to make one. . . .

"Oh, is it?" Pruitt asked unpleasantly. "Why is that?"

"They're not troublemakers," I replied, injecting an earnest note into my voice. "They wouldn't do anything like that."

"They say they didn't do it. They're lying," he said flatly. His bushy eyebrows needed trimming. And the nose hair — yuck!

I looked indignant. "My brothers don't lie!" Of course, we all lie like rugs when we have to, but I wasn't going to tell him that.

"All children lie." Mr. Pruitt sneered. "Children are born knowing how to lie. They're dishonest, disrespectful, unhousebroken animals. Until we get to them."

Which made me question his career choice. *Nice school you picked out, Anne.* Sheesh.

I raised my chin. "Not my brothers. Our parents are missionaries, doing the Lord's work. We would never lie."

This seemed to give Mr. Pruitt pause, and again I congratulated myself on the brilliant backstory I'd given us. "Did anyone *see* them set off a stink bomb?"

"What *is* a stink bomb, anyway?" Gazzy asked, all blue eyes and innocence.

"There, you see?" I said. "They don't even know what one is."

Pruitt's small eyes narrowed even more. "You're not fooling me," he said with clear venom. "I know your brothers are guilty. I know you're protecting them. And I know something else: This is the last time you'll get away with anything at this school. Do I make myself clear?"

Actually, not really, but I was going to let it slide.

"Yes," I said crisply, and motioned to Gazzy to get up. When Iggy heard him, he rose also. I moved purposefully toward the door. "Thank you," I said, right before we slipped out.

We slunk out into the hall, and I started marching them to their classrooms.

"We're going to talk about this later, guys," I said under my breath.

After I dropped off Iggy, I realized I had a throbbing headache. One that seemed to have been caused by regular garden-variety tension, rather than by, say, a chip, or a Voice, or some wack-job whitecoat torturing me. What a nice change.

47

"You ignorant little *sah-vages,*" Gazzy said, puffing and screwing up his face. As usual, his imitation was uncanny. I almost wanted to turn around to make sure the headmaster hadn't snuck up behind us.

Angel and Nudge were cracking up at Gazzy's recounting of the tale.

"You malignant little *fiends,*" he added, and I couldn't help laughing.

"But sir," Gazzy went on in my voice, "our parents are missionaries. Lying is the Tenth Commandment. They're *innocent* of all wrongdoing. What's a stink bomb?"

Now even Fang was laughing, his shoulders shaking. In his white dress shirt he hardly even looked like himself.

"Is lying really the Tenth Commandment?" Iggy asked.

"No idea," I said. "Let's cut into the woods. This road's making me nervous."

We'd walked along the main road until we were out of sight of the school. Now we headed into the woods at an angle, knowing we would meet up with one of Anne's orchards soon.

"So who really did set off the stink bomb?" Nudge asked.

I rolled my eyes. "They did, of course." I glared at Gazzy, frustrated that my look was lost on Iggy. "I don't know how, I don't know why. I just know they did."

"Well, yes," Gazzy admitted, looking a tiny bit embarrassed. "This kid was a total jerk to me on the playground, and someone stuck a Kick Me sign on the back of Iggy's shirt."

"I told you I'd take care of that," Fang said to Iggy.

I sighed. "Guys, you're going to meet jerks in every situation. For the rest of your lives." However long that would be. "But you can't be doing stuff like stink bombs — not right now. We're trying to blend, remember? We're trying to not make waves, to not stick out. So making a stink bomb, setting it off, and getting caught was *not* the right way to go."

"Sorry, Max," said Gazzy, sounding almost sincere.

Inside, I understood why they'd done it. I even wished I'd been able to see the headhunter's face when he'd found out about it. But this stunt had been totally uncool. And dangerous.

"Listen, you two," I said sternly, as we crested a ridge and found ourselves at the edge of Anne's property. "You put us all at risk. From now on you're going to toe the line at that stupid school or you're going to answer to me. Got it?"

"Got it," Gazzy mumbled.

"Yeah, got it," Iggy said reluctantly. "We'll be more stupid and idiotic in the future. We'll blend."

"Good."

48

Anne was not thrilled with us when we got home.

"I got a phone call" were her first words as we hung our jackets up neatly in the hall. "I guess you're all adjusting. Well, anyway. Come on into the kitchen. There's hot chocolate and cookies."

Way to reward the buggers, Anne. Great mothering. I took the opportunity to give Gazzy another glare, and his small shoulders hunched.

"Let me just say that I'm very disappointed in your behavior," Anne said, as she started pouring mugs of hot chocolate. She plopped two marshmallows in mine, and I tried not to think about the time Jeb had done the same thing for me, not too long ago.

She opened a package of chocolate-chip cookies and put them on a plate on the table. We all dug in — lunch had been hours before, and we'd had only normal-sized meals.

"I could show you how to make cookies from scratch," I said, then blinked in surprise. Had those words really left my mouth? Everyone else looked surprised too, and I felt defensive. So, what, I was never nice to Anne?

"There's a recipe on the back of the chip package," I mumbled, taking another cookie.

"I'd like that, Max. Thanks," said Anne, her voice softer. She gave me a pleasant smile, then went to the sink.

"Stink bomb," Total chortled, in between bites of cookie. "That must've been great."

49

No. The bigger playground. Angel looked into her teacher's eyes and pushed the thought at her gently. They were supposed to go to the younger kids' playground at recess, but Angel wanted more room. There was no reason they shouldn't play on the big field.

"I guess there's no reason you can't play on the big field," Angel's teacher said slowly.

"Yes!" said one of Angel's classmates, and they turned and ran through the gates and onto the big playground.

"Ariel! Come play with us!"

Angel ran over and joined Meredith, Kayla, and Courtney.

"Can we play Swan Lake?" Angel asked. Their teacher had just read them that story, and Angel had loved it. Her whole life was like Swan Lake. She was a swan. Fang and Max were hawks, kind of big and fierce. Iggy was a big white seabird, like an albatross or something. Nudge was a little pheasant, smooth and brown and beautiful. Gazzy was something sturdy — an owl?

And she was a swan. At least for today.

"Yeah! Let's play Swan Lake!"

"I'm Odette," Angel called, holding up her hand.

"I'm the second swan," said Kayla.

"I'm the littlest swan," said Meredith, holding out her uniform skirt to make it more tutulike.

Angel closed her eyes and tried to feel like a swan. When she opened them, the whole world was her stage, and she was the most beautiful ballerina-swan ever. Gently she ran in graceful circles around the other kids. She took big, soft running leaps, staying in the air as long as she could. Then she landed, raised her arms over her head, and twirled in little circles.

The other girls were dancing too, tiptoeing across the browning lawn, swishing their arms in slow movements to look like wings. Again Angel tripped lightly over the grass, spinning and jumping and feeling just like Odette, cursed to live as a swan because of Rothbart's spell.

Another spin, another arabesque, another long leap where Angel seemed to hang in the air for minutes. She wished so much that she could take out her wings and really do Swan Lake the way it should have been done, but she knew she couldn't. Not now, anyway. Not here. Maybe after Max saved the world. After Max saved the world, most of the regular people would be gone. Jeb had told Angel so, when she'd been at the School again, last month. Mutants like them had a greater chance of surviving. They'd been designed to survive. So maybe when most of the regular people were gone, Angel wouldn't have to hide her wings anymore, and she could just fly around and be Odette anytime she wanted to.

She could hardly wait.

50

Study Hall was my favorite class. The school had a great library, with seemingly endless books and six computers for kids to do research on.

The school librarian was this nice, smart guy named Michael Lazzara. Everybody seemed to like Mr. Lazzara a lot, even me. So far, anyway.

Today I was in research mode. Maybe if I hit some code-breaking sites I could figure out a different approach for how to find our parents.

All six computers had kids sitting at them. I stood there a moment, wishing I could just tip a kid out of a chair.

"Here, I can get off."

I looked over at the guy who'd spoken. "What?"

The guy got up and gathered his books. "I don't need the computer. You can have it."

"Oh, okay. Thanks."

"You're new," the guy said. "You're in my Language Arts class."

"Yeah," I said. I'd recognized him — years of paranoia had honed my ability to remember faces. "I'm Max."

"I know. I'm Sam." He gave me a warm smile, and I blinked, realizing he was cute. I'd never really had the luxury of noticing cuteness or lack thereof in guys. Mostly it was the lethal/nonlethal distinction that I went with. "Where did you move from?"

"Uh . . . Missouri."

"Wow. Midwest. This must be pretty different for you."

"Yep."

"So, are you doing schoolwork or more of a personal project?" He nodded at the computer. I started to say, What's with the questions? but then I thought, *Maybe he's not interrogating me. Maybe this is how people interact, get to know each other. They exchange information.*

"Um, more of a personal project," I said.

He smiled again. "Me too. I was checking out this kayak I want to buy. I'm hoping my Christmas money will give me enough."

I smiled, trying to act as if I knew what Christmas money was. Voice? A little help here? The Voice was silent. After mentally reviewing possible responses, I went with: "Cool."

"Well, I'll let you get to it, then," he said, looking like he wanted to say something else. I waited, but he didn't — just picked up his stuff and split. I felt like a Vulcan, studying these odd, quaint humans.

Sighing, I sat down at the computer. I would never fit in. Never. Not anywhere.

51

Fang and I had checked out what we thought were the coordinates of addresses in the coded pages from the Institute. But there had been a few words too, in addition to our names. Today's mission: Google them. I typed in the first phrase, even though it looked like a typo, a pair of nonsense words: *ter Borcht.*

Something moving outdoors caught my eye, and I glanced out the window just in time to see Angel practically floating across the main playing field. She and a bunch of other girls were twirling around like ballerinas, but Angel was the only one who could leap eight feet in the air and hang there as if suspended by wires.

I gritted my teeth, watching them. What part of "blend in" did these kids not understand? For crying out loud.

A list of results popped up on my computer screen. How weird. Apparently *ter Borcht* wasn't gibberish. I clicked on the first result.

Ter Borcht, Roland. Geneticist. Medical license revoked, 2001. Imprisoned for unauthorized criminal genetic experiments on humans, 2002. A controversial figure in the field of genetic research, ter Borcht was for many years considered a genius, and the leading researcher in human genetics. However, in 2002, after being found guilty of criminal human experiments, ter Borcht was declared insane. He is currently incarcerated in the "Dangerous-Incurable" wing of a rehabilitation facility in the Netherlands.

Well, holy moly. Food for thought. I tried to remember what other words had shown up in the coded pages.

"Sit up!" a voice snapped, and I turned to see the headhunter, Mr. Pruitt, leaning over some terrified kid at a study table. The kid quickly sat up straight. In the background, Mr. Lazzara was rolling his eyes. Even he didn't seem to like Pruitt. Mr. Pruitt banged his walking stick against the table leg, making everyone jump. "This isn't your bedroom," he said snidely. "You may not lounge about like the do-nothing slug you no doubt are at home. In this school, you will sit up straight, as if you actually had a spine."

He was going on and on, but I very quietly picked up my books, slithered out of my chair, and slunk out the library's side door.

I could do without a dose of hateful today, thanks.

52

I walked down the hall as quickly as I could without making any noise.

Ter Borcht: evil genetic scientist. Gee, one of the family. Had I ever heard that name before? Clearly he must have been involved with Jeb, the School, the whitecoats, at some point. I mean, how many *independent* evil genetic researchers could there be? Surely they all kept in touch, exchanged notes, built mutants together. . . .

This was a huge breakthrough — or another horribly disappointing dead end. Whichever it was, I couldn't wait to talk to the flock about it. Just as I hurried past an empty classroom, I caught sight of Fang. Excellent — I had five minutes till my next class. I started to head in, then realized he wasn't alone. A girl was with him, talking to him, looking earnest. Fang was standing there impassively as she went on, brushing her long dark red hair over her shoulder.

I grinned. Poor Fang. Was she selling something? Asking him to join the Chess Club?

In the next moment, the girl had put both her hands on Fang's chest and pushed him against the wall. I strode forward, reaching out to yank open the door. Even if she was an Eraser, Fang and I could make mincemeat out of her.

Then I froze. It wasn't an attack. The girl had pressed herself against Fang like static cling, and she went on her tiptoes and kissed him, right on the mouth.

Fang stood there for a moment, then his hands came up, holding her around the waist. I waited for him to push her away, hoping he would be sensitive about it, not hurt her feelings.

But I watched, dumbfounded, as Fang's hands slid slowly up her back, holding the girl closer. He angled his head so they could kiss better.

I stepped back, not breathing, feeling like I was going to hurl.

Oh, God.

Spinning on my heel, I raced down the hall and into the girls' bathroom.

I locked myself in a stall and sat down on the closed seat. Cold sweat was beading on my forehead, and I felt shaky and chilled, as if I'd just fought for my life. The image of Fang holding that girl closer, tilting his head, popped up in my brain. Closing my eyes did nothing to stop it.

Okay. Get a grip. God. What are you doing?

My breaths were shallow and fast, and I felt rage roiling in my stomach like acid.

No, calm down, calm down.

I forced myself to take several deep breaths, in and out, in and out.

Okay. Just calm down. So he kissed someone. Big deal. Why should I even care anyway? Why should I even care if he kissed every girl in this whole school? He was like my — brother. I mean, he wasn't my brother, not really. But he was *like* a brother. Yes. That was it. I'd been surprised, but now I was over it. I was fine.

Standing up, I left the stall and splashed cold water on my face. I was fine. I mean, why would I even care?

Maybe you have feelings for him, said my Voice. Nooo, the Voice couldn't ever respond when I really *needed* it to. But give me a sensitive situation where I'd really rather just deal with it alone? It was all over me.

Maybe not, I thought snidely.

You can't stay children forever, said the Voice, gently mocking. *People grow up, have kids of their own. Think about it.*

I suppressed a shriek of frustration, gripping the edge of the sink hard so I wouldn't ram my head into the wall. Like I was going to think about anything else, *now.*

53

"There they are."

Ari focused the binoculars on the small group on the road, maybe a quarter mile away. Walking to their perfect home from their perfect school. Wasn't that *special.* He looked into the back of the van. Six Erasers, already morphed and eager for action, sat waiting for him to give the word. The new Max was sitting in the back with them, wearing headphones.

"She's up on her soapbox again," the new Max said.

Ari snorted. Max — the original Max — was so full of herself, so tougher-than-thou. She ran those kids around like they were her slaves.

Slaves. There was a fun idea. Picturing the mutant bird freaks as his personal slaves cheered Ari up. He would make them do everything — take care of everything. They would bring him food and remind him to take his pills, and Max would rub his shoulders where his wings hurt. That would be so great. A tiny buzzer went off —

his watch timer. Ari popped a handful of pills and reset the timer.

Unfortunately he wasn't going to get to make them his slaves. Fortunately he still got to kill them.

"I swear, that girl wouldn't be happy anywhere," the new Max said, sounding disgusted.

"Let's give her something to be unhappy about," Ari said, and hit the gas pedal. His heart started pumping with anticipation. He hated Max, but he loved fighting her. No one else was as exciting, as much of a challenge — not even Fang. And every time they fought, he learned more about how to defeat her. Someday he would have the last punch, see the surprise on her face. . . .

In seconds the van had caught up to the group, and they wheeled around at the sound of the tires.

"Want a ride, kids?" asked the Eraser in the passenger seat, who hadn't morphed yet.

"What, no candy?" the original Max practically snarled. Then her eyes fell on Ari.

A laugh rose from his chest as he slammed on the brakes. He loved it! Seeing the flare of hatred and fear in her eyes when she looked at him. "Showtime, folks!" he shouted. "Max is mine!"

Erasers poured out of the back of the van before it had even stopped.

Time to play.

54

So, again, Ari was alive? Ari was back? I needed to think about that later.

"Happy now?" Fang muttered at me, and I took a second to scowl at him before launching myself at the closest wolf boy.

The sad thing was, I *was* happier. Well, not happy, exactly — just more on solid ground. A boy from class talking to me? Complete washout. Kicking Eraser butt, especially pathetic, off-balance Erasers with too-big wings? It was just more *me,* somehow.

Within moments I had cracked one's kneecap with a hard side kick, and he crumpled to the ground. Very cheering. *Watch it!* said the Voice, just before another one clipped my jaw, swiveling my head. *Go with the flow.* Okay. I went with the momentum, completed the turn, and came out swinging with a hard right that smashed his jaw. Howling with pain, he fell to his knees, holding his face. Seconds later he bounced up, his eyes red with fury, in time to have Gazzy smack both hands over his ears, blowing his eardrums. Screaming, he went down again.

Fang had taken one out and was working on Ari. A quick glance showed me that Angel was dealing with a female Eraser — using her mind control to make the Eraser run headfirst into a tree, hard. Yowch. Then Angel flashed me an angelic smile, and I remembered again that we had to have a clear-the-air ethics talk sometime soon.

Max — focus! A huge thud against my back knocked the wind out of me. Wheezing for air, I whirled to see Ari, grinning, swinging hard at my head. I ducked, whirled, and put all my weight into a roundhouse kick that spun him sideways and almost knocked him off his feet. The other Erasers were mostly down for the count: It was me against him. Slowly we circled each other. Ari grinned, and fury washed over me, coloring everything red. Out of the corner of my eye, I saw Fang herd the younger kids into the woods and then up into the air.

"Cute uniform." Ari sneered, showing his sharp canines. "It's a good look for you."

"Where'd you get those wings?" I countered. "Wal-Mart?" I kept my weight centered as we circled each other like tigers.

The other Erasers were staggering back to the van, piling into it like circus clowns. Ari saw them.

"Guess it won't be today, guys," Ari called to his team. "Next time I'll let you eat the little one. I hear they taste like chicken."

Angel.

Growling, I lunged for Ari. He stepped aside and swung at me. I easily ducked. Rage fueled my fight, and I did a quick running start, then hit him with a flying side kick, both feet ramming hard against his ribs. He fell over heavily, banging his head on the road.

I jammed my foot against his neck and leaned over him. "How many times do I have to kill you?" I snarled. "Rough estimate."

I saw fiery hatred in his eyes, and it really hit me: This wasn't even Ari any longer, the little kid who'd watched us from a distance when we were at the School. His own father had turned him into a monster, and any Ari that was left was being burned away from the inside. The idea made me feel sick, and I took my foot off his neck and stepped back.

Ari sat up quickly, gagging. "Point to you this time," he said, his voice raspy as he rubbed his neck. "But you have no hope of winning." He jumped to his feet. "I'm just playing with you, like a cat with a mouse."

I was already backing toward the woods, unfolding my wings, ready to leap into the air. "Yeah," I said, my voice dripping with hostility. "An awkward Frankenstein puddy-tat against a fierce, bloodthirsty, undefeated, *well-designed* mouse."

His lip curled and he lunged at me again, but I'd already done an up-and-away and was hovering about fifteen feet off the ground. I rose higher and watched Ari stomp heavily to the van and throw himself in through the back doors. Inside the van, I caught the barest flash of blond-streaked hair.

None of the Erasers had long streaked hair.

55

"What happened to you?" Anne cried.

We trailed into the house and automatically hung up our jackets, most of which were blood-spattered. Total trotted around our feet, sniffing and growling. Angel reached down and hugged him, talking gently, and I just barely heard Total say, "Those *wankers.*"

"Erasers," said the Gasman. "I'm hungry. Is there a snack?"

"What are Erasers?" Anne asked, sounding genuinely confused.

Could she possibly not know? Or maybe she just didn't know the hip insider's slang for them. "We're human-avian hybrids," I said, walking down the hall to the kitchen. I could smell popcorn. "Erasers are human-lupine hybrids."

"Rabbits?" Anne asked, still sounding confused. She followed me.

I giggled. "That's *lapin.* Or, more correctly, *leporid.* Not *lupine.*"

"Oh. Wolves," Anne said, getting it.

"Give the lady a prize," I said, entering the kitchen.

"Popcorn! And hot apple cider!" Gazzy said happily.

"Wash your hands," Anne said, then took a good look at him. Gazzy had a couple bruises but looked okay. Angel and Nudge were fine. Iggy had a split lip. Fang's nose was bleeding. I had a sudden flash of him kissing that girl and shut it down hard.

"Get cleaned up," Anne said. "I'll get some bandages. Is anyone hurt seriously?"

"No," said Nudge, digging into the popcorn. "But an Eraser tore my sweater. Jerk."

"There's milk too," said Anne, taking a glass bottle out of the fridge. She put it on the table and went to get the first-aid kit.

I helped Angel pour herself a glass of milk, and then I noticed: This was a different brand of milk than before. The other had been in cartons. Cartons with missing-kid pictures on them. This bottle had a smiling cow but no missing kids. Hmm.

Later I sat at the table doing my homework, which is just another term for "grown-up-imposed yet self-inflicted torture," IMHO. Anne sat down next to me.

"So Erasers are human-wolf hybrids," she said. "And they attacked you? Have they ever attacked you before? Where did they come from? How did they know where you were?"

I looked at her. "Isn't all this in your reports?" I asked. "Your files? Yeah, of course the Erasers attacked us. They always do. They're everywhere. They were created to be . . . weapons, kind of. Back at the School, they were the guards, the security. The punishers. Since we escaped,

Erasers have been tracking us. I was wondering when they'd show up. This is the longest we've gone without them finding us."

"Why didn't you tell me?" Anne asked, concern on her face.

I shook my head. "I really thought you knew. You knew a bunch of other stuff about us. I mean, I wasn't keeping Erasers a secret or anything."

Anne let out a heavy breath. "We'd heard only vague rumors. They seemed so far-fetched that we didn't believe them. You say these Erasers track you? How?"

Probably my chip. The one *somebody* put in my arm.

I shrugged and looked back at my world studies textbook.

At least, I feared it was my chip. I wasn't positive, but it made the most sense. This was my chance to tell Anne about my chip. Maybe with her FBI resources, she could find a way to take it out. But something held me back. I just couldn't bring myself to trust her. Maybe in about five years, if we were still here. God, what a depressing thought.

Also, these days, I was wondering if it might *not* be my chip, might be something else. Like, if Total was chipped. Or even one of the flock. Angel? We just didn't know.

Anne stood up. "Well, I'm going to make some phone calls," she said firmly. "Those were the last Erasers you'll see."

I almost chuckled at her naïveté.

56

"Night, Tiffany-Krystal," I said, grinning, and Nudge grinned back. We stacked our fists on top of each other and tapped the backs with our other hands.

"Night," said Nudge, lying back on her comfy pillows. "Max? We are going to stay for a while, aren't we? We're not leaving, like, tomorrow, right?"

"No," I said quietly. "Not tomorrow. Just — be on your toes, and try to blend, okay?"

"Okay. I do blend pretty good, I think," Nudge said. "I have three friends I sit with at lunch. My teacher seems to like me."

"Of course she likes you. How could she not?" I kissed Nudge's forehead and left, heading down the hall to tuck in Angel.

Pushing open her door, I saw that Anne was already there, pulling the covers up to Angel's chin.

"You had a long day, sweetie," said Anne, stroking Angel's hair off her face. "Get some good sleep now."

"Okay," said Angel.

"And Ariel? Don't let Total up on the bed," Anne said. "He has his own bed."

"Uh-huh," said Angel agreeably. I rolled my eyes. Total would be on the bed before Anne was five steps down the hall.

"Good night, sleep tight," Anne said, standing up.

"Don't let the bedbugs bite," Angel answered cheerfully.

Anne smiled at us and went out.

Total hopped up on the bed. Angel held up the covers for him and he wriggled underneath them, resting his head on a corner of Angel's pillow. I tucked them both in.

"Would it kill her to turn up the heat?" Total grumbled sleepily. "This place is an icebox. You could practically hang meat in here."

Angel and I grinned at each other.

"You all right?" I asked.

She nodded. "I hated seeing the Erasers today."

"You and me both. Ari really creeps me out. Do you pick up anything from him?"

Angel thought. "Dark. Red. Angry. Torn. Confused. He hates us."

I frowned at this grim picture of what was happening inside Ari's head.

"And he loves you," Angel added. "He loves you a lot."

57

I backed out of Angel's room, trying not to look shocked. Jeez. Ari loved me? Like a little kid? Like a big Eraser? Was that why he kept trying to kill me? He needed to read an article about how to send clearer signals.

A sound behind me made me turn around fast, to see that I'd almost run into Fang coming down the hall.

"They down?"

I nodded. "They're beat. School really takes it out of them. And then, of course, Erasers."

"Yeah."

We saw Anne come out of Nudge's room. She smiled and mouthed "Good night" at us, then headed downstairs. I thought about her being the last person Nudge would see before she went to sleep, and my jaw tightened.

"Let them enjoy it while they can," said Fang, reading my expression in that irritating way he had.

"She's taking my place," I said without meaning to.

Fang shrugged. "You're a fighter, not a mom."

I almost gasped, stung. "I can't be both? You think I'm

a lousy mom? What, because I'm not girly enough, is that it?" I was really mad, the tensions of the day boiling over in me. "Not like that girl with the red hair, stuck to you like glue!" My hands came up and, without thinking, I shoved Fang hard.

Since this was Fang, he didn't just take it like a gentleman. He immediately shoved me back, almost making me hit the wall. I was mortified — not only because I was attacking my best friend, but because I'd sounded like a jealous idiot. Which I *wasn't*. At *all*.

I stood there, breathing fast, feeling my cheeks flame with humiliation and anger. My hands clenched and unclenched, and I wanted to disappear.

I felt his dark eyes looking at me and waited for him to tease me about being upset over the Red-Haired Wonder.

He stepped closer to me, till his face was only inches away from mine. We'd been the same height for most of our lives, but in the past two years he'd shot past me. Now my eyes were level with his shoulder.

"You're girly enough," he said quietly. "As I recall."

New embarrassment washed over me — he was referring to when I'd kissed him at the beach, weeks ago. He just had girls throwing themselves at him left and right, didn't he?

I gritted my teeth and didn't say anything.

"And you've been a great mom. But you're only fourteen and you shouldn't have to be a mom. Give yourself ten years or so."

He went past me, brushing my shoulder as I stood there stiffly. He meant a real mom, with my own kids. I definitely considered the flock my own kids, but Fang meant kids I made myself. Like the Voice had said earlier.

Right then, I just hated my life, in a whole new, refreshing way.

"By the way," Fang called from down the hallway. "I've started a blog. I'm using the computers at school. Against all the rules, of course. Fang's Blog." He chuckled, as only Fang can chuckle. "Check it out sometime . . . *Mom.*"

58

It was cold out tonight, but the new Max didn't even feel it. She edged back on her branch, pressing her spine against the rough bark of the tree trunk. The binoculars were heavy on their cord around her neck. Drawing her knees up, she hugged herself, feeling a warm tear escape her eye and roll down her cheek. She was watching the other Max all the time, watching and learning. But it was hard. It was painful.

"Oh, Max," she whispered, seeing the other Max far away, through the window of Anne's house. "I know just how you feel. You and I are always alone, no matter how many other people are around."

59

At school the next morning, we were greeted by the sight of several large tour buses taking up practically the whole parking lot. I saw my new friend J.J., and she waved and came over to me as the rest of the flock melted into the crowd.

"This is a special treat," J.J. said cheerfully. "A field trip."

"Field trip?" I pictured us all out in the fields, tracking something.

"Yep, field trip. The whole school is off to the White House, home of our beloved leader. Which means no classes, no lectures, and probably no homework."

I smiled at J.J. I liked her style. She wasn't all stuck-up and stiff. Didn't take things too seriously. Like, well, *I* did, for instance.

"All righty, then," I said. "Field trip it is."

"Our class is over here," a girl's voice said.

Iggy frowned. He was concentrating on sounds, listening

for the scrape of Fang's boot against the pavement. One second he'd been there, and the next, Iggy had been surrounded by a sea of voices he couldn't sort through.

A hand gently touched his arm. "Our class is over here," the voice said again, and he recognized it. This girl sat eight feet away from him, due northeast, in their classroom.

Iggy was embarrassed, standing there like a blind idiot, not knowing where to go.

"Our teacher changed direction on us with no warning," the girl explained. He remembered her name was Tess.

"Oh," Iggy muttered. He moved where she was subtly tugging him. "Thanks."

"No prob," Tess said easily. "You know, I was so relieved when they put you in our class. Now I won't stick out so much."

Because you're a blind mutant freak? Iggy thought, confused.

"You know, tall for my age, like you. People always say, Oh, be glad about it — you can be a basketball player, or a model or something. But when you're fourteen, a girl, and five ten, the whole thing pretty much sucks," she finished. "But now I'm not alone. We match."

Iggy laughed, and then he heard Fang's step, felt Fang barely brush against his jacket, telling him where he was.

"Tess?" the teacher called.

"Got to go — room leader and all," said Tess. "I'll find you later, when we're walking around, okay?"

"Okay," said Iggy, feeling dazed. He heard Tess's light step hurry away. What had just happened? He felt like he'd been hit by a truck.

"You're slayin' 'em, big guy," said Fang.

"Of course, there's far too much to see and do in Washington DC for us to cover everything today," said one of the teachers, standing at the front of the bus. She raised her voice to be heard over the engine. "This morning we'll tour the Capitol and see where the House of Representatives and the Senate meet. Then we'll spend half an hour at the Vietnam Memorial, the Wall. After lunch, we'll go to the White House."

Angel's seat buddy, Caralyn, oohed and looked excited.

"I can't wait to see the White House," Angel said, and Caralyn nodded.

"I wish we were going to the Museum of Natural History," Caralyn said. "Have you been there?"

"Uh-uh."

"It's really cool. It has dinosaur skeletons, and a huge stuffed whale hanging from the ceiling, and meteors and diamonds."

"Sounds cool," said Angel. Maybe she would ask Anne to bring them there. Maybe she should just get her teacher to think of detouring there today. No, maybe not. If Max found out, she would be mad. Angel patted Celeste, tucked into the waistband of her plaid school skirt, and decided to just go with the program. For now.

60

If you're ever feeling a lack of middle-aged white men, just pop into the Capitol. Not so much the House of Representatives, which has a bit more color and texture, but the Senate — jeez. Yes, let's have *more* testosterone running the country.

In the Capitol building we watched a short movie about our Founding Fathers and how they tried to create a perfect system of government. They sounded so freaking sincere, the whole "perfect union" and "all men are created equal" thing. Except of course for the men they owned as household property. Not to put a fly in the ointment.

But despite all that, hearing their words, seeing the Constitution, getting the whole story of what they were trying to do — well, you gotta give 'em credit. They really were trying to set up something good and fair. Kind of in a way that no other country, before or since, had tried to do.

Long and short of it: Democracy gets a big thumbs-up from me.

The Vietnam Wall was awful. A huge, smooth black granite monolith covered with names of people who died in a war. Very depressing. I saw Nudge make the mistake of touching the Wall. She almost doubled over — her ability to sense people and emotions through leftover vibrations must have been mind-blowing here. A couple of her new friends put their arms around her, and I saw one pull out a tissue. I would talk to her about it later.

Then the White House.

Well. It is one big, fancy hacienda, let me tell you. Not a castle. Not as froufrou as the Taj Mahal or Graceland. But still mucho impressive.

You know, being in the White House — surrounded by invisible state-of-the-art security systems, as well as extremely visible guards with guns — I felt the safest I had in ages. If anyone wanted to get to us, they'd have to go through White House security first. Which I was comfortable with.

We saw the "Parrot" collection of rooms (Red, Blue, Green), as well as the gi-normous State Dining Hall. The library was weensy, as libraries go. There was a whole room just for presidential china, which I got a kick out of. What next? The presidential pantry?

After a while, even with the different colors, the rooms started melding together: undersized antique furniture, fancy curtains, famous paintings of famous people I sometimes recognized. When I thought about all the history that had actually happened where I stood, I almost got a little chill. Or it could have been the inadequate heating.

It just cracked me up that here I was, Maximum Ride, in person, on a school field trip. I mean, how freakish was that? This past week was the first time I'd ever gone to school in my life. I'd grown up in a dog crate. I had freaking *wings.* But here I was, commingling with the best of 'em, playing nicely with others. Sometimes I just impress the *h* out of myself.

Finally our guide rounded us all up in the visitors' center.

"Come on, we have ten minutes to get souvenirs," said J.J., heading to a display case. I had no one to buy souvenirs for: We can't collect stuff. It would weigh us down too much.

I saw Nudge and Gazzy looking through the books.

"Wasn't this great?" Nudge asked excitedly. "I can't believe we're in the White House! I want to be president someday."

"I'll be vice president," the Gasman offered.

"You guys would be great," I said politely. Yes, they could run on the Mutant Party ticket, with a freak-of-nature platform. No prob. I'm sure America is ready for that.

I looked around and saw Fang. The Red-Haired Wonder was hovering by him, of course, and it irked me to all get-out. How could he even stand her, with her smiles and her agreeableness? I didn't get it. I also saw Iggy talking to a girl — she was touching some State Department silk scarves and laughing with him. I hoped she was nice. And not an Eraser.

But where was the ever-so-adorable-and-scary Angel?

I surveyed the crowd. Besides our school group, there were random assorted tourists, another tour group, and . . .

no Angel. Not anywhere. That little girl sure had a talent for disappearing.

"Nudge. Where's Angel?"

Nudge looked around. "I don't see her. Maybe the bathroom?"

I was already walking toward Fang. "Excuse me," I said tightly, interrupting the Red-Haired Wonder's adoration, "I don't see An— Ariel."

Fang scanned the crowd. The Red-Haired Wonder smiled at me.

"You're Nick's sister, right?"

Please, someone save me. "Uh-huh."

Fang turned back to me. "I'll go look."

I followed him, heading for the doorway we'd all come through. This was all I needed. We were trying to blend, to not stand out, and she went and got lost in the freaking White House. Where getting lost would no doubt cause somewhat of a hullabaloo. Should I ask her teacher? Alert a guard? Maybe she was just lost, *or* maybe she'd been kidnapped by Erasers. Again. So much for my feeling of security. *Dang* it.

There were three entrances to this room, a guard at each one. Where to start?

Then an excited ripple spread through the crowd, a soft murmur of voices. I was taller than a lot of the other kids and I quickly scanned the faces I could see. The crowd parted, and Angel came toward me, a little smile on her face. Celeste dangled from one hand, and I noticed incongruously that we had to send that bear through the wash but soon.

Then I saw who was holding Angel's other hand.

The president. Or a stunning facsimile.

My jaw dropped as I stared at them. Several black-suited men with earphones scurried into the room, looking alarmed.

"Hi, Max," said Angel. "I got lost. Mr. Danning brought me back."

"Hi, uh, Ariel," I said weakly, searching her face. I glanced up at the president. He looked so lifelike, much more so than he did on TV. "Uh, thanks. Sir."

He gave me a warm smile. "No problem, miss. Your sister knew you'd be worried. You've got yourself a remarkable little girl here."

Yeah? You mean the wings? Or was it the infiltrating-your-brain part? Oh, God, I had a bad feeling about this. I studied Angel, but as usual she looked wide-eyed and innocent. Not that that had ever meant anything.

"Yes, we certainly do," I said. "Thank you for finding her. And bringing her back."

Angel's teacher fell all over herself, shaking the president's hand and thanking him and apologizing all at the same time.

"My pleasure." The president — the authentic president of the United States — leaned down and smiled at Angel. "You take care now," he said. "Don't go getting lost anymore."

"I won't," Angel said. "Thanks for finding me."

He patted her blond curls, making them bounce, then waved at the crowd before turning and heading out of the visitors' center. The black-suited men hurried after him like ants on speed.

Every eye in the room was on us. I kneeled down to Angel's level and spoke through a clenched smile. "I can't believe this happened," I said. "Are you okay?"

Angel nodded. "I was worried, 'cause I looked up and my whole class was gone. So I went down a hall, and then another hall, and then the president met me. But nothing weird happened. None of those guys turned into Erasers or anything."

"Okaaay," I said, my heart still beating fast. "Just stick close from now on. I don't want to lose you again."

"Okay, Max," Angel said solemnly, taking my hand.

I also didn't want her playing mind-puppet with the leader of the free world, but I was going to save that conversation till later.

61

"Zoom in." Jeb leaned closer to the black-and-white monitor.

Ari wordlessly rewound the tape and zoomed in. Again he watched as the crowd in the visitors' center rippled outward like a school of fish. Again the smiling countenance of the president appeared in the top left corner of the screen. Ari zoomed the focus in on the president and the blond kid by his side.

Jeb examined the screen intently, touching the glass as if he could touch the images themselves. Ari watched Jeb's eyes focus on Angel, on Max, on the president. His gut tightened. What would it take to make Jeb look at him like that? He'd never cared about Ari when he was just a regular boy. Then Ari had been turned into a mutant freak, just like the bird kids. And still his own father had no time for him, no interest in him. What would it take? Not even dying had helped, which, face it, would have been most people's trump card.

It was time. Past time. Time to take the freaks down.

When they were completely gone, just footnotes in a science text, then Jeb would have to realize how important Ari was.

He watched as Max's eyes widened on the screen. With those jackets on, you could hardly tell these kids were mutant freaks. Ari knew he himself was pretty identifiable. His retrofitted wings were too large to fold neatly up against his spine. His skin was rough from morphing in and out. And his features — Ari couldn't quite put his finger on it, but there was something odd about his features, maybe from having a seven-year-old face stretched to fit a man-sized Eraser.

Max smiled at the president nervously. Even on a tiny black-and-white screen, she was striking. Tall, lean, sandy-streaked hair. He knew that under her jacket her arms were whipcord tough, strong. He could still feel the bruise from her last kick on his ribs. He scowled.

And there was his father, watching the screen as if looking at a Thanksgiving dinner. As if they were his kids, instead of Ari. As if he was proud of them and wanted them back.

But he wasn't going to get them back. Not ever. Ari was going to make sure of that. Plans had been made. Wheels set in motion. Jeb would be angry at first. But he would come around.

Ari covered his mouth to hide his smile.

62

"Max?"

I looked up to see Nudge standing in the doorway of my room, shifting from foot to foot with excitement.

"Yeah?"

"I think I know the secret of the code."

"Do tell," I said, once we'd all gathered in her room.

"I think it's from a book," she said. "I mean, okay, it could be some computerized code, in which case we'll never break it. But I think they want us to break it — want *you* to break it, as part of your testing."

"Yeah, I guess I'm failing this particular test."

"Not yet," Nudge said. "There're still a couple of things we haven't tried. Like if the numbers all relate back to a book."

"Which book?" asked Iggy.

"A big book, with lots of words. A book that wouldn't be hard for you to find," said Nudge. "Something all over the place, that a lot of people have."

"*The Da Vinci Code?*" the Gasman suggested.

Iggy made a pained expression. "No. Like the Bible, nimrod. It's everywhere. In hotels, people's houses, schools. It's something Max could find easily. Right, Nudge?"

"Yeah," Nudge said.

"I don't understand," said Angel.

"Like, there's strings of numbers, right?" said Nudge. "It would be like what Fang saw with the maps. But now one number is a book, another one is a chapter, another is a verse, and another would be one word from that verse. Then you take all the words and see what they add up to."

"Huh," I said, thinking. "Do we have a Bible here?"

Nudge reached down and pulled out a thick volume. "Anne had one downstairs. I'm borrowing it. Trying to strengthen my relationship with the Lord."

Four hours later my brain was fried. Anne had made the younger kids go to bed. Iggy, Fang, and I were still trying to make the freaking numbers work with the Bible. But no matter how we played it, nothing was panning out.

"Maybe it's the wrong version of the Bible," Fang said tiredly. "There are different versions."

"This is the King James," said Iggy, rubbing his forehead. "The most common one in America."

"And what do we have?" I rolled my shoulders and rotated my head from side to side.

Fang looked at his notes. "*Thou. Upon. Fasting. Round. Always. Saul. Dwell. Fruit. Affliction. Didst. Delight. Dwell* again."

I frowned, shaking my head in frustration. "Nothing. No pattern, no meaning. The Bible was a great idea, but maybe we're doing it wrong."

"So I guess we just kiss the world good-bye," Fang said after a pause.

I gave him a look. "So funny. You're quite the wit."

He gave the barest hint of a smug smile. "The ladies like it."

Iggy burst out laughing, but I just stared at Fang, appalled. How could he joke about something like that? Sometimes I felt as if I didn't even know him anymore.

I stood up, letting my pages fall to the ground. "I'm beat. See you in the morning." I stood up and left without another look at either of them.

"I don't suppose you took a look at my blog yet?" Fang called out. I didn't bother to answer . . . *that I had.* And it was good. The boy had some poetry in him.

63

"Cool," said the Gasman. "Glad I ran into you." They were surrounded by an interweaving stream of voices, as kids all around them changed classes. It was before lunch, and Iggy had been on his way to the library when Gazzy had touched his arm.

Iggy nodded. "We'll have to remember we have the same recess on . . . what day is this?" The voices around them thinned and started to fade away as he and Gazzy turned a corner.

"Friday. C'mon, let's check this out."

Iggy heard Gazzy open a door. From the sound of the echo, he knew they were facing a big space that went down. "What is this, the basement?"

"Yeah. I've been wanting to explore a bit."

"Cool."

Gazzy touched the back of Iggy's hand, and Iggy concentrated on what was echoing barely perceptibly around him. At the bottom of the stairs, air currents and the slightest sounds told him they were in a large, relatively empty space.

"What's it like?" he said, lowering his voice.

"Big," said Gazzy. "Basementy. There're some doors. Let's see what's behind 'em."

Iggy heard the Gasman turn a doorknob and felt the breeze as the door swung toward them.

"Um, school supplies," the Gasman said, moving a few feet away. He paused, and Iggy heard another door open.

"Sports equipment."

"Anything good?"

"It's all too big to carry — couldn't hide it. Unless we had our backpacks with us."

"Note to self," said Iggy.

"Right."

Iggy's hand shot out and touched Gazzy's shoulder. He held one finger to his lips and listened hard. Yes: footsteps.

"Someone coming down," he said in the barest whisper.

Gazzy took Iggy's sleeve and they walked quickly and silently a few yards down the hall. Another door opened, and the Gasman pulled Iggy inside and shut it behind them with a slight *snick.*

"Where are we?" Iggy breathed.

"Looks like a file room," whispered Gazzy. "Let's get behind some cabinets, just in case."

Iggy followed Gazzy to the back of the room, sensing tall things on either side of them. He felt Gazzy hunch down on the floor and crouched down too, just as they heard voices, getting louder.

"But what do you want me to do, Mr. Pruitt?" a woman asked, sounding flustered.

"I want you to make sure those files are lost," said the headmaster in his horrible, sneering voice. "We can't destroy them, but we can't have them found either. Is that totally beyond your comprehension?"

"No, no, but —," said the woman.

"But nothing!" the headmaster snapped. "Surely you can handle this one simple task, Ms. Cox. Put the files where *you* can find them but no one else can. Or is that too much for you?"

Iggy shook his head. The headmaster was such a total jerk. He hated him. Someone should teach him a lesson.

"No," said the woman, sounding defeated. "I can do it."

"Very well then."

Iggy heard the headmaster turn and stalk off, and Ms. Cox sighed right outside the file room. Then the door opened. Iggy heard the slight crackling buzz of the overhead fluorescent light coming on. He felt Gazzy tense beside him.

A metal drawer opened. Papers rustled. The drawer closed. *Come on, leave,* Iggy thought. But instead the footsteps came closer, in their direction. *No, turn around, leave,* Iggy mentally urged her. If only he could do mind control like Angel. Next to him, Gazzy was holding his breath, not making a sound. If she found them, it would be very bad.

The light snapped off. Footsteps left the room, and the door closed again. The Gasman breathed out at last.

"Close call," he whispered, and Iggy nodded, his mouth dry. "Let's split."

They were almost back to the stairs when the door at

the top of the stairs opened. They froze, with Iggy straining to hear what was happening. The next moment, they heard voices coming from the other end of the hall. They were trapped, with people coming from both sides.

"Crap!" Gazzy whispered.

"Do you have the thing?" Iggy asked tensely.

"Yeah. But Max said —"

"We're going to get caught!" Iggy interrupted him. "Get the thing!"

64

"Okay, now you're creeping me out," I told Nudge. We were in the school library, and it was like she was able to extract information from the computer by osmosis, practically. We didn't even need Mr. Lazzara the librarian's help. First, we went on Fang's blog and saw that he was adding stuff on a daily basis — *his* point of view on what had happened to us so far. Now he was adding drawings as well. Next, I had Nudge search for more ter Borcht mentions and also for any notices about missing infants during any of the years we were born. We couldn't narrow down the months, but the years we were pretty sure about.

"Okay, fourteen years ago," Nudge said, concentrating on the screen. "We might have the most luck with that, because there's three of you." She scrolled down. "Unless, you know, one of you was born in the fall of one year and the others were born in the spring of the next year. But in general I think we —"

"Is this school related?" The chilly, hate-filled voice,

quivering with suppressed rage, could belong only to . . . the headhunter.

"We're looking up newspaper articles," Nudge said innocently. "For civics class."

That's my girl. Able to lie on a moment's notice.

"Really?" Mr. Pruitt sneered, his lip curling. "And exactly what part of the curriculum —"

Boom.

The whole library shuddered slightly. Mr. Pruitt and I looked at each other in surprise, then his fuzzy eyebrows came together. The next instant, the school's fire alarms started clanging, making us all jump.

For a moment we just stood there, too stunned to react. Then a loud hiss came from overhead. My head snapped up just in time for me to see the ceiling's sprinkler system cranking on, showering us with icy water.

"What?" shouted Mr. Pruitt. "What is the meaning of this?"

My guess was it meant that Iggy and the Gasman had just shot to the top of my "so in trouble" list, but I didn't say anything.

Everyone scrambled for the doors, yelling and pushing.

Mr. Lazzara cupped his hands around his mouth. "Orderly, please! Fire drill forms! Children!"

Mr. Pruitt charged toward the doors, practically mowing kids down in his effort to get out from under the sprinklers.

Nudge grinned at me, water dripping off her curly hair. "I didn't know school would be this much fun," she said.

65

"This is grounds for expulsion!" Mr. Pruitt screamed, veins popping out on his forehead.

I watched him with interest, calculating the chances of his keeling over from a heart attack within the next five minutes. Right now it looked like 60, 65 percent for.

The six of us were standing soggily in his office, half an hour after the last fire truck had left. Pruitt had insisted on seeing all of us together. We were chilled and bedraggled, and just wanted to get our butts home.

But nooo.

First we had to listen to the headhunter chew us out. Granted, being chewed out by someone as horrible as the headhunter was a walk in the park compared to, say, having Erasers try to kill you. But still, an afternoon-ruiner, for sure.

"The stink bomb was reason enough!" Mr. Pruitt shouted. "But I stupidly gave you a second chance! You're nothing but a bunch of street rats! Vermin!"

I was impressed. *Vermin* was a new one on me, and I'd been called everything from arrogant to zealous.

Mr. Pruitt paused to suck in a breath, and I jumped in. "My brothers didn't do the stink bomb! You never proved it. Now you're accusing us again with no evidence! How — how un-American!"

I thought the headhunter was going to pop a vessel. Instead he reached out and grabbed the Gasman's hands, holding them in the air.

My heart sank as I saw the smudges of black powder, ground into his skin when the bomb went off.

"Besides that!" I blustered.

The headhunter seemed to swell with new rage, but just at that moment, the assistant showed Anne into the office.

She didn't work for the FBI for nothing — somehow she managed to calm the headhunter down and shooed us out of the office and into her Suburban.

For half a mile there was silence in the car, but then she started in.

"This was your big opportunity, kids," she began. "I'd had higher hopes. . . ."

There was a bunch more, but I tuned it out, gazing through my window at the fading autumn color. Every once in a while words floated into my consciousness: *grounded, big trouble, disappointed, upset, no TV.* And so on.

None of us said anything. It had been years since we'd had to answer to any grown-up. We weren't about to start now.

66

What Anne didn't get was that only weeks ago we'd been sleeping in subway tunnels and scrounging for food. So being "grounded" and not able to watch TV was, like, meaningless.

"We still have this whole house," Nudge pointed out in a whisper. "It's full of books and games and food."

"No dessert, though," Total said mournfully. "And I didn't do anything!"

"Yeah, no dessert," said the Gasman indignantly.

I glared at him. "And whose fault is that, wise guy? You and Iggy screwed up *again.* For God's sake, quit bringing explosives to school!"

"We did hear the headhunter telling Ms. Cox to bury some files," the Gasman reminded me. "If we could find them, it might give us something to use against him."

I sighed. "How about we just stay under the radar until we leave? Don't retaliate, don't do anything else. Just quietly get through the rest of our time here."

"How long will we be here? Did you decide when you want to leave?" Angel asked.

"Yeah," I said drily. "Two weeks ago."

"Can we just stay through Thanksgiving?" Nudge asked. "We've never had a Thanksgiving meal. Please?"

I nodded reluctantly. "If no one else *messes up,* that should be okay."

I went upstairs and headed to my room. As I passed Anne's open door, I heard the TV. The words *missing children* caught my attention, and I paused, listening.

"Yes, the recent disappearance of several area children has brought back difficult memories for other parents who have lost children, whether recently or years ago. We're talking now with Mr. and Mrs. Griffiths, whose only son was taken from a local hospital right after his birth."

I froze. Griffiths was Iggy's last name — we thought. I remembered that much from the legible papers we found at the Institute in New York — before they disappeared. But the Institute file had also said that Iggy's father was dead. So these people couldn't be his parents — could they? Riveted, I edged my way forward a few inches so I could watch the TV through the partially open door. I heard Anne in her bathroom, brushing her teeth.

"You'd think that after fourteen years, it would get easier," said the woman sadly. "But it doesn't. It's the same pain, all the time."

My breath caught in my throat. Fourteen years? Griffiths? The reporter's image cleared and was replaced by a couple. The man had his arm around his wife's shoulders. They both looked sad.

One other thing.

The woman looked just like Iggy.

67

Fang looked intently at me, peering through the strands of hair that always covered his eyes.

"They were standing in front of their house. I saw enough to recognize it if I saw it again," I told him in a fast whisper. It was late, and everyone else was asleep. I'd waited till now to tell Fang what I'd seen. "Their name was Griffiths. Their kid disappeared fourteen years ago. And the woman was the spitting image of Iggy."

Fang shook his head slowly, thinking. "I can't believe you would just happen to see that."

"I know. But how could it possibly be a setup? We weren't even allowed to watch TV today. I just — I think we have to check it out."

Fang shook his head again. "How many houses are there in the DC area?"

"This house had a big, dark church behind it, like on the next block. It was old-fashioned, and the spire was really tall. How many of those are there?"

Fang sighed. "About a million."

"Fang! This is a huge break! Of course we should go check it out!"

He looked at me. "But we're *grounded,*" he said with a straight face.

I stared at him for a second, and then we both burst out laughing.

68

"What's wrong?" Fang had been acting a little off all night. Now we were flying high over the lights of DC, and he kept wiping his forehead and rolling his shoulders.

"I'm way hot," he muttered. "But I don't feel sick. Just — way hot."

"Like I did?" I raised my eyebrows. "Huh. Give it a week; you'll be flying like the Concorde. I think. Or, you know, you're dying." I shot him a grin, which he didn't return. "What? You feel really bad?"

"No. But I just thought of something. I have your blood in me."

I looked at him, his wide, dark wings moving smoothly, powerfully through the night air.

"So? It was just blood."

He shook his head. "Not our blood. The red cells have DNA, remember? I got transfused with your DNA."

I thought. "Uh, so?"

He shrugged. "So maybe that's why this is happening. Maybe it wasn't supposed to happen to me."

"Hmm," I said. "And we don't know if that's bad or good or nothing."

"Guess we'll find out," he said.

Turns out there are practically hundreds of freaking tall church steeples in the DC area. Though finding the right one tonight seemed amusingly unlikely, we cruised around, looking for a steeple in a residential neighborhood. We dropped down more than a dozen times, but once I had scanned all the close-by houses, we took to the air again.

After three hours of this, we were hungry and tired. We didn't even have to speak — just looked at each other, shrugged, and turned in unison to head back to Anne's place.

It was around 3:00 a.m. when we got back to Anne's. We headed toward the window we'd left open, in a little-used storeroom on the second floor.

"Fang." He looked at me, and I gestured at the house with one hand.

We could see Anne's silhouette clearly in the window of her room. She was awake and looking for us at 3:00 a.m. Didn't that woman ever sleep?

Was Anne just a spy? For the FBI or someone else?

Suddenly I felt exhausted. We coasted down to the house, tucked our wings in at the last second, and zipped through the window. We stacked hands and tapped them, then went to our separate rooms. I kicked off my shoes and fell into bed in my clothes. I didn't expect Anne to come to my room.

She'd already seen everything she needed to see.

69

The next couple of weeks were the most surreal ones of my life, and that's saying something, since it beats growing up in a cage, being on the run, finding other mutants in a lab deep below the subways of New York City, and, oh yeah, having *wings.*

This was way weirder than that.

Nothing awful happened.

We went back to school, and it was business as usual, except that Gazzy and Iggy somehow managed to get through their days without detonating anything. A first.

The headhunter stayed out of our way, perhaps for health reasons, trying to avoid an apoplectic fit.

Angel's teacher seemed to behave pretty normally — like, she didn't suddenly take her class to a toy store and buy them anything they wanted. That would have been a tip-off for me.

Nudge got invited to a birthday party. A nonmutant birthday party. Anne promised to help her find an outfit that would hide her wings but still look normal.

And — brace yourself. I saved the best and the worst for last:

That guy Sam asked me on a date.

"You what?" Iggy burst out.

"I got asked on a date," I repeated, flinging mashed potatoes onto my plate.

"Oh, Max!" Nudge said.

"You're kidding," said the Gasman with his mouth full. He laughed, trying not to spit food. "What a loser! What'd he say when you shot him down?"

I busily cut my steak.

"You said yes, didn't you?" Nudge asked.

"Oh, my God," said Iggy, his hand on his forehead. "Max on a *date.* I thought we were trying to *avoid* tears and violence and mayhem."

Yet another frustrating instance of dagger glances not working on Iggy.

"I think it's great," said Angel. "Max is beautiful. She *should* go on dates."

"What are you going to wear?" Anne asked with a smile.

"Don't know," I muttered, my face getting hot.

And did you notice who didn't say one word?

Right.

70

"Just think of it as a recon mission."

Fang leaned against my door frame, watching me stare at myself in the dresser mirror.

"What?" I asked testily. "I'm fine." I tucked my shirt in and pulled on the oversize velour hoodie that would hide my wings. I hoped.

"Uh-huh. Usually when you look like that, I know you're about to hurl."

"I'm *fine,*" I said tightly, trying not to hyperventilate. What was I doing? How stupid was I to agree to this? Maybe I should call him and cancel. I could say I was sick. I could —

The doorbell rang. Fang gave me an unholy grin and headed downstairs.

"Gosh, five brothers and sisters," Sam said.

"Yeah. What about you?" We were waiting in line to buy movie tickets.

"Three older sisters," he said. "They make my life a

living hell. Fortunately, the two oldest are off at college now."

I smiled. Talking to Sam was easier than I'd expected. And for the next two hours, I wouldn't have to talk at all.

The film we saw was an incredibly violent military-espionage-action thing that looked like home movies from my childhood. Mostly I sat in the dark, analyzing fight scenes and praying that Sam wouldn't try to hold my hand. What if my palms were sweaty? I nervously rubbed them on my jeans.

When the movie was over, we decided to get ice cream at a little shop down the block. As I was trying to think of something to say, Sam reached over and took one of my hands.

Just like that, we were holding hands.

It wasn't bad.

At Ye Olde Ice Cream Shoppe, we got our orders and sat down at a little marble-topped table. I was wondering how far I could throw the table, if necessary, when Sam asked, "So what are you doing for Thanksgiving?"

"Just having dinner with Anne, I think," I said.

"It's too bad you won't be with your parents."

"True." I nodded and applied myself to my sundae.

"We're going to have hell dinner with the relatives," Sam said. He held up his maraschino cherry. "Want mine?"

"Yep." He put it on top of my sundae and smiled. I smiled back. "Why is it hell dinner?"

He made a face. "My two oldest sisters will be back. There will be much hogging of the bathrooms, phone, and TV. My uncle Ted will talk nonstop about his business, which is insurance."

I winced in sympathy.

"Mom will try to keep Aunt Phyllis away from the liquor, but it won't work. Dad will be trying to watch the football game, so he'll be shouting at the TV and spilling corn nuts on the carpet." Sam shrugged. I liked the way his chestnut hair sort of fell over his forehead. And he had nice eyes. Hazel colored. Kind of tortoiseshell.

"Sounds pretty bad," I said. Was that kind of Thanksgiving common? I had no idea. I only knew what I'd seen on TV. What kind of Thanksgiving would my old friends Ella and Dr. Martinez have?

Sam shrugged again. "It'll suck. But then it'll be over, and I'll have four weeks to brace myself for Christmas."

I laughed, and he grinned back at me. A slight movement behind him caught my eye. Sam had his back to the big plate-glass window, and someone had walked past it. No — someone was still there.

My hand froze in midair, and my heart felt encased in ice.

Ari was outside, giving me a predator's grin and a thumbs-up sign.

71

Right in the middle of my freaking *date.*

Quickly I glanced around the shop. There was an exit behind the counter. I could knock over this table to slow him down . . .

"Max? Are you okay?"

"Uh-huh," I muttered absently, my eyes locked on Ari. He grinned again at me, then walked past the window. I saw a flash of streaked hair next to him, and then I saw my reflection in the window.

Sam turned to see what I was looking at just as Ari slipped out of sight.

I sat very still, waiting for Erasers to burst through the window, drop through the ceiling.

Sam was still looking at me quizzically. "You okay?" he asked again.

"Um-hmm." I tried to look normal. "Just thought I saw something."

Believe what you know, not what you see.

Okay, so not only Erasers butting in, but don't you just

hate it when the little Voice inside your brain starts talking at you during a date? I know I sure do. And what did it mean? I already knew Ari was still alive.

"Max?"

I gave Sam my attention again. "Sorry — got distracted." I smiled apologetically at him. I was on full alert, ready to spring into action, but nothing was happening.

"I like how you're eating a whole sundae," said Sam. "Some girls would be like, Oh, just a small fat-free scoop in a cup. But you're all over that thing."

I laughed, startled, wondering if I should feel embarrassed. "I don't worry about what I eat." Just, you know, *if* I'm going to eat.

"I like it," Sam said again.

And I am liking you, I thought.

72

We got a ride back to Anne's with Sam's third-oldest sister, who'd just gotten her license. Sam walked me up to Anne's front porch.

"Thanks," I said, feeling awkward and at a loss again. "I had a really good time."

"Me too," said Sam. "You're not like other girls I've met."

You can say that again, pal.

"Is that good or bad?" I asked.

"Good. Definitely good." Sam really did have a nice smile. He moved closer to me, put one hand on my shoulder and the other under my chin. My eyes went wide when he kissed me. We were almost the same height, and he wasn't as lean and hard as Fang. He kissed me again, angling his head the other way, and he put his arms around my waist.

You know what? My wings didn't even cross my mind. I closed my eyes and just went with it. Oh, my God, kissing.

Go with the flow, Max.

For once, the Voice had something worthwhile to say.

An irritated little beep came from the car — Sam's sister wanted to get home.

We broke apart, both of us wide-eyed and laughing a little.

"Whoa," Sam said, and I nodded in agreement.

"You better go," I said. "But thanks again, for everything. It was great."

"Yeah." Sam looked like he wanted to kiss me again, but his sister tapped the horn once more. Looking regretful, he went down the steps and across the dark driveway. "Talk to you tomorrow," he called back over his shoulder.

"Yeah."

They drove off, leaving me alone with feelings I didn't even have words for.

73

Anne was waiting for me inside. "How was it?" she asked, standing up and smiling.

"Fine," I said. "Well, good night." I kept walking and went up the stairs. I wasn't trying to be rude, not that that usually bothers me, but I just couldn't talk to her about anything that mattered. I went up to my room and sat on my bed, reliving the last ten minutes.

My door opened slightly, and Fang put his head around it. He came in holding one hand over his eyes. "Whoa," he said. "Your happy glow. It's blinding."

I rolled my eyes at him, then pulled off my hoodie. I wiggled my shoulders and let my wings untuck a little bit. Ahh. That felt better. I'd been holding them in tight all night. I wondered if Sam had felt them at all. He hadn't screamed or looked horrified, so I guessed not.

Fang shut the door. "They wanted to stay up to wait for you, but Anne made them go to bed."

"Good thinking on Anne's part," I said.

"So? How was it?" Fang leaned against my desk and

crossed his arms over his chest. I heard something in his voice and looked up at his face. As usual, he looked completely impassive, but I knew him so well that I could read the almost indiscernible twitch of his jaw muscle, the slight tightening around his eyes.

"I saw him — what's the phrase? oh, yeah — 'stuck to you like glue.' So I guess you got along all right." Fang waited as I tried to figure out what was going through his head.

"Yeah," I said finally. "There's a lot of that going around."

He looked a little embarrassed, and I kicked off my sneakers. Fang sat down next to me, leaning against my headboard. "So you like him. I don't have to kill him." His voice was tense.

I shrugged. "Yeah. He was really nice. We had a good time."

"But . . . ?"

I rubbed my temples with my hands. "But so what? He could be the nicest guy in the world, but it doesn't change anything. I'm still a mutant freak. We're still in a situation I hate more every day. We can't trust anyone. We can't solve the code mystery. We can't find our parents — not that it would help if we did."

Fang was quiet.

"I saw Ari tonight," I said, and his head came up. "He was standing outside the ice cream shop. He smiled at me. And there was someone with him. . . ." I paused, thinking back to that flash of blond hair. "I saw —" Then it hit me. I'd thought I'd seen my reflection in the window. But I hadn't.

I turned slowly and looked at Fang. "Ari had me with

him. There was a me outside the window." My stomach took a dive.

Fang blinked: his version of complete astonishment.

"I saw a flash of blond-streaked hair in the van that day they attacked us," I said. "And tonight I saw that same hair, outside with Ari. I thought it was my own reflection in the window. But it wasn't a reflection. It was a *me*."

He didn't bother asking me if I was sure. He knew he didn't have to.

"Holy crap," he said, trying to process this. "A Max on the dark side. Pretty much the worst thing I can think of. Jesus. Another Max. A bad Max. Crap."

"That's not all," I said slowly. "You know how I said if I went bad, I'd want you to — do anything you had to, to keep the others safe?"

He looked at me warily. "Yeah."

"The reason I asked about that . . ." I took a deep breath and looked away. "A couple times, when I've looked into a mirror, I've — seen myself morph. Into an Eraser."

Fang didn't say anything.

"I touch my face, and it feels just the same. Human, smooth. But the mirror shows me as an Eraser." I looked down. I couldn't believe I was admitting this out loud.

There was a long silence. Seconds ticked by like hours.

"I bet you looked kind of Pekingesey," Fang said finally.

I snapped my head up to look at him. He seemed very calm, very normal, despite what I'd just told him. "What?"

"Bet you were kind of cute, pup girl." He bared his

teeth as if they were fangs and made a little growling sound. "Rrrff!" he said, and made a pouncing motion at me.

I smacked him upside the head. He dodged to one side, laughing, but I jumped to my feet, angry. He held his hands up in surrender and with difficulty stopped laughing.

"Look," said Fang, trying to keep a straight face. "I know you're not an Eraser. I don't know why you saw that in the mirror, and I don't know who the other Max is, but I know who you are, all the way through. And you're not an Eraser. And even if I saw you as an Eraser, I would still recognize you. I know you're not evil, no matter what you might look like."

I thought of the Voice telling me to believe what I knew rather than what I saw, and tears started to my eyes. I sank back down onto the bed, just wanting to go to sleep and not think about anything.

"Thanks," I told Fang in a broken voice.

He stood up, then smoothed my hair with his hand. "You're fine," he said quietly.

"Don't you *dare* put any of this in your blog," I warned him. "Don't even think about it for a millisecond."

"Don't flatter yourself," he said, and left my room.

PART 4

THERE'S NO PLACE LIKE HOME

74

"Please."

"It isn't time yet, Ari." Jeb didn't look at him, just kept reading printouts of reports from the field.

"It'll never be time!" Ari exploded, pacing angrily around the room. "You keep telling me it's almost time, but you never let me take them out! What are we waiting for?"

His wings ached and burned where they were attached, and Ari reached into his pocket for his pills. He downed four, dry, and turned back to his father.

"Be patient," said Jeb. "You know we need to stick to the plan." He looked up at Ari. "You're letting your emotions color your decisions. That isn't good, Ari. We've talked about this."

"Me!" Ari burst out. "What about you? You know the reason you can't off her? 'Cause you're all wrapped up in her! You love Max! You love Max best! That's why you won't let me kill her."

Jeb didn't say anything, just looked at him. Ari could

tell Jeb was mad and trying not to show it. Just once, Ari wanted to see Jeb show the same love and admiration for him as he did for Max. When Jeb looked at Max, even pictures of Max, his face softened, his eyes grew more intent. When he looked at Ari, it was as if he were looking at anyone.

And Jeb hated the new Max, for some reason. He couldn't stand to be around her — everyone had noticed it. So Ari was making a big point of hanging out with her as much as possible. Anything to get under Jeb's skin, make him take notice.

Jeb finally spoke. "You don't know what you're talking about. You don't know the big picture. You have a part to play in this, but you have to do what I tell you. If you don't think you can do that, I'll find someone who can."

Rage ignited inside Ari. His hands gripped at his sides so he wouldn't reach out and grab Jeb's throat. He wanted to throttle the life out of him — almost. Just until Jeb realized he loved Ari and should respect him more.

But right now he had to get out of here. Ari spun and crashed out the door, letting it slam behind him. Outside, he took a running jump off the roof of the trailer — he still wasn't great at taking off right from the ground. Awkwardly and painfully, he flew high and headed for one of his favorite alone places — the top of a huge tree.

He landed clumsily on a branch and grabbed the trunk to hang on. Furious tears sprang to his eyes. Closing them, he leaned back against the smooth, mottled bark of his tree. It all hurt so much. His wings, how much Jeb loved Max, how Max looked right through Ari . . .

He remembered how she'd smiled at that pale twig last

night when they were eating ice cream. Who was that guy? A nobody. A fragile little human. Ari could rip him in half without even trying.

A low growl rose in his throat as he remembered how Max had kissed that loser on the front porch. Max had kissed him! Like she was some normal girl! If that guy only knew — he wouldn't go near Max in a million years.

But maybe he would. Maybe he would love Max even if he knew she was a mutant freak. Max was special that way. People cared about her. Boys loved her. She was so strong — so strong and beautiful and fierce.

A choked sob burst out of Ari's chest. Tears streaming down his cheeks, he brought his arm up to his face, pressing his tears into his jacket.

Ari made another muffled sound against his sleeve, and then it all became too much. He felt himself morph full out into an Eraser, and his powerful jaws opened. Feeling his tears streaking through his fur, Ari stifled a sob and clamped his teeth down into his arm. He closed his eyes and hung on tight, making sure no sound escaped. He felt his teeth pierce his jacket, felt them scissor into his skin and muscle. He tasted blood, but he hung on.

Because actually, this felt better.

75

"I think that's it. I am freaking *amazing.* We found it." I peeped out from behind the yew shrub and looked across the street again. "No wonder you worship me."

Clearly I had snapped out of my malaise of the previous night. Let's keep those fourteen-year-old mutant-bird-kid hormone swings coming, eh?

Fang gave me a long-suffering and not very worshipful glance, then looked past me at the modest suburban brick house. It was dinky, old-fashioned, but, given how close it was to DC, probably worth almost half a million dollars. *Note to self:* Invest in DC real estate. Save up your allowance.

"Really? And that's the church in the background?"

I nodded. "Yep. So what now?"

He looked at me. "You're the leader."

I narrowed my eyes at him, then grabbed his shoulder and marched him across the street with me. I rang the bell before my annoying common sense could kick in.

We waited, and I heard footsteps coming to the door.

Then it opened, and Fang and I were staring at the woman who may or may not but really looked like she could have been Iggy's mother.

"Yes?" she said, and she was — get this — drying her hands on a kitchen towel *just like a mom.* She was tall and slender, with very pale strawberry-blond hair, fair skin, and freckles. Her eyes were a light sky blue, like Iggy's, except of course hers actually worked because they hadn't been experimented on by mad scientists. Mad as in crazy, not as in anger-management classes.

"Can I help you?" she asked.

"Ma'am, we're selling subscriptions to the *Wall Street Journal,*" Fang said with a straight face.

Her expression cleared. "Oh, no thanks. We already get the *Post.*"

"Okay then," said Fang, and we turned and skedaddled right out of there.

She absolutely, positively, definitely *might* have been Iggy's mom. So what now?

76

“Still smells kind of like explosives,” Iggy muttered to the Gasman.

The Gasman sniffed. “Yeah. I like that smell. Smells like excitement.”

“God knows we could use more of that,” Iggy said.

Gazzy’s footsteps were almost silent on the hard concrete floor, but Iggy could follow him with no effort. Even without Gazzy, Iggy could have found his way to the file room by memory. He bet he could even find his way back to the Institute if you dropped him into a subway tunnel in New York. It almost made up for being completely without any kind of freaking sight *at all.*

Yeah, right.

“Here we go.” Gazzy soundlessly opened the file room door, and Iggy heard the flick of the light switch. Now he got to stand around like a coatrack while Gazzy did all the work.

“She put those files someplace toward the front of the

room," he reminded the Gasman. "On the right side. Is there a metal cabinet?"

"They're all metal," said Gazzy, moving over. He opened one, riffled some pages, then closed it. "I don't even know what I'm looking for. All the files look alike."

"None of 'em are marked Top Secret in big black letters?"

"No."

Iggy waited while the Gasman opened and riffled through and closed several more file drawers.

"Hey, wait a minute," Gazzy said. "Huh. This is something. It's a bunch of files lumped together with a rubber band. They're a different color, and they look older, beat-up."

"So read them."

The sound of the rubber band being pulled off. Pages rustling.

"Whoa."

"What?" This was the kind of thing that made Iggy crazy: other people getting all the info much sooner because they could see. He always had to wait to be told stuff. He *hated* it.

"These are files on, like, patients," said the Gasman. "Not students from this school. These are patients, and they're from the . . . Standish Home for Incurables."

"What is that? Sounds like a whole bunch of not-fun."

Gazzy read, and Iggy forced himself to be patient.

"Wait —," said Gazzy, and Iggy thought, *Oh, like I have a lot of freaking choice.*

"This is weird. I mean, as far as I can tell, *this* school used to be, like, an insane asylum, until maybe just two years ago. These files are on patients who used to live here. But why is the headhunter saving them?"

"Maybe he had something to do with them? Did he run the nuthouse? Maybe he was a *patient* and he killed all the others and opened this school —"

"Can't tell. There's a lot of stuff here. Too much to read right now. Let's show these to Max. I can stuff them under my shirt."

"Cool. We better be heading back."

"Yep."

Iggy followed Gazzy to the stairs. *Let's see, almost lunchtime. Wonder where Tess will sit today* — Then Gazzy paused for a second, and Iggy almost ran into him.

"That's funny," Gazzy muttered. "There's a door here I never noticed."

Iggy heard him step forward and open it. Dank, cool air wafted out at them.

"What is it?"

"A tunnel," said the Gasman, sounding taken aback. "A long, dark tunnel going farther than I can see. Right under the school."

77

I was kind of dreading seeing Sam again at school. Would he blow me off? Had he told anyone about us kissing? Would I get teased and therefore have to kick serious butt?

It was fine. I saw him in class, and he gave me a discreet and yet special smile. No one seemed to be watching him or me to see us interact as gossip fodder. During free period, we sat at a table across from each other and talked and read and studied, and not even the headhunter came down on us.

It was cool. For almost that whole day, I felt like life didn't totally suck. And that lasted all the way till I got back to Anne's, so we might be talking new record here.

"A tunnel?" I looked at Gazzy and Iggy in confusion. "Why would there be a tunnel under the school?"

"Excellent question," the Gasman said, nodding. "Plus the secret files."

I flipped through the files again. "Nudge? Do a check

on the school. Didn't I see something that said it had been there for, like, twenty years?"

"All the brochures said that," Fang confirmed. "Plus there's a plaque in the front hall that says Founded in 1985."

Nudge got onto the laptop we'd more or less appropriated from Anne. I kept flipping through the files, which were all about patients who had entered the sanitarium and never come out. The files were dated mostly from the last fifteen years or so, until just two years ago. In other people's lives, ending up at a school that used to be a mental hospital and had a tunnel under it would be very interesting but coincidental.

In our lives, it was like a great big red warning light blinking on and off.

"Huh," said Nudge. "The school's Web site says it's been in that building since 1985. But when I Google it, nothing shows up before two years ago."

"Did they change the name?" Iggy asked.

Fang shook his head. "Don't think so — it doesn't say that anywhere."

I double-checked the mystery files. "The Standish Home had the exact same address. And look at this office stationery — it has a little drawing of the building." I showed it to the others. It was a drawing of our school, exactly.

I looked up at the flock. "This can't be good," I said, with my natural gift for understatement.

"Should we ask Anne about it?" Iggy asked.

Fang and I met eyes. He gave the tiniest shake of his head.

"What for?" I said. "Either she knows about it and is

in on everything, so we don't want to tip her off that we know, or she only knows what they told her and so can't help us."

We were quiet for a few moments, each of us thinking. I heard the TV click on in the kitchen. Anne took out pots and opened the fridge. The news was on, talking about an upcoming cold snap and who had won a recent college football game. Then a male newscaster said, "And in our nation's capital today, the president made a surprising announcement that has many politicos scratching their heads. Only three days before this year's budget was supposed to be presented, President Danning announced a stunning revision: He has taken back almost a billion dollars allotted to the military and is channeling it into public education, as well as nationwide shelters for homeless women and children."

I froze.

Fang and I exchanged looks of disbelief, then I looked at Angel. She was grinning. I heard Total laugh, and then Angel and Total slapped high fives. Well, Total slapped a high four.

I dropped my head and rubbed my temples, which had suddenly started pounding. We had to get out of this town. Next Angel would be making the president ban homework or something.

78

That night, at exactly 11:05, six windows on the second floor of Anne's house opened. One by one we jumped out of our respective rooms, fell about eight feet, then snapped our wings open and got some uplift.

The six of us flew through the dark, chilly night. There were no clouds, and the moon shone so brightly that the trees below us cast long shadows.

The bat cave looked satisfyingly like something from a horror movie. Fang had discovered it weeks ago. It was set into an old limestone ridge a couple miles from the house. Overgrown vines, dead with approaching winter, obscured the entrance. We flew through them, trying not to get tangled, and braked to a fast stop inside. The cave was full of stalactites hanging down like teeth from the ceiling, and somewhere in the darkness there was an ominous drip of unseen water. About thirty feet in, the air became thick with the acidic smell of guano, so we stayed near the opening.

"I bet no people have ever been in here," said Gazzy,

sitting cross-legged in the entrance. "They'd have to rock climb just to get up here."

"I wish we could see what's farther back," said Nudge.

"Yeah, me too," said Iggy brightly.

"Okay, guys," I said. "Listen, I've been thinking, and I really think it's time for us to move on. This has been a great break, but we're all rested, healed up, and we should disappear again."

This announcement was not met with confetti and noisemakers.

"I mean," I went on in the deafening silence, "Ari knows we're close by. He attacked us on our way home from school — he probably has cameras trained on Anne's house. The headhunter has it in for us. Now the weird files from the school, the mystery tunnel — it's all adding up to an ugly picture." *Not to mention what Angel might be doing to the leader of the free world.* I shot her a hard glance, in case she was listening in on my thoughts, and she grinned at me.

"We should clear out of here before all this stuff starts hitting the fan."

I saw Nudge and Gazzy glance at each other. Angel leaned her head against Iggy's shoulder. He patted her hair. More silence.

"I mean, maybe this is where we learn to think smart, stay one step ahead of the game instead of having the game bite us in the ass."

Or maybe this is the time you learn how to stay and make it work.

I scowled. *This isn't a relationship, Voice. It's a trap, or a test, or at best a surreal side trip on a journey that's already been fairly mind-blowing.*

"It's just that . . . ," Nudge began, looking at Gazzy. He gave her an encouraging nod. "Well, Thursday's Thanksgiving. We only have half a day of school Wednesday, and then it's Thanksgiving."

"We've never had a real Thanksgiving dinner before," said Angel. "Anne's going to make turkey and pumpkin pie."

Frustration made me snide, in that endearing way I had. "Yeah, and *that's* worth staying in town for — Anne's home cooking."

The younger kids looked abashed, and I felt like a jerk, raining on their parade.

"I'm just — really antsy," I explained carefully. "I'm twitchy and nervous and feel like I want to be screaming through the sky on the way out of town, you know?"

"We know," Nudge said apologetically. "It's just — she's going to make sweet potatoes with raisins and little marshmallows on top."

I bit my lip hard in order to keep from saying, "Well, God knows *that's* worth sacrificing our freedom for! Why didn't you mention it earlier?"

Instead I tried a smile that turned into a grimace, and turned around for a minute, as if I were examining the night sky. Through the vines. When I'd gotten more of a grip, I turned back to them.

"Okay, so we'll stay for Thanksgiving," I said reluctantly. Their faces lit up, and I felt an anvil settling on my chest. "Those better be some good sweet potatoes."

79

"Did the thing pop yet?" Anne peered anxiously over my shoulder into the oven.

"Uh, not yet," I said. "But it looks like it's doing okay." I compared the turkey in the oven to the picture on the stuffing package. "See? It's the right color."

"Well, it's supposed to be done when that thing pops up."

"I know," I said reassuringly. I'd heard her the first fifty times.

"What if it's defective?" Anne looked stricken. "What if it never pops? What if it's my first turkey and our first Thanksgiving together and it's awful and dry and we all hate it?"

"Well, no doubt that would be symbolic of our whole lifetime together," I said solemnly, then made a "kidding" face. "Uh, maybe you could supervise Zephyr with setting the table? He looked a little lost with all the extra silverware."

Anne looked at me, nodded, glanced again at the oven window, then went into the dining room.

"How's that stuffing coming?" I asked Nudge.

"Okeydokey," she said, fluffing it in a pot with a large wooden salad fork. She read the package again. "I think it's done."

"Looks good," I said. "Just set it aside. There's no way to make sure all this stuff comes out ready at the same time."

"Cranberry sauce is good to go," Iggy said, jiggling the can so it slid out with a wet plop into a bowl. "I could have made some from scratch."

"I know." I lowered my voice. "You're the only one here who can cook at all. But let's just go with the program."

"I want a drumstick," said Total, from right under my feet.

"Get in line," I told him, and went over to Fang. I watched what he was doing for a minute, and he turned to me with an "I dare you to say something" expression.

"You're an artist," I managed. He turned back and surveyed the neat rows of marshmallows lined up across the casserole of mashed sweet potatoes.

"We've all got crosses to bear," he said, and went back to work.

I leaned down and looked into the oven again. "Anne? The little white thing popped up. I think it's ready."

"Oh, my God!" Anne exclaimed from the other room. She rushed into the kitchen and grabbed some oven mitts. "It popped?" She was lunging for the oven door when suddenly she turned to me. "What if the popper thing is wrong? What if it's not really ready?"

I looked at her. "Take the turkey out of the oven."

She breathed out. "Right. Okay."

Sheesh. Grown-ups.

80

Fifteen minutes later, we were all sitting around the dining-room table. Everything looked very schmancy. We had a white tablecloth and cloth napkins. Candles were lit. The food was on the table, looking like all the pictures on the packages.

Gazzy was holding his fork and knife upright on the table, and I frowned at him and shook my head. He put them down.

"How about we go around and each give thanks individually?" Anne said. "Ariel? Why don't you go first?"

"Uh . . ." Angel looked at me, and I smiled tightly.

Just do your best, sweetie, and don't give anything away. She gave me a tiny nod.

"I'm thankful for my family," she said, gesturing at all of us. "I'm thankful I have a dog. I'm thankful I have Max to take care of me." And then, as if realizing that Anne was sitting right there, Angel added, "And I'm thankful that we've had this good time here. I really like this place."

Anne smiled at her. "Thank you. Now Zephyr?"

"Um, I'm thankful for all this food," said Gazzy. "And you know, my family. And being here."

"Krystal?"

"I'm thankful for food and my brothers and sisters," said Nudge. "And I'm thankful I have big brown eyes and long lashes. I'm thankful that we could stay here for a while. I'm thankful for MTV. And gummy worms."

"All right," said Anne. "Jeff?"

"Uh, what Zephyr said." Iggy's fingers drummed on the table. "Fnick's turn."

Fang looked like he'd rather be at the dentist. "Me too. Family, food. Place to stay." His dark eyes met mine and his face flushed, like he was having one of those heat attacks.

My turn. I *was* thankful for stuff — but not anything I wanted to mention in front of Anne. Silently I was thankful for all of us being together and being healthy. I was so thankful we had Angel back, and that we were free and not at the School. I was thankful we weren't being attacked by Erasers at this very minute. Bad things had happened to us, could happen again, but weren't happening now, and I wasn't stupid enough to take it for granted.

"Uh, I'm thankful that we've had this time here," I said. "It's been really great. And, you know, thankful for my family, and for having plenty of food."

Anne paused, as if waiting to see if anyone would add anything. "My turn, then. Thank you all for helping make our Thanksgiving meal. I never could have done it myself."

You ain't whistling Dixie, I thought.

"To me, it's even more meaningful that we all worked

together to make our dinner," Anne continued. "I've never had children, never been that domestic. But these last weeks with you here, well, I've gotten a real idea of everything that I've been missing. I like the fact that my life is centered around yours. Amazingly, I like having a household of children."

Total licked my leg under the table, and I almost yelped, then heard him chuckle softly.

"It's chaotic, and tons of work, and expensive, and I get called to the school, and every night I fall into bed completely exhausted and know that I have to do it all again the next day." She looked around at us and smiled. "And now I wouldn't have it any other way."

As speeches went, it was a pretty good one, I'll give her that.

"So I sincerely hope that this Thanksgiving is only the first in a long line of Thanksgivings we'll share together." Again she smiled at us, letting her gaze linger on Angel. "Because I would like to adopt all of you."

81

"Yes, let's give thanks for what we have by *leaving* it," the Gasman muttered.

"Gazzy, I told you — you don't have to come," I said.

"Of course I have to come," he said, tying his sneakers — new ones that Anne had bought.

"I just can't believe it," said Angel, bouncing a little on my bed.

"It's what we've all waited for," said Nudge, sounding wistful. She looked over at Iggy quickly. "I'm glad it's happened to you, Iggy. I mean, it would be nice if it happened to all of us, but for the first one, I'm glad it was —" She stopped, as if realizing she was running on.

"Thanks." Iggy was sitting tensely, shoes and coat already on. His face was flushed, and his long, slender fingers drummed nervously on his knees.

Last night, after some of our Thanksgiving bloat had eased, Fang and I had told the others about possibly finding Iggy's parents. They'd all been stunned.

"Do you want to go see them?" I'd asked Iggy.

"Yeah, of course!" Iggy had said, then his eyebrows came together. "I'm not sure."

"What?" Nudge shrieked. "How can you not be sure?"

"It's what we've talked about before," Iggy said, looking self-conscious. "I mean, I'm blind now. I have wings. I'm a weird, mutant hybrid, and they've never seen anything like me. Maybe they would want the original, all-human me, but . . ."

That was exactly what I was thinking. Personally, I thought that even if we found info on my parents, I probably wouldn't want to go ring their doorbell. And they probably wouldn't want me to either.

"I understand," I said. "But it's up to you. We'll support you, whatever you decide."

"Let me sleep on it," Iggy had said.

"No prob," I'd said.

So he'd thought about it and decided to go, and here we were.

Fang opened my bedroom window wide. Nudge clambered onto the windowsill and launched herself into the air. The sun lit her tawny wings as she caught the wind and rose into the sky. One by one the rest of us followed, with me going last.

It felt weird to be flying out in the middle of the day, but today was special. Today we were taking Iggy to see his parents, his real parents.

I had no idea what would happen. Today could be filled with unbelievable joy or tearful heartbreak. Even if it ended with happiness for Iggy, the rest of us would get the heartbreak. Because we would be telling him good-bye. Which for me was too painful to begin to comprehend.

We hadn't really talked about Anne's offer to adopt us. As far as I was concerned, it wasn't even worth thinking about. I wondered if any of the younger kids felt differently, and guessed I'd find out sooner or later. Probably sooner.

After twenty minutes of flying, we were across the street from the house Fang and I had gone to several days before. It was the day after Thanksgiving, so we hoped they would both be home.

"You ready?" I asked Iggy, taking his hand in mine. The only way I could get through this was to not think about the bigger picture. I could take only one second at a time.

Iggy nodded stiffly, his sightless eyes staring straight ahead, as if by looking hard enough, he could make his parents' house come into view. He leaned down to whisper in my ear. "I'm scared."

I squeezed his hand and whispered back, "If you weren't, I'd know you were nuts. But I think if you don't do this, you'll wonder about it forever."

"I know. I know I have to do it. But . . ."

He didn't have to say any more. Fourteen years ago, his parents had lost a perfect little baby. Now Iggy was almost six feet tall and blind, and "genetic hybrid" was the kind description.

He shook his head and put his shoulders back. "Let's do this thing."

The six of us crossed the street. It had clouded over a bit, and the wind was cold. I pulled Angel's coat tighter around her chin and tucked in her scarf. She looked up at me solemnly, her blue eyes expressing the same hopes and fears we were all feeling.

I rang the doorbell. We were wound so tight it sounded like an enormous gong. A few moments later, the door opened, and the same woman as before looked out at me. Her brow furrowed slightly, as if she remembered my face but not from where.

"Uh, hello . . . ma'am," I began, in that smooth handle-everything manner I have. "I saw you on TV, where you said you'd lost your son?"

A look of sadness crossed her face. "Yes?"

I stepped back so she could see Iggy. "I think this is him."

Okay, so I'm not known for subtlety.

For a second the woman frowned, about to get angry at me for yanking her chain, but then she looked at Iggy and her frown changed to a look of puzzlement.

Now that I saw them both together, the similarities were even more obvious. They had the same coloring, same body type, same cheekbones and chin. The woman blinked. Her mouth opened, but no sound came out. She put her hand to her chest and stared at Iggy. I gave Iggy's hand another squeeze — he had no idea what was going on and just had to wait in painful suspense.

Then a man appeared. The woman stepped back and motioned silently to Iggy. Though Iggy looked very much like the woman, he did share some features with the man as well. They had the same nose, the same shape mouth. The man stared at Iggy, then looked around at all of us.

"Wha . . . ," he said, looking stunned.

"We saw you on TV," I explained again. "We think this might be the son you lost, fourteen years ago." I put my arm through Iggy's and pulled him forward a little bit.

"We call him Iggy. But I think his last name is really Griffiths, like yours."

Iggy's fair face flushed, and he lowered his head. I could practically feel the pounding of his heart.

"James?" the woman whispered, starting to reach out to Iggy. She stopped and looked at her husband. "Tom — is this James?" she asked wonderingly.

The man swallowed visibly. He stepped back from the door. "Please, come in, all of you."

I started to refuse — we never went into strange places where we might get trapped or caught. But I realized that this was where Iggy might stay, forever, and if I thought it was a trap, then we better get the heck out of here.

So I swallowed hard and said, "Okay."

As the others filed into the house, I shot a glance at Angel to see if she looked at all concerned or suspicious. But she just walked right in, so, with a tight feeling in my chest, I followed her.

The inside of the house was nice, but not as fancy or big as Anne's. I looked around, thinking, *This might be where Iggy will live from now on.* He might eat dinner at that table and listen to that TV. It was starting to seem as if we'd fallen down the rabbit hole, you know? Weird, half-wolf mutants chasing us? Totally believable. The idea that Iggy might be moving into a normal existence? Totally mind-blowing.

"Um, sit down," the woman said, watching Iggy.

He hesitated until he felt me sit down, then he sat next to me.

"I don't know where to begin," said the woman. She sat on Iggy's other side, and she finally seemed to get it that he wasn't looking around, wasn't meeting her eyes.

"Um, I'm blind," said Iggy, his fingers plucking nervously at the hem of his sweatshirt. "They, uh — well, I can't see anymore."

"Oh, *dear,*" said the woman, looking distressed. The man sat across from us, and I saw a look of pain on his face.

"We don't know what happened," he said, leaning forward. "You — our son was taken out of this house fourteen years ago. You were — he was only four months old. There was no trace. I hired detectives. We —" He stopped, as if the memory was too painful for him to go on.

"It's a long, weird story," I said. "And we're not one hundred percent positive. But it really does look like Iggy's the baby you lost."

The woman nodded and then took Iggy's hand. "I feel he is. You might not be positive, but I feel it. I can tell. This is my son."

I couldn't believe it. How many times had we had this fantasy? Now it was all coming true for Iggy.

"I have to say — I think you're right." The man cleared his throat. "He — it sounds funny, but he really looks just the same as he did when he was a baby."

Any other time, Gazzy and Fang would have been all over that, riding Iggy and teasing him mercilessly. But they sat there stone-faced. It was starting to sink in, what was happening, what was about to happen.

"I know!" Mrs. Griffiths sat up suddenly. "James had a small red birthmark on his side, toward the back. I asked the doctor about it, but he said it was fine."

"Iggy has a birthmark," I said slowly. I'd seen it a hundred times.

Iggy wordlessly pulled up his shirt on the left side. Mrs. Griffiths immediately saw the birthmark. She gasped and put her hand over her mouth.

"Oh, my God!" she said, tears starting to run down her cheeks. "Oh, God. James! It's James!" In the next moment, she had leaned over and pulled Iggy into a tight hug. One hand stroked his strawberry-blond hair. Her eyes were closed, and her tears left a wet spot on Iggy's shoulder. "James, James," she whispered. "My baby."

My own throat was closing up. I glanced over and saw that Angel and Nudge were both fighting tears. Jeez. It was turning into a real weep-fest.

I cleared my throat. "So, well, you think this is James, the son you lost?"

The man, tears in his own eyes, nodded. "That's my son," he said, his voice breaking.

I hate stuff like this, where everyone's overwhelmed and weeping with joy and emotions are splashing all over the place. Ugh.

"Wh— who are you?" Mr. Griffiths asked me, as his wife pulled back to look at Iggy's face. He gestured at all of us.

"We're — friends," I said. "We — were taken too. But you're the first parents we've found." I hadn't meant to say *that*. What was wrong with me? Usually I was much stealthier and more secretive.

Mr. and Mrs. Griffiths looked even more surprised and concerned.

"So, uh, what now?" I asked briskly, rubbing my palms on my jeans.

The two grown-ups shot quick glances at each other. Mr. Griffiths gave his wife a subtle nod, and she turned to me. "James belongs with us," she said firmly. "I thought I'd lost him forever. Now that we have him back, I'm never letting him go. Do you hear me?" She looked positively fierce, and I held up my hands in the universal "Whoa, Nelly" gesture.

"No one's going to try to stop you. I think he's James too. But you know he's blind."

"I don't care," said Mrs. Griffiths, looking at Iggy with love. "I don't care if there are a million problems. We can handle anything, if we have him back."

Okay, that *might* cover the whole wing wrinkle. . . .

"Iggy? Do you want to stay?" I asked.

His face flushed again, but underneath his reserve I saw the hint of an unbelieving happiness. My heart squeezed painfully, and I thought, *I'm losing him.*

Slowly Iggy nodded. "I guess this is where I belong."

I patted his arm. "Yeah," I said softly.

"Do you have — things?" asked Mrs. Griffiths. "We'll move a bigger bed into what used to be your room. I haven't changed anything in there — just in case you came back to us someday." She touched his face gently. "It's a miracle. I can't believe it. If this is a dream, I hope I never wake up."

Iggy smiled faintly. "I don't have much of anything, actually," he said. He held up the small backpack that we'd filled with a few crucial supplies from Anne's house.

"Fine," said Mrs. Griffiths. "We can get you anything you need."

Spoken like a real parent.

82

And that's how one of us found his real parents. I won't bore you with the whole heartrending good-bye scene. Suffice it to say that mucho tears were shed. There was much going on in the "lamenting" department. I really don't want to talk about it.

Okay, I'll give you one little insight. I'd grown up with Iggy, known him my whole short, horrible life. I'd known him back when he could see, helped him learn how to fly. He was less obnoxious than Fang, quieter than Nudge, and a better cook than any of us. He was the Gasman's best friend. And yeah, friends move away, and it's sad and then you get over it. But there were only five people in the entire freaking world that I cared about and trusted, and I had just lost one of them. I'd had to walk away knowing that Iggy was standing in the doorway as if he could actually watch us leave, watch us leave him behind forever.

Basically, I felt like my heart had been stomped on by a soccer team wearing cleats.

But enough about me. I said I didn't want to talk about it.

83

Anne was quite the panicky mother hen about losing one of her chicks, especially since we wouldn't tell her squat about it.

All weekend she made hysterical phone calls and hovered over us, alternately begging, pleading, crying, and threatening. But all we would say was that he had left because he wanted to and he was safe. End of discussion.

Except Anne didn't understand what "end of discussion" meant. Saying "end of discussion" really only works if the other person actually shuts up about it. Anne didn't.

By Monday morning, our nerves were all stretched pretty thin. For one thing, I felt like my left arm had been cut off, because Iggy was gone. I'd found Nudge crying in her room twice; and Gazzy seemed practically catatonic without his favorite partner in crime. Angel didn't try to be stoic but climbed into my lap sobbing. Which meant that Total joined us.

"I'm such a marshmallow," he sobbed, tears making wet spots on his fur.

It took a lot to make any one of us cry. Losing Iggy was plenty. So with all the tears and heartache and sleeplessness, and then Anne riding me, trying to find out where Iggy was, by Monday morning I was pretty much ready to snap.

I mean, I was happy for him. Way happy. But more than sad for the rest of us. And knowing that this could happen again, to any of us, made me feel like the *Titanic,* plowing right toward an iceberg.

"I'm going to report Jeff missing at school," Anne told us as we filed out to the car.

"Okay," I said wearily, knowing it wouldn't help. We all piled into her Suburban and she headed to school, back as rigid as a steel pipe.

"I'm going to call the police," she said, looking at me in the mirror.

"Whatever," I said, ready to explode. "Why don't you put his face on a milk carton? He's just another one of those missing kids, isn't he? This place is full of them."

Anne's face in the mirror looked taken aback, almost — was it afraid? Interestingly, after that she dropped it.

Which meant what?

84

"Right! You all have your orders," Ari barked. He rolled his shoulders under his black leather coat. Another Eraser was driving, and twelve more crouched in the back of the van. "We go in, we grab the mutants, we clear out. Like surgery, right?"

"Right," several Erasers muttered.

Take the mutants alive, his Voice reminded him.

"Remember — take the mutants alive," Ari said. He grinned, looking forward to what was about to happen. "And no one touches Max! She's mine." He waited for the Voice to jump in with more advice, but it was silent.

He rubbed his hands together, already itching to feel his fists connect with Max's face. Sure, Dad had said to bring Max back alive — there was more he wanted to learn about her. But the only thing Ari wanted to learn was what size coffin she'd need. He knew how he'd play it: Despite his orders, another Eraser had "gone crazy," killing everything in sight. Before Ari could stop him, he'd ripped out Max's throat. Then Jeb would kill that

Eraser, Max would be dead, and Ari would be sitting pretty.

There were no downsides.

On the other hand . . . what if Max "disappeared"? What if Ari took Max and stashed her somewhere where no one could find her and she couldn't escape? He thought he knew a place. If Max was trapped, if she had no hope of escaping, and if Ari was the only one keeping her alive with food and water — then she'd get used to him, right? She'd be grateful to him, even. It would be just the two of them, with no one telling them what to do. They would become friends. Max would like him. They could play cards. She could read to him. They could play outside.

This was sounding more and more like the best idea he'd had all year. And he knew a good place to take her. Someplace she couldn't escape from. That is, once he'd cut her wings off.

85

"I have one more announcement," said Mr. Pruitt, staring balefully at the entire student body. It was Monday-morning assembly, and we were all trapped in the school auditorium, listening to the headhunter spew bile at us. At least it was equal-opportunity bile — not aimed at just the flock. So far he'd vented his feelings about how messy we left the lunchroom, how we thieving little punks had stolen school supplies, and how he doubted our ability to use the restrooms like normal human beings.

The man definitely had issues.

"One of our students has gone missing," Mr. Pruitt said, seeming to stare right at me.

I put on an innocent "Who, *moi?*" expression.

"Jeff Walker," the headhunter went on. "From ninth grade. Though he was a new student, I'm sure you all know whom I'm talking about. We're calling in a special detective unit," he said, narrowing his eyes at me. I kept my face carefully blank. "But if any of you have seen him, or know anything, or have any information whatsoever, come forward now. If we later find out that you *did* know something and did *not* come forward, it will be very bad for you. Am I making myself clear?"

Lots of confused nods.

Many kids turned to look at me, Fang, and the rest of the flock because we were Iggy's "siblings." I realized I should look upset and worried, and tried to change gears.

"Dismissed," spit the headhunter, making it sound like a terminal sentence.

I leaped up, anxious to get out of the crowded auditorium. In the hallway, my friend J.J. caught up to me.

"I'm so sorry, Max," she said, looking concerned. "What happened?"

Amazingly I had no story prepared. In my twisted freak-show world, people appearing out of nowhere and disappearing into nothingness was kind of everyday fare. Somehow, the idea that Iggy's absence would actually upset and concern people other than Anne had never occurred to me.

Okay, I'd dropped this ball. I admit it.

"Uh . . . ," I said, stalling. I didn't have time to think through all the possible stories to see if they had loopholes or bear traps further down the line. Several other kids crowded around us.

"I can't talk about it," I said. And just like that, thinking about Iggy's really being gone made actual, unfake tears come to my eyes. I let 'em rip. "I mean . . . I . . . just can't talk about it right now." I added a tiny sniffle and was rewarded with concerned understanding.

"Okay, everyone," J.J. said, waving her arms. "She can't talk about it. Let's back off, give her some space."

"Thanks," I told her. "I still can't believe he's really gone." Completely true.

"I'm so sorry," said J.J. "If only they had taken *my* brother instead."

She actually made me smile, just like a real friend.

"I'll see you later," she said, heading toward her locker. "Let me know if I can help — if you need anything."

I nodded. "Thanks."

The other kids were still looking at me, and paranoia made the hairs on the back of my neck stand up. Sitting in the auditorium, kids following me to ask me questions — I was way too twitchy to deal with any of it.

I turned and strode off in the other direction. But in the next hall, more kids looked up and, after glancing at one another, started toward me. Then the headhunter turned the corner. He hadn't seen me yet and was barking at other students. It was only moments before I would come under his fire. This was feeling bad.

I reversed direction quickly and headed down a third hall, and then I saw a door marked Teachers' Lounge. I'd never been in there. I pushed the door open and ducked in, already preparing my story about being lost.

Still facing the closed door, I let out a breath I hadn't realized I was holding. Then I turned around, ready to start sucking up to any teacher who might be in here.

There were quite a few teachers here, I observed with surprise. Including a bunch I'd never seen before. One was standing at the front of the room, as if telling a story, and others were grouped at tables. I quickly glanced at their faces, looking for someone I knew. Oh, good, Mr. Lazzara.

But — my heart took a beat and froze.

These were teachers, in the teachers' lounge.

Why were three of them pulling out Tasers?

86

Because they were whitecoat plants, ready to capture a mutant bird kid? I'm just guessing here.

In a split second I opened that door and whirled to run —

— right into the headhunter.

His ugly face split in an unholy grin, and he grabbed both my arms with an iron grip. "Leaving so soon? Surely you're not tired of our *hospitality,*" he snarled. He shoved me back into the teachers' lounge as I wrenched my arms free.

"Why, what's happening?" Mr. Lazzara asked in surprise.

"Keep away!" one of the other teachers barked at him.

I backed up and looked at the headhunter, disappointed but not surprised to see him pulling a plastic cord out of his pocket, no doubt intended for my wrists.

"I always knew there was a reason I hated you," I said tightly. "Besides just your personality, I mean." Then I leaped into the air, aiming a kick at his head. I caught him off guard and whipped his head sideways, but he sprang up and came for me. I jumped onto a table, grabbed the light fixture hanging from the ceiling, and swung fast, hard kicks at everyone coming toward me.

Guess what, Voice? I thought. *This time I'm believing what I'm seeing.*

The headhunter grabbed for me again. "Oh, no you don't, you wretched little blister," he spit at me. "You're my prize, my *reward* for suffering through day after day of ignorant, pestilent little swine."

"I miss the gold-watch tradition, myself," I said, then I spun out of the way, kicking him hard as he lunged for me across the table. He fell and slid sideways, knocking down some other teachers, including the ones with Tasers. *Note to self:* Crack up later.

Some teachers were huddled against a back wall, looking terrified. Michael Lazzara looked as though he was about to throw himself into the action on the good-guy side. But the bad-guy teachers were closing in on me from all angles, pointing their Tasers at me. I didn't know who they were or who they worked for, but a good general rule of thumb is to avoid people with electric stun guns.

With a huge jump, I cleared several teachers and crashed through the door into the hallway. I wasn't sure exactly which classrooms the flock would be in at this time, so I just streaked down the hall, shouting at the top of my lungs.

"Bandada! Bezheet! See-chass! Move, move, move!"

87

I ran as fast as I could down both classroom halls, yelling, and saw Nudge and then Fang burst out of their rooms. I felt both frantic and incredibly pissed: Here was the proof I'd needed all along to convince the others to leave *before now.*

Other kids were streaming into the hallway, wondering what all the commotion was. Angel! Thank God, there she was, racing out of her classroom in front of me. She looked back, nodded, and poured on the speed toward the exit.

"Max! In here!" I saw Sam twenty feet ahead, standing in the doorway of an empty classroom. He motioned urgently with his hand. "Come on! Through here!"

But was he starting to look kind of Erasery around the edges — teeth a tiny bit too long, hair a shade thicker? I couldn't tell and couldn't take a chance.

"You can trust me!" he said, as I saw the Gasman rush out of his room, almost running into Nudge.

Sam stepped forward as if to intercept me, but I made

one of my famous split-second decisions. I plowed right through him, knocking him to the ground.

"The thing is," I said, "I can't trust *anybody!*"

"Max!" Fang shouted, standing at the exit doors. The four of us raced toward him, and together we burst through to the parking lot. Behind us, the whole school was in chaos — kids filling the halls, people screaming, yelling, running around.

Looks like school's out, I thought.

"Up and away!" I shouted, hearing a car's engine race. The rest of the flock took to the air just as I realized the headhunter's fancy car was screeching toward me at full speed. He was going to run me down — if he could.

I ran straight at the car and, right before it crashed into me, I jumped into the air. As my wings gathered wind beneath them, I kicked hard, shattering the headhunter's windshield. Then I was ten, fifteen, twenty feet in the air, looking down.

Within seconds the headhunter had lost control of his car, and it squealed, sliding sideways right into several parked cars.

"Cool!" said the Gasman.

Pruitt spilled out of his wrecked car, his face almost purple with insane rage. "This isn't the end of this!" he screamed, shaking his fist up at me in time-honored custom. "You're accidents, stains, mistakes! And we'll get you!"

"If I had a nickel for every time I've heard *that,*" I said, shaking my head.

As we rose higher, teachers poured out of the school, pushing aside screaming kids, who cowered and tried to hide. Some of the teachers were clearly working for Pruitt, while others looked terrified and confused.

Then I saw an all-too-familiar gray van careen into the parking lot, spitting gravel as it leaned dangerously around a corner. Sure, let's add some Erasers to the mix! The more the merrier! Were they in league with Pruitt or had things just gotten interesting?

"Go!" I said to the flock, and surged upward as fast as I could. Ari and some of the other Erasers could fly, but we had a head start. I saw Ari jump out of the van, barking orders, swearing, watching us escape.

"Later *much,*" I said, and we soared into the sky, right into the weak autumn sun.

88

"Where to now?" the Gasman asked. We hovered in midair, our wings beating rhythmically, just hard enough to keep us in place. We'd kept a steady lookout, but so far no one seemed to be after us.

"We need to go back to Anne's," said Angel.

"Yeah, just real quick, to get some stuff," Nudge agreed.

"Actually," I said, "I hid our packs in the bat cave a few days ago. Just in case something like this happened. And I didn't forget to lift one of these," I added, wagging one of Anne's countless credit cards in front of them. "She'll never miss it."

"Great," said the Gasman in relief. "That was really smart, Max."

"That's why they pay me the big bucks," I said. It was taking everything I had to not yell *I told you so!* But now wasn't the time. Later, when we were safe, *then* I would rub it in.

"We still have to go back to Anne's," Angel said urgently.

"Ange, we just can't take the risk of saying good-bye," I said.

"No," Angel said. *"Total's there."*

Oh, crap. I took two seconds to judge the likelihood of Angel leaving Total behind, which was *none,* and then Fang and I looked at each other and sighed.

"We'll try," I said, and saw relief flood her face.

"Oh, *thanks,* Max," she said. "We'll make it fast, I promise."

It took three minutes to fly to Anne's big, comfortable farmhouse, where we'd lived for almost two months. Where at least some of us had felt relatively happy and safe.

Where at least thirty Erasers were swarming over the land, the orchards, out of the barn, all around the house.

Jeezum, that was fast.

Meanwhile, Angel was peering down at the yard, looking through the trees in the orchard.

Please don't let Total be snoozing in front of the fire, I prayed silently. *Let him be paying attention.*

"There!" said Angel, pointing over to the pond. Sure enough, Total's small black body was racing excitedly around the edge of the water. An Eraser was chasing him, but Total was amazingly fast on his short legs.

Angel tucked her wings in and dived.

"Fang!" I said, and Fang immediately went after her.

The sound of an engine made me turn, and I saw Ari's van tearing up the long driveway.

Over by the pond, Angel was rocketing down. Erasers nearby were shouting for backup and starting to run toward her. Fang was right on her tail, ready to attack if necessary.

"Total!" Angel shouted. "Come!"

Instantly Total raced toward her, and when he'd gotten up speed, he bunched his small muscles and leaped into the air with all his might. I saw him sail upward as if he'd been shot out of a cannon, higher than any dog had ever leaped. Fifteen, twenty, almost thirty feet into the air, the height of a three-story building. Angel swooped down, scooped him into her arms, then surged upward, her beautiful, pure white wings working with hard, smooth precision.

The Erasers roared below. Fang took Total from Angel, making a "yuck" face as Total licked him happily. They rejoined me, Nudge, and the Gasman.

"About time you got here," Total said, wiggling against Fang. "I thought I was going to have to bite some ankles!"

89

"Okay, guys — it's time to get the flock outta here." I'd been wanting to say that for ages.

"Wait —," said Nudge, watching Anne's yard.

"No, we have to *go,*" I said more strongly. "Ari and the rest will be after us any second. Let's get a head start." *For once.*

"There's Anne," said Nudge, pointing.

Sure enough, she was on the front lawn, striding toward an Eraser. Not something most humans would do. She shouted at Ari, waving her arms angrily, not afraid of him.

A nondescript black sedan pulled to a stop by the house. A black sedan. *What a cliché,* I thought acidly.

The door opened and Jeb Batchelder stepped out. Wonderful. His arrival added the perfect touch of anguish that had been missing from this picture.

Jeb walked up to Ari, who was now yelling back at Anne.

Anne, get out of there, I thought, unable to look away.

True, I didn't think she was totally on the up-and-up, but she didn't deserve to get her throat ripped out. She was holding her own, though, even poking a finger into Ari's chest. With a loud snarl, he grabbed her hand and twisted, making her cry out. Jeb smashed Ari's hand away. Anne stepped aside, rubbing her wrist, looking furious.

Jeb pushed Ari, forcing him to back up. Ari looked crazed with fury, his jaws snapping, beady red eyes burning. He kept pointing at us, high up in the air, and seemed to be arguing with Jeb. I was torn — I wanted to race out of there, put as much distance between us and the Erasers as possible. But, as usual, seeing Jeb created all sorts of mixed emotions. Rage being the primary one.

Jeb, Anne, the Erasers, Pruitt, the other teachers. They were all parts of a bigger picture, but right now the picture looked as if it had been painted by drunken monkeys — nothing added up.

"Look, we just have to go," I began, when a voice behind us said, "Yo."

In case you're wondering, it *is* in fact possible to jump a foot in the air when you're already hovering in the air. Gasping, heart pounding, I whipped around and gaped.

"Oh, my God! Iggy!"

90

"Iggy! Iggy!" All of us were shouting and trying to rush him at once. He made a wry Iggy-face that I interpreted as deep happiness to be here. I edged closer and tried to hug him without getting our wings tangled. We managed sort of an arm's length air kiss. The boys slapped high fives with him, and Nudge and Angel managed air kisses too.

"I went by the school," he said. "They seem to be having a bad day."

I gave a dry laugh. "Yeah, you could say that."

"Do I hear a ruckus down below?" Iggy asked.

"You do indeed," I said, then I realized that he was *here*. "Oh, no — Iggy. What happened?"

"Well," he said, his face grim, "they didn't mind the wings. In fact, they loved the wings. Especially since they got eight different publishers and magazines into a bidding war for the all-exclusive rights to my life story, complete with photographs and interviews with the freak himself." His voice was indescribably bitter.

"Oh, no," I said. "They were going to tell people?"

"They were going to turn me into a sideshow freak," Iggy said. "I mean, a really public one."

I beat back the rush of joy I felt at having him here and let my sympathy get some air.

"I'm so sorry, Ig," I said, reaching out to rub his shoulder. "I thought they were the real thing."

"That's just it," he said, anger showing on his face. "Maybe they were. I don't know. Maybe they weren't. But they *felt* like the real thing, and the real thing wanted to make money off me."

I couldn't help reaching out to touch him again. "I'm so sorry, Iggy, really. But I'm so happy you're back."

"I'm glad to be back too," said Iggy. "Even before they went nuts on me, I just missed you guys too much."

"This is great, and we'll have a group hug later," Fang interrupted, "but can we pay attention to what's happening below?"

Oh, right. Way down below, Jeb, Ari, and Anne were still shouting at one another. Teams of Erasers were starting to report back, since obviously we weren't on the premises. Several of them shaded their eyes to look up at us, five hundred feet in the air.

"Hmm," I said. "Something's missing down below. Some important puzzle piece. Oh, I know: It's me. Hang on, guys." I folded my wings and aimed myself downward.

91

I shot toward the ground at two hundred miles an hour. It was a total rush, over in a split second, and then I was braking, snapping my wings out to catch the air. I began running before my feet hit the ground, and came to a stop fifteen feet from the Terrible Trio.

Aware of the Erasers at my back, I walked up to Anne, Jeb, and Ari.

"Well, looks like the gang's all here," I said, crossing my arms over my chest. "Anne, meet Jeb. Jeb, meet Anne. Oh, *sorry* . . . looks like you two already know each other *really well!*"

"Hello, sweetheart," Jeb said, gazing at me as if I held the secret to the world. Oh, wait, I guess I did.

"I'm not your sweet anything," I said.

"No — you're *mine,*" Ari spit, pacing angrily.

"In your nightmares," I said, sounding bored, and he lunged at me, snarling. Jeb shot out an arm and held him back. Anne looked at me with concern.

"Are you all right?" she said. "I got a call from the school —"

"I bet you did," I said. "Their school emergency plan went to heck in a handbasket. Well, they were too rigid anyway." I turned back to Jeb. "What do you want? Every time you show up, my life nose-dives. And believe me, it's not that far till I hit rock bottom."

"You got that right." Ari sneered.

"Shut up, dog boy," I said. I felt sorry for the seven-year-old Ari who'd been victimized. This creature shared no part of him.

"Max, as always, I'm here to help," said Jeb, channeling sincerity. "This . . . experiment isn't working out. I'm here to help you get to the next phase."

"You're out of bounds here," said Anne angrily. "This is my situation."

Jeb's anger flared. "*You* don't know what you're doing. Max is a multimillion-dollar, finely tuned instrument. You've almost *ruined* her. She's not a lapdog! She's a warrior — the best there is. *I* made her what she is and I won't let you destroy her."

"Whoa," I said, holding my hands up. "This is getting a little dysfunctional, even for me. I have an idea: How about the three of you take flying leaps off a cliff? That would solve most of our problems right there."

"That would suit me just fine," Ari snarled. "Then it would be just you and me."

"Please. The way you fly? There wouldn't be enough left to fill a garbage bag."

He lunged at me again. Both Anne and Jeb stopped him.

"I'm going now," I said, "and I'm going to stay gone.

If I see any one of you again, I'll take you out. And that's a euphemism, by the way."

Jeb sighed and shook his head. "It's not that simple, Max. There's nowhere for you to go. This whole planet is one big maze, and you're the rat running through it."

My eyes narrowed coldly. "That's what you think. You and your psycho-scientist pals can play out Act Three by yourselves. As far as I'm concerned, this experiment, this *training scenario,* is over. Way over. Don't come knocking again. I mean it."

"The decision, unfortunately, isn't yours to make," Jeb said patiently. "But you don't have to believe me. You can ask my boss, the one who's pulling all the strings."

"Jeb . . . ," Anne said, a warning tone in her voice.

"Yeah, right." I sneered. "Call him on your cell phone. I'll wait."

"I don't have to. She's right here," Jeb said with a gentle smile.

Well, the only other "she" around was Anne.

She was his boss, the one who was running things.

The one who was running me.

92

I should have known.

Maybe, deep down inside, I had known. Maybe that was why I had never been able to trust Anne, to relax. Or maybe that had just been my total paranoia coming in handy again.

"You're the lead dog?" I asked Anne, then shook my head. "No, I can't even pretend to be surprised. Nothing you guys throw at me could surprise me anymore."

"Let's put that to the test," Ari said tightly. His whole body was rigid, his eyes bloodshot. His ragged claws were curling up into his palms over and over.

"Down, boy," I said, expecting him to snap at any second.

"It's not like that, Max," said Anne, her face sincere and concerned. "I wanted to be part of your becoming. You're not just an experiment. To me, you're almost like a daughter." Her eyes were warm and pleading. I thought of all the nights she'd tucked us in, the many disastrous attempts to put dinner on the table. How she'd bought us clothes, books, art supplies. She'd held Nudge when she cried, she'd patched up Gazzy's skinned knees.

You know what? I'd done all that stuff too. And I was better at it. And, bonus, I wasn't *evil.*

"I'm guessing that *almost* is the operative word here," I said. "Part of my *becoming?* Congratulations. You're part of my becoming *pissed off.*" I realized how crushed Gazzy, Nudge, and Angel would be when they found out Anne was in this mess even deeper than the spawn of Satan, Jeb himself. Suddenly I'd had enough, more than enough. I shook my head, subtly loosening my wing muscles. "You can't even make decent cookies," I told her, and then jumped straight up into the air, the way we'd practiced so many times. With one bound, I was over their heads, and then I unfurled my wings and pushed down with all my might. I almost clipped them — I have a thirteen-foot wingspan. I soared up to where my flock was waiting.

"*Vámonos,*" I said. "There's no one here but people to leave."

93

That would have been too easy, right?

Within seconds, Ari's control broke. Even as I was speeding away, I heard him shouting orders. Glancing over my shoulder, I saw a swarm of heavy, clumsy Erasers rising darkly into the air. Only — hello — these weren't that clumsy.

"Uh-oh — this is a new batch, guys," I called. "These Erasers can actually fly. Move it!"

"Through the woods!" Fang called, and I nodded.

"Rendezvous at the bat cave," I added. "Make sure you aren't followed!"

The six of us dived into the trees, effortlessly slipping among the branches and trunks. We'd practiced moves like this hundreds of times, and it was exhilarating, like playing a video game, only, you know, in real life. In less than a minute we heard crashes and yells behind us. Several Erasers had already misjudged their wingspans and almost ripped their wings off on unforgiving tree trunks.

It was pretty funny.

"No one touches Max! She's mine!" I heard Ari shout, and thought, *Oh, brother.*

We split up, each leading a bunch of Erasers on a crazy zigzag path. Together again, Iggy and Gazzy flew in tandem, with Iggy able to mimic Gazzy's moves within milliseconds. Angel was a blur of white through the green and brown of the forest. I knew Fang was holding Total and hoped that didn't cramp his style too much.

"This is where it ends," I heard Ari snarl, surprisingly close. I took a split-second look back and saw that he was barely thirty feet behind me. Okay, time to pour on the power. I sucked in a deep breath and surged forward, putting some of my newfound speed into action.

And practically almost *killed* myself, because trees were popping in my way faster than I had ever practiced. *Get it together, Maximum,* I told myself grimly. *React faster. You can do it.*

Concentrating fiercely, I aimed myself like a bullet through and over and between the thick trees and scrubby undergrowth. All sound faded away as I focused intently on finding a path for myself through the woods. Again and again I flipped sideways, shooting through impossibly narrow gaps. Several times I clipped my wing tips against something and even ripped some feathers out, making me hiss in a breath.

There was no way Ari could keep up with me at this speed, being such a bad flyer, with patched-on wings. I slowed, and time slowed with me. Sound reached my ears again — I was far away from everyone. Uh, too far, actually. I turned around and headed back.

I came up behind Ari, all stealthy wings, where he was perched on a branch.

"No! I told you — she's mine!" Ari was shouting into an earpiece. "This time no one's going to stop me. You take care of the others. I'll find Max."

He tapped his com unit off and took out a small pair of military binoculars. He peered through them, and I was practically holding my sides to keep from laughing. Finally he turned enough to see me — a hundred miles wide, filling his vision.

"Ah!" he cried in surprise, and dropped the binoculars.

Then I laughed. "So, what plans do you have for me, dog boy?"

I expected him to snarl and lunge, as usual. But he sat back on his branch and looked at me, seeming almost calm and roughly in the neighborhood of sane.

"Plans," he said. "I don't want to kill you. But I will if I have to. If you don't cooperate."

"Cooperate? This is *me* you're talking to."

Ari reached behind him and took a large, lethal-looking knife out of his pack. "I'm going to ask you once, nicely. What happens after that is up to you."

What was he up to? "Uh, okay. Ask away."

"You come with me. The two of us disappear. We never have to deal with Jeb and the whitecoats and everyone else again."

"Disappear where?" You know what they say: Curiosity killed the mutant bird kid. But I couldn't help myself.

"A place I know."

"And I would be stuck there? With you as my guard? I have to tell you, this isn't among my top-ten offers."

"Not as your guard. As your friend."

"You and me." This was throwing me for a loop — and then I remembered Angel telling me that she'd picked up on Ari actually loving me. In a hateful, twisted way, of course.

"Yes. This is your one chance."

"Uh-huh." I couldn't for the life of me see where this was headed in his mind. Unless — ick. "Ari, I can't leave the flock," I said, straight out. "Not for you, not for Jeb, not for anyone."

"I'm sorry to hear that," Ari said evenly, then he lunged at me with the knife.

I let myself fall backward off my branch, doing a flip in the air and unfurling my wings as I came right-side up. I didn't even look back as I took off through the woods again, fast, heading back to the general area where the flock had split up. I felt sorry for Ari. Or, at least, I potentially felt sorry for him, if he would quit trying to kill me.

94

"Max!" It was Fang. Immediately I zoomed upward and burst through the treetops into the open sky above. He was up there, fighting three Erasers at once. I streaked over and chopped one right where his neck met his shoulder. He cried out, and then I grabbed his wings and pulled them together, hard, in back of him. He shrieked in pain and started to drop like a rock. It was a little trick we'd learned back when we were first starting to fly. I'd forbidden us to do it to one another.

That Eraser crashed down into the trees below and disappeared from sight.

"Where's everybody else?" I called to Fang as I moved in.

"Gone — Total too," he said. "This is all that's left." He circled up to the right and then fell down sideways, landing hard on an Eraser's wing. Their wings were heavier than ours but not nearly as smoothly integrated into their bodies. This one folded also and fell clumsily downward. He tried to get aloft again, but just as his wings extended, he hit the trees. We heard him screaming all the way down to the ground.

"That had to hurt," said Fang.

"Should we go —," I began, but just then Ari shot out of the trees and smashed right into Fang at full speed. He wheeled around surprisingly quickly and hovered in the air, facing us.

"We end this now!" he growled.

"I agree," said Fang in a low, deadly tone, and he rushed Ari.

Remembering what had happened when they'd fought on the beach, I got ready to fling myself between them, but Fang zipped in like a hawk and managed a snap kick to Ari's chest so hard that Ari started coughing. Before I could even say, "Good one," Fang had circled and chopped the side of his hand down on Ari's neck. Ari dropped about ten feet because he momentarily forgot to flap, but then his face set in anger and he surged upward again. His wingspan must have been eighteen feet, because he was a full-size Eraser. I could only imagine how hard he had to work just to stay aloft.

Fang whirled in a tight circle, like a hawk ballet, and flew in sideways before Ari could even react. His fist crashed against the side of Ari's face, and I saw Ari's nose start to bleed. I guessed Fang was remembering the beach incident too.

Ari roared and came right at Fang, claws slashing the air, teeth bared, eyes burning. He had power, hatred, and Eraser strength on his side. But Fang was fast and nimble, and had a truckload of resentment and hunger for revenge.

It was a pretty even match.

I wanted to jump in and help, but I sensed it was one of those boy things and I should stay out of it unless Fang was really getting his butt kicked. So I hovered nearby, scanning the horizon, hoping the rest of the flock was safe at the bat cave. No other Erasers seemed to be around, amazingly, and choppers didn't suddenly appear. It was just your basic one-on-one mutant-vs.-mutant fight.

Which Fang seemed to be winning. I mean, let's hear it for resentment and revenge. Even though Ari was probably actually stronger than Fang, Fang was so quick and so, so mad.

I winced as I heard the bone-jarring *crack* of Fang's fist against the side of Ari's head. The blow spun his head sideways, and Fang darted in with a fast side kick right to Ari's ribs. I saw Ari's grimacing face and hoped this would be over soon, before he got in a lucky hit.

Again Fang swung a hard left punch. Ari turned at the last minute and caught it right in the muzzle. Blood started dripping out of his mouth. "You —," Fang said as he punched him from the right. "Quit —" Ari tried to back up, but he was clumsy with his wings and ended up dropping several feet. Fang dropped also, with precision, and rammed an uppercut into Ari's ribs. I heard Ari's breath leave in a *whoosh.* "Attacking —" Finally Fang drew back, gave one big beat of his wings, and shot forward, feetfirst. Both feet connected forcefully with Ari's stomach, and Ari wheezed for air. "Us!" Fang finished, delivering an uppercut to the chin that literally made Ari spin backward through the air.

And he kept tumbling. I got a glimpse of his battered, rage-filled face as he fell toward the treetops, sixty feet below. He tried to catch himself, working his wings, but it was too late. He crashed into the greenery, and we heard branches snapping from up where we were.

He'd hardly managed to touch Fang.

I looked over at Fang. He was panting, sweating, watching Ari's fall with a look of cold satisfaction.

"So — working out some issues here, are we?" I said.

He gave me a dry look. "Let's go find the others."

95

Fang and I kept a lookout all the way to the bat cave. We had no way of knowing if someone was tracking us with a telescope or whatever. But we took a complicated, mostly hidden route, and ended up shooting quickly in through the overhanging vines at the cave entrance.

"Max!" Nudge said, jumping up to give me a hug. Then we were all hugging one another, and Total was jumping up and down with excited little yips.

"Are they gone?" Gazzy asked.

"For now," I said. "Fang kicked Ari's butt."

"Way to go!" Iggy said, holding up his fist. Fang bumped fists with him, trying not to look too pleased with himself.

"He has issues," Nudge whispered knowingly out of the side of her mouth. I laughed.

"Okay, guys," I said. "New agenda. Forget looking for our parents. We've hit a dead end. And besides, I don't think I could bear to give one of you up again right now. How about moving on to saving the world?"

"Yeah, let's get out of here," said Total, looking up at me.

"But where to?" asked Nudge.

"I've been thinking about that," I began.

"Florida," said Angel.

"What? Why?" I asked.

"I just feel like Florida is where we should go," Angel said, shrugging. "Plus, you know, Disney World."

"Yes! Disney World!" said Gazzy.

"Swimming pools, sunshine — I am so there," Total agreed.

I looked at Fang. He shrugged. And actually, I didn't really have any other plan.

Go with the flow, Max. Ride the flow.

After that pithy nugget from my Voice-turned-travel-agent, I said, "Well, okay, then. Florida it is. Grab your packs."

PART 5

BACK TO SAVING THE WORLD

96

"I see. You had a plan." Jeb poured himself a cup of coffee.

"Yeah," Ari said sullenly. He wasn't sure if Jeb was mad at him or not. Sometimes Jeb didn't seem mad, but then it would turn out that he was. Ari hated that.

"You were going to steal Max for yourself."

"Yeah."

Jeb took a sip of his coffee. "And why were you going to do that?"

Ari shrugged. "I just want to have her to myself. I'm tired of chasing the others. I don't care about them."

"But you care about Max. How old are you now?"

"Seven." Which was another thing. Jeb *never* remembered his birthday. "But I'm big. Bigger than you."

"Yes." Jeb made it sound totally unimportant. "Ari, I'm proud of you."

"Wh-what?"

Jeb turned and smiled at him. "I'm proud of you, son. I'm impressed that you made a plan for yourself, and that you chose Max."

Ari felt like the sun was shining warmly on his shoulders. But — was this a trap? He looked at Jeb warily. "Oh, yeah?"

"Yes. You're only seven, but you're thinking like a grown-up. It's incredibly interesting. Tell you what — I want to see where this takes us. We're going to find out where the flock has gone, and when we do, you can put your plan into action again."

"My plan?"

"Yes, your plan to steal Max. I'll help you make it happen. We'll take out the rest of the flock, but you have to grab Max. Where were you going to take her?"

"A place."

"We'll work out the details later. In the meantime, get some rest, eat something. I've already got people tracking the flock."

Slowly Ari turned and left the room. If this was true . . . An almost painful burst of joy exploded inside him. Dad was going to help. Dad had said he was proud of him. He was going to get Max all to himself. It was like Christmas and his birthday and sort of Halloween, all rolled up into one.

97

Have you ever — no, I guess you never have. If you've never flown with hawks, there's no way you'd be able to understand what it's like. Maybe if you've swum with sharks or something, not like at SeaWorld but in the ocean. That might be kind of close to this feeling.

I looked over at Nudge. Her face was serene, curly hair streaming behind her. We had just crossed the border from Virginia into North Carolina. The Appalachian Mountains rose beneath us, not as high and not nearly as pointy as the Rockies. These were older ranges, and time had softened them. See? Some of that geography stuff stuck with me after all.

We were high, high up, where oxygen was pretty thin. The sun was hot and bright on our backs and wings, and we had nothing but open sky all around us in every direction. Best of all, we'd spotted a flock of broad-winged hawks and joined them.

At first they'd scattered, wondering who the heck these huge, ugly raptors were dropping down on them, but then they'd cautiously circled back. Now we were wheeling in and among them, flying in a loose formation, the six of us and maybe twelve of them. I'd already hissed at Total to be very quiet and not make a sound. He huddled in Iggy's arms, nose quivering, small black paws twitching as he chased them in his mind.

"This is incredible," the Gasman said, tilting one wing down to soar in a huge circle around us. I grinned at him. Just two hours ago we'd been screeching out of Anne's yard as Erasers swarmed out of vans, aiming their sights at us. Now we were free, breathing thin, pure air, surrounded by creatures who showed us what to aim for: their fierce, proud beauty, awesome grace and flying skill, and unjudging acceptance of beings so incredibly different from them.

It was a huge change from, say, Erasers, who mainly showed us how to not be clumsy, predatory idiots. And I for one was thankful.

"Maybe we could just live with them," Nudge said wistfully.

"Yeah," said Gazzy. " 'Cause you love eating raw squirrels and snakes and stuff."

"Eew. I forgot about that," said Nudge.

"Anyway, guys, we can't live with them," I said, stepping up to my role as full-time rainer-on-parader. "We need to get farther away."

"I want to go to Florida. You *said*," Total chimed in, and though the hawks had warily accepted our speech, Total's voice made them realize that he was alive. Several of them sheared off, effortlessly tipping a few feathers downward to shift their whole position in the airstream.

It was so completely streamlined, the way they did it, and I practiced it myself.

We flew out of the hawks' territory, and they left us with hoarse cries. One by one we sheared off, soaring in huge, symmetrical arcs and then joining up again.

"It's like synchronized swimming," Gazzy said, pleased.

"No, it's like exhibition jets," said Iggy. "Like the Air Force Thunderbirds. We need stuff so we can leave huge trails of colored smoke behind us."

"Oh, yeah!" said Gazzy, totally psyched. "Like, we could get sulfur and —"

"And this would help our whole 'lie low, disappear' act how?" I said, bringing them back to reality.

"Oh, yeah," said Iggy.

"Maybe someday," I said, hating to see him and the Gasman so disappointed. "In the meantime, let's do a vertical stack!" I said, angling upward into position. Fang put himself directly below me, carefully out of range of my feet, because he's just paranoid that way. Iggy was below him, then Gazzy, Nudge, and finally Angel on the bottom, as white as the clouds we were flying over. We were six stacked bird kids, flying in unison, making only one shadow on the clouds. Totally cool.

Of course it was too freaking peaceful to last, right? I mean, there was no way I was going to wallow in serenity for more than two seconds, right?

No, *of course not.*

What happened was, Gazzy suddenly pushed upward into Iggy, wanting to knock him off balance, the way all of us have done to each other a million times. It would have been fine, and even funny, if Iggy hadn't been holding, say, a mutant talking dog. For example.

But he was. And when Gazzy bumped up into him, he knocked Total out of Iggy's arms. Total gave a startled yip and then he dropped like a piece of coal, right through the clouds and out of sight.

98

Angel reached for Total as he plummeted past her, but her fingers only grazed his fur.

"Total!" she cried, and Total started barking and howling, dropping farther away, his voice trailing off.

"Oh, crap," I muttered, then veered down past Fang. "If I'm not back in two minutes, do *not* let Angel have another pet." Then I tucked my wings behind me and started to drop.

"Max! Get Total!" Angel shouted after me, her voice panicky.

"No, I'm dropping straight down through clouds just for *fun*," I said to myself. I know people always fantasize about dropping through clouds or walking on clouds, landing on clouds. The thing is, clouds are wet. Wet and usually chilly. And you can't see anything. So, not as high on the fun scale as you might think.

I followed the sound of Total's howling, letting myself fall toward the earth. Suddenly the mist cleared and I saw the ground, green and brown, below me. Plus a bunch of white —

"Aaahh!" I cried, as I dropped out of the cloud and practically onto the back of a glider plane. My feet actually brushed its thin skin before I pulled my knees up and angled my wings sharply. I slightly scraped the plane's right wing before I could pull enough to the side, then I moved my wings powerfully and rose up several yards, out of the way.

Gliders are virtually soundless. That was the lesson for today. This close I could hear the wind whistling against the smooth, streamlined plane, but there had been no sound to tip me off. That had been close. If I'd dropped in front of it . . .

I could no longer hear Total. Dang it! My eyes raked the air below me. I tucked my wings back and aimed downward again, shooting like a rocket instead of just letting myself fall. I poured on my new supernatural speed and roared toward the ground, and suddenly Total was in view and getting larger fast.

He was still howling pathetically. There was no time for me to slow down, so I just shot toward him, scooped him into my arms, then pulled out of the steep, steep dive about two hundred feet from the mountainside. Raising my face to the sun, I rushed upward, my wings feeling like steel, like fusion rockets. I looked ahead to make sure there was nothing above me, then I finally glanced down to check on Total.

He was crying. Large tears made wet streaks through his black fur. "You saved me," he choked out. "I couldn't fly. I was falling. But you got me."

"Yeah, I wouldn't let you fall," I told him, and rubbed

behind his ears. Still weeping, he licked my cheek gratefully. I clenched my teeth.

The rest of the flock was circling overhead — Fang had made Angel stay with him. She was peering down anxiously, and as soon as she saw me coming she hurried to meet me. "You got him!" she shouted happily. "You saved him!"

Total wiggled excitedly in my arms, and I let him go over to Angel's embrace. He weighed almost half as much as she did, so she couldn't hold him long, but right now they were crying in each other's arms. Fine. Let him lick *her.* I rubbed my cheek against my sweatshirt shoulder.

Angel was actually crying herself, I realized. She almost never cried — none of us cried easily, and Angel was unnaturally stoic for a six-year-old. The fact that she was crying because she'd almost lost Total told me that she was majorly attached to him. Which wasn't great. I mean, I liked Total fine, but we still didn't know much about him. I wasn't 100 percent sure we could trust him.

Or me, actually. My chip.

"Oh, Total," Angel cried, her tears soaking his head. "I was so scared!"

"*You* were scared!" Total said, burrowing deeper into her arms. "I thought I was gonna plotz!"

"Okay, I better take him," said Fang, holding out his hands. Total crept cautiously into his arms and tucked himself neatly into the crook of Fang's elbow.

"I need wings," said Total, still sniffling. "I need my *own* wings. Then things like that wouldn't happen."

Yeah, that was all I needed. A *flying* talking mutant dog.

99

At last, at last. Ari strode through the doors of a Best-Mart, feeling huge and powerful. Dad was going to let him have Max. She would be all his. Dad could have the others. Ari would have a chance to make Max like him. He remembered when they had fought in the sewer tunnel, in New York. That had been really bad. Max had acted as if she hated him. But now they would be friends. Soon. Very soon.

The Best-Mart was crowded — Atlanta was a big city. Ari and a couple of Eraser troops had hunkered down at a cheap hotel on the highway, waiting for dark. In the meantime, Ari had decided to celebrate.

Now he looked around the store. It was huge. Too bright, too noisy. Hot and full of people, all around. He wished he could drop a bomb on this whole place, watch it light up like a bonfire. He *could* do it — but he would probably just get in trouble. Again. And get the "don't call attention to yourself" lecture. Again. Ari felt like, Hellooo, I have *wings!* I turn into a *wolf! Blending* is out of the question!

But anyway, this place was full of cool stuff. Ari

deserved to have something really cool. This was the clothes department. Bor-ing.

Housewares. Bor-ing.

The automotive section, which seemed as if it should be interesting but was actually bor-ing because all it had was, like, oil and windshield cleaner.

Oh, so *gross,* the underwear department. There was a lady right there, holding a *bra!* Out in the open! Oh, my God — was she crazy? Ari turned away and kept walking, fast.

Finally — here, at the back of the store. Electronics. Ari's heart sped up as his eyes darted past the rows of TVs, all tuned to the same station. Maybe thirty of them. It was so awesome. Ari could sit here all day, watching them. But that wasn't all. There were boom boxes, cool phones, Walkmans, MP3 players. It would be great to be able to listen to cool music all the time.

Then he saw it. The huge Game Boy display. There were eight Game Boys, all different colors, cabled to a shelf. Next to them was a TV, and it was playing videos of all the different Game Boys, like, having adventures. The blue one was surfing, and the red one tried to break out through the TV, and the silver one got a tattoo. It was the coolest thing Ari had ever seen. He stood there, mesmerized, for a long time.

"Uh, sir?"

Ari turned and saw a salesman wearing a red vest.

"Can I help you, sir? These babies are really hot. Can't keep 'em on the shelves. Would you care to see one?"

"Yeah."

The salesman blinked at the sound of Ari's gravelly, morph-roughed voice. But he regained his composure and managed a smile. "Certainly." He pulled a set of jingling keys from his pocket. "Now, what color would you like, sir? They all have their merits."

"The red one." The one that had tried to break out of the TV.

"I like this one too." The salesman unclipped the red Game Boy from its cable and handed it to Ari. "You'll see it has all the advanced features, including — hey, wait a minute, sir."

Ari was already walking down the aisle toward the exit.

"Sir — wait! You can't take that out of this department! If you want one, I have to ring it up for you!"

His voice sounded like a gnat buzzing around Ari's head. Ari opened the Game Boy and pressed the on button. The screen flickered to bright, colorful life. He smiled.

The salesman caught up with him and grabbed his arm. Ari shrugged him off easily. He thumbed through the menu and chose a game. Another man, larger, stood in front of him, arms crossed.

"You're not going no —," he began, but Ari snapped out his fist and punched him without even looking. The man's breath left him in a *whoosh* and he doubled over.

Ari walked right through the exit doors. Alarms sounded. A tinny voice said, "You have triggered our security system. . . ." That was all Ari heard because he was out in the parking lot. His thumbs started working the controls. This was a good day. A favorite song popped into his head, and he started rapping under his breath about "a kid who refused to respect adults."

Ari had his Game Boy. It was incredibly awesome. And he'd gotten it for himself. He didn't need anyone to give him stuff.

He became vaguely aware of a ruckus behind him. Turning, he saw an unarmed rent-a-cop holding a billy club, and four store employees, vests almost as red as their faces. Ari sighed. They always had to make things difficult. Well, he could simple things up real fast.

Whirling, he went for a full-out morph. As always, it was kind of uncomfortable, like getting pulled in all directions till his joints popped. His jaw elongated, his eyes yellowed, long, sharp canines pushed down through his gums. He raised his hairy, claw-tipped paws high, one of them incongruously holding a red Game Boy.

"Arrgh!" He'd practiced this in the mirror, the raised claws, snarling muzzle, angry expression, the roar. It all came together in a terrifying, grotesque picture, and now it had the intended effect: Everyone stopped dead. They gasped in fright.

Ari grinned, knowing how horrible he looked when he gave a morphy grin. He looked like a nightmare, like anyone's worst nightmare.

"Arrgh!" he roared again, raising his claws higher.

That did it. The employees scattered, and the rent-a-cop put a hand over his chest and turned pale.

Ari laughed and loped out of the parking lot, waiting until he was out of sight to unfurl his heavy, awkward wings and take off.

He loved his Game Boy.

100

That night we crashed in General Coffee State Park, not far from Douglas, Georgia. Fang and I scouted around for a few minutes and found a scooped-out indentation in the face of some limestone rock.

"Not as good as a cave, but decent," Fang said.

I looked at it and nodded. "This will keep us out of the wind, and it probably won't rain. Looks pretty clear." I turned to get the others, but Fang put his hand on my arm.

"You okay?" he asked. "What happened back there at Anne's?"

Just like that, it all came rushing back — my day. Being trapped in a school full of — enemies, teachers, Pruitt. Thinking Sam was an Eraser. Leaving Anne's house, knowing she was responsible for a lot of our situation.

Suddenly I was exhausted. "It was pretty much business as usual." Which was the sad truth.

"What's in Florida?" Fang asked. "Why does Angel want to go there?"

"I don't know. Maybe just Disney World?" I looked at him. "You think it's something else?"

He frowned, then shook his head. I noticed his hair was getting long again, growing out from his funky New York haircut. That seemed like a lifetime ago. "I don't know what to think," he said, "I'm tired of having to think about it, you know?"

"I totally know," I said, rubbing my temples. "Finding our parents, figuring out the whole whitecoat thing. Me saving the world, and so on. I'm tired of all of it."

Fang looked away for a moment. "I'm ready to forget all that stuff. Look what happened with Iggy. I don't even want to know at this point. I just want to quit running. I also miss having somewhere to make entries in the ol' blog. I really do."

"Let's think about it, think about how we can do it. From Florida, we'd be in a good place to head out over the ocean, find some deserted island somewhere. We could do some research." The more I thought about it, the more it seemed like a great idea. We would be safe. We could rest. We could relax on a beach and eat coconuts, and Angel could talk fish into committing suicide for our dinner. It would be heaven.

And the fact that I was even entertaining this idea as a possibility only showed how pathetically desperate I was. And how out of touch with reality.

101

"Come on, one more time," Iggy wheedled.

"No," said the Gasman.

"One more time."

"No. It's no fun. You always win, like, right away."

Fang and I looked at each other and rolled our eyes. Those two had been at it all morning.

"I guess Iggy feels okay again," I said out of the side of my mouth. Fang nodded. Iggy, of all of us, had faced the most disappointment lately. We'd actually found his parents: They were real. And they had turned out to be traitors, betrayers. All of Iggy's hopes and dreams about one day finding his parents and having them not care that he was blind and a recombinant life-form — they'd all come true. And then they'd all been torn away.

It was much worse than for the rest of us, who hadn't even gotten close.

Iggy had been silent and stoic since he'd come back to us, but now he had recovered enough to make Gazzy's life miserable, so I knew he was getting back to normal. I shifted Total in my arms and rolled my shoulders.

"How long till we get to Florida?" Nudge asked. "Are we really going to Disney World? Do you think we'll see anyone famous? I want to go to the Swiss Family Treehouse. I want to see Beauty and the Beast and get their autographs. I want to see the Tree of Life —"

I held up a hand. "Okay, hang on. I'm hoping we can go to Disney World, but we have to get down there first, check everything out. We just crossed the Georgia-Florida border, so —"

"The ocean!" said Gazzy, pointing. Way to the east, we could see the dark gray-blue of seemingly endless water. "Can we go to the beach? Please? Just for a minute?"

I thought about it. We'd had some really good times and some really bad times at beaches. "It's almost winter," I hedged.

"But the water's not cold," Iggy said.

I looked at Fang. He shrugged helpfully: my call.

Max, you need to stay focused.

My Voice. *I'm . . . somewhat focused,* I thought defensively. I could practically hear the Voice sigh.

If you're going to Florida, go to Florida, said the Voice. *Pick a goal and follow it through. When you're saving the world, you can't exactly take commercial breaks.*

That did it.

"Hey, guys, wanna go to the beach?" I called.

"Yeah!" said Gazzy, punching one fist in the air.

"Yes, yes," Angel said happily.

"I'm up for it," said Total, in Fang's arms.

Nudge and Iggy cheered.

"Beach it is," I said, swerving in a graceful arc, heading east.

Max, you're acting like a child, the Voice said. *You're above rebelling against your fate just to rebel. You've got a date with destiny. Don't be late.*

I brushed some hair out of my eyes. *Is that a movie quote? Or is it an actual date? I don't remember destiny asking me. I never even gave destiny my phone number.*

The Voice never displayed emotion, so I might have imagined the tense patience I heard. *Max, sooner or later you have to take this seriously. If it was just* your *life, no one would care if you bothered. But we're talking about saving everyone's lives.*

For some reason that really stung. My jaw set. *Shut up! I'm tired of you! Tired of my so-called destiny! I'm acting like a child because I* am *a child! Just leave me the hell alone!*

I felt tears forming in my eyes, which burned from the constant wind. I couldn't take this anymore. I'd been having a rare decent day, and now the Voice had ruined it, dropping the whole world onto my shoulders again.

"Yo."

I looked over to see Fang watching me. "You okay? Is this a headache?"

I nodded and wiped my eyes, feeling like I was about to explode. "Yeah," I said. "A huge, freaking, unbearable *headache!*" I was practically shouting at the end, and five heads turned toward me. I had to get out of here. And, thanks to my supersonic power, I could, in the blink of an eye.

102

"See you at the beach," I muttered to Fang, and then I hunched my shoulders and poured on the speed. In seconds I had shot way past the flock, the wind making my eyes water more. It was funny, but going this fast almost made me want to put my arms out in front of me, like Superman, as if it would split the air out of my way or something.

What the hey — no one could see me. I stretched my arms out in front, feeling like an arrow, a spear, slicing through heaven.

I was at the beach in four minutes. I braked and slowed down, but not enough, and ended up running too fast through the sand and then tripping onto my face. Slowly I got up, spitting out sand, and brushed myself off. I was burning up and pulled off my sweatshirt.

I had maybe twenty minutes till the rest of them came. I walked along the beach, keeping my wings out so they would cool off. I felt desperate and scared and angry. "I don't even know *how* to save the world," I said out loud, hating how pathetic I sounded.

By existing, said the Voice. *By being strong. By lasting.*

"Shut *up!*" I yelled, kicking a piece of driftwood so hard it practically flew out of sight.

I'd had it, totally had it. No more. I ran to the water's edge and looked down at the sand. In moments I had found it — a piece of broken shell, sharp on one side.

It was time for the chip to go. The Voice came from the chip, I was sure of it. No chip, no Voice inside my head that I couldn't get away from. I pressed my lips together hard and started sawing at my forearm, where I had seen the chip on an X-ray, three lifetimes ago, in Dr. Martinez's office.

The first slice brought blood and a surprising amount of pain. I clenched my teeth harder and kept sawing. Blood ran down my arm. I would have to cut through tendons and muscles and veins to get to the chip. Dr. Martinez had said that if I tried to take it out, I could lose the use of my arm.

Too bad.

I heard skidding, running footsteps behind me, and then Fang was panting over me.

"What the hell are you doing?" he shouted, and grabbed my wrist, smacking my hand to make me drop the piece of shell. "Are you *crazy?*"

I glared at him, then saw the rest of the flock approaching slowly. I realized what they must be seeing: me kneeling on sand stained red with blood. I was beyond being upset.

"Want the chip out," I said brokenly. I looked down, feeling a thousand years old. Just over a week ago, I'd been a fourteen-year-old girl on her first date, getting her first kiss. Now I was me again, a mutant freak running away from a fate that was closing around me like a net.

"Look where you're cutting!" Fang snapped. "You're going to bleed to death, you *idiot!*" He threw my hand down and took off his backpack. In the next moment he was dumping antiseptic into my wound, making me wince.

Nudge lowered herself to the sand next to me. "Max," she said, her eyes huge, "what were you doing?" She sounded horrified, shocked.

"I wanted to get the chip out," I whispered.

"Well, forget it!" Fang said angrily, now starting to bandage my arm. "The chip stays in. You don't get off that easy! *You* die when *we* die!"

I looked up at him, his face pale with anger, his jaw tight. I had scared him. I had scared them all. I was supposed to be the solution, not the problem. I wasn't supposed to make things *worse.*

"I'm sorry," I barely managed, and then — get this — I burst into tears.

103

I could count on one hand how many times these kids had seen me cry. I'd learned to swallow my feelings because they needed me to be strong. Invincible Max. Saving the world, one bird kid at a time. For the first six years of Angel's life, I don't think she saw me cry once. In the last few months? I was about to run out of fingers to count on.

I didn't even have the strength to run off and hide. I just knelt in the sand, my hands over my face. My cut hurt like hell.

Then strong arms were around me, a gentle hand was pressing me into a wiry, rock-hard shoulder. Fang. I pulled my wings in, leaned against him, and sobbed. Soon I felt other, tentative hands patting my back, stroking my hair. Someone said, "Shh, shh." Nudge.

"It's okay, Max," Iggy said, sounding shaken. "Everything's okay."

Nothing in our world was okay. Except that we had one another. I nodded into Fang's shoulder.

I don't know how long this touching scene rolled on,

but eventually my sobs gave way to shuddering breaths, and finally I was spent. Fang's shirt was soaked.

I was *so* embarrassed. I was the leader, and here I was breaking down like a baby. How could I boss them around if I was so weak? I sniffled and sat back, knowing I must look like a train wreck. Fang let me go, not saying anything. Slowly I raised my eyes, turning slightly to see the flock. I was way too embarrassed to look at Fang.

"Sorry, guys." My voice sounded rusty.

Total came and rested his head on my leg, his black eyes sympathetic.

The Gasman looked frightened. "We didn't *have* to go to the beach, Max."

A sort of choking laugh left me, and I reached out to ruffle his hair. "It wasn't that, Gazzy. Just other stuff, getting to me."

"Like what?" Iggy asked.

I sighed heavily and wiped my eyes. "Stuff. The Voice in my head. Everyone chasing us. School. Anne. Ari. Jeb. They keep telling me I'm supposed to save the world, but how, and from what, I don't even know."

Angel reached out and patted my knee. "From, you know, after everything gets blown up and most of the people are gone. We'll be stronger, and able to fly, so we can leave the blown-up parts and find some nice land that isn't blown up or contan— contama—"

"Contaminated?" Iggy provided, and Angel nodded.

"Yeah, that. Then *we* can keep on living, even if there are hardly any people left."

104

There was silence after this little bombshell. I stared at Angel.

"Uh . . . where did you hear that, sweetie?" I asked.

Angel sat back on her heels and trailed her fingers through the cool sand. "At the School. I wasn't supposed to hear it, but that's what they thought." She sounded nonchalant and started digging out a moat for a sand castle.

"Who's going to blow up the world?" the Gasman asked indignantly.

Angel shrugged. "Lots of people can — they have big bombs. Countries and stuff. But the people at the School kept thinking it would be just one company, a business company. They think it's going to blow up the world, mostly. Maybe even by accident."

Well, this was an interesting turn of events.

"And what company was that?" I asked.

Angel looked off into the distance, frowning. "Don't

remember," she said. "Like, the name of a deer or something. A gazelle. Can I go swim?"

"Uh, sure," I said faintly.

Happily pulling her swimsuit out of her backpack, Angel raced Total down to the water. Within seconds he came trotting back, shaking his fur. "That water's freezing," he said. He raised his nose, sniffed the air, then headed off to investigate some rocks.

Gazzy, after a nod from me, also ran down to the water, shedding clothes. Nudge and Iggy moved over to sit on a big rock. They fished around in their backpacks and pulled out some protein bars.

"So, *huh?*" I said to Fang when the others were gone.

He shook his head, stuffing the remaining bandages back into his pack. "Yeah. Surprise."

"How long has she been sitting on this? Why hasn't it come up *before?*"

"Because she's six and more concerned with her stuffed bear and her dog? I don't know. Plus, we don't even know if she understood what she heard. There's a chance she got it wrong."

I thought for a moment. "Even if aspects of it are wrong, I don't see how she could misunderstand the whole blowing-up-the-world concept. And the fact that we were designed to outlast a catastrophe. It fits in with what Jeb keeps telling me."

Fang let out a breath. "So what now?"

"I don't know. I need to think."

We were silent for a while. My arm was throbbing.

"So what was that about?" Fang said finally.

I couldn't pretend to not know what he was talking about. "I'm just — really tired. The Voice was ragging on me about my destiny and how I have to get on the stick about saving the world. It just feels like too much sometimes." I never would have admitted that to the others. Sure, I could tell them that things were getting to me, but let them know I wasn't sure I could handle it? No way.

"I've been running on adrenaline, without a master plan. Every day it's just, keep the flock safe, keep us together. But now everything else has been dumped on me, all these bits and pieces that aren't adding up to a whole picture, and it's too much."

"Pieces like Ari and Jeb and Anne and the Voice?"

"Yeah. Everything. Everything that's happened to us since we left home. I don't know what to do, and it's so freaking hard even pretending that I do."

"Walk away from it," Fang said. "Let's find an island. Drop off the screen."

"That sounds really good," I said slowly. "But we'd have to get the others on board. I'm pretty sure the younger kids still really want to find their parents. And now I want to find out what this company is that Angel heard about. What if — you do research on an island possibility and I'll focus on this other stuff?" It was the closest I'd ever come to sharing my role as leader. Actually, it didn't feel so bad.

"Yeah, cool," Fang said.

For a few minutes we watched Angel and the Gasman playing in the shallow surf. I was amazed they weren't cold, but they seemed fine. Iggy and Nudge were walking down the beach. Nudge was putting different-shaped shells in Iggy's hands so he could feel them. I wanted time to freeze *here,* right here, right now, forever.

There was something I needed to say. "Sorry. About before."

Fang shot a sideways glance at me, his eyes dark and inscrutable, as always. He looked back out at the water. I didn't expect any more acknowledgment than that. Fang never —

"You almost gave me a heart attack," he said quietly. "When I saw you, and all that blood . . ." He threw a small rock as hard as he could down the beach.

"I'm sorry."

"Don't do it again," he said.

I swallowed hard. "I won't."

Something changed right then, but I didn't know what.

"Hey!" said Angel, standing up in knee-high water. "I can talk to fish!"

That wasn't it.

105

"You can what?" I called, getting up and walking toward the water.

"I can talk to fish!" Angel said happily, water dripping off her long, skinny body.

"Ask one over for dinner," Fang said, joining us.

The Gasman shook his head like a wet dog. "You can *not,*" he said.

"I'll prove it!" Angel dived back under the water.

By this time, Nudge and Iggy were walking up.

"She talks to fish now?" Iggy asked.

Then, with no warning, a six-foot shark surfaced, mouth open, maybe two yards away from Gazzy. None of us made a sound — we were conditioned not to yell in a crisis. I'm sure we were all screaming in our heads. I sprang into the water, grabbed Gazzy's arm, and hauled him toward shore. He was frozen with fright and seemed like dead weight. I kept expecting to feel the huge tug of the shark taking off my leg.

Angel popped back out of the chest-high water. I motioned her urgently to do an up-and-away. She laughed.

"He's my friend!" she shouted. "He's saying hi!" The shark had circled and was now moving right toward her. My heart was in my throat — what if she only *thought* she could talk to fish? "Go on, maybe you should wave," Angel said to the shark, as I tensed to fly out over the water to snatch her up.

Before our eyes, the shark literally turned on its side, came a little bit out of the water, and waved a fin slightly.

"Holy cra—," the Gasman began, but I said, "Gazzy!"

"Would someone please tell me what the heck is going on?" Iggy said.

"Angel just made a shark wave its fin at us," Nudge told him breathlessly.

"Uh — wha . . . ?"

Then three more sharks appeared in the shallow water around Angel. Together, the four sharks turned on their sides and waved their fins.

Angel was laughing. "Isn't that so great?"

Total trotted up next to me, his little feet kicking sand. "That's awesome! Make them do it again!"

My knees felt weak. I needed to sit down. "That was neat, sweetie," I said, trying to sound calm. "Now please ask the sharks to leave, okay?"

Angel shrugged and talked to the sharks again. Slowly they turned and headed back out to sea.

"That was *so awesome*," Total said, as Angel splashed toward shore. He licked Angel's leg, then spit. "Ugh! Salt."

"So, Angel talks to fish, is that right?" Iggy said carefully. "And this is useful how?"

106

We had to keep on the move. It was going to be dark soon, and we needed shelter. Most kids my age would be bummed about their next math test or that their parents cut their phone calls short. I was more concerned with shelter, food, water. The little luxuries of life.

We were over northern Florida now. All along the coast we saw a million twinkling lights of homes and stores and cars moving in threads like blood cells in a vein. If blood cells had, you know, weensy little headlights.

But there was a huge unlit area below us. In general, dark = no people. I looked over at Fang, and he nodded. We started to descend.

A few minutes' reconnaissance informed us that this was the Ocala National Forest. It looked like a good place, and we dropped down out of the twilight and aimed ourselves carefully through small gaps in the umbrella of treetops. And landed in water.

"Yuck!" I was calf-deep in muddy water, surrounded

by cypress knees and towering pines. Looking around, I saw land a couple yards away and slogged over to it. "To the left!" I called, as Nudge and Iggy swooped in.

"This is good," I said, looking around in what was rapidly becoming the pitch-darkness. "Easy to get out of, straight up through the trees, but almost impossible for anyone to track us overland."

"Home, sweet swamp," said the Gasman, and I smiled.

An hour later we had a small fire going and were roasting things on sticks. I was so used to eating this way that even if I were, like, a grown-up making breakfast for my 2.4 children, I would probably be impaling Pop-Tarts on the ends of sticks and holding them over a fire.

Now Fang pulled a smoking, meaty chunk off a stick and dropped it onto an empty Baggie, which was Nudge's plate.

"Want some more raccoon?" he asked.

Nudge paused in midbite. "It is *not!* You went to the store. Didn't you? There's no way this is raccoon." She examined the meat critically.

Fang shrugged. I rolled my eyes at him.

"Oh, maybe you're right," he said seriously. "Maybe *this* is the raccoon, and I gave you the possum."

Nudge choked and started coughing.

"*Stop* it," I told Fang, reaching over to pat Nudge's back. He looked at me innocently.

"He's just kidding, Nudge," said the Gasman. "Last time I checked, Oscar Mayer wasn't making squirrel dogs." He held up an empty package, and Nudge wheezed a bit and swallowed.

I was trying not to laugh, and then I felt the hairs on the back of my neck prickle. I glanced around — we were all here. But I felt like someone was watching us. I see incredibly well in the dark, but the fire was too bright to see much beyond it. Maybe I was imagining it.

Next to me, Angel straightened up. "Someone's here," she whispered.

Or maybe not.

107

Well, it had been a whole day without an Eraser crashing — literally — our party.

I snapped my fingers softly twice, and five heads turned toward me, alert and tense.

"Someone's here," Angel repeated softly.

Fang kept turning things in the fire, but his back was taut and straight, and I knew he was reviewing escape plans.

"What are you getting?" I asked Angel out of the side of my mouth.

She frowned, her blond curls glinting in the firelight. "Not Erasers." She cocked her head to one side, concentrating. "Kids?" She looked puzzled.

I got slowly to my feet, scanning the darkness around the fire. Moving to the edge of our little circle, I peered intently into the woods. Then I saw them. Two small, skinny forms, inching toward our fire. Much too small to be Erasers. And human, not animal.

"Who's there?" I said strongly. I stood tall and put my

shoulders back, making myself look bigger. Fang got up and came to stand next to me.

The two little forms slunk nearer, more quickly.

"Who are you?" I asked, sounding mean. "Come closer, where I can see you."

They crawled into our small area, two dirty, skinny, big-eyed children. I mean, all of us bird kids looked really long and slender compared to other kids our ages, but our bones didn't really stick out. Theirs did.

They gave us all wary glances but seemed riveted by the fire and the smell of food cooking. One of them actually licked her lips — they were a boy and a girl.

Hmm. They didn't seem like the biggest threat I'd ever seen. I leaned over, put some hot dogs onto a paper bag, and placed it in front of them.

Yo. I thought Gazzy and Iggy were repulsive eaters. I made a mental note to not ever let them get this close to starving. Those two kids fell on the hot dogs and virtually shoved them whole into their mouths. It made me think of a TV special I'd seen that showed hyenas ripping apart their prey.

I put two slices of bread in front of them, then two more, then two more, then two more hot dogs. They all disappeared in instants. After that I gave them candy bars, and their eyes widened as if I'd just handed them — uh . . . candy bars when they were starving. Finally their chewing slowed. Now they seemed to savor every bite. Fang passed them a canteen of water. They drained it.

They crawled closer to the fire and sat in front of it, looking sleepy and unafraid, as if it would be fine if we killed them now, because they weren't hungry anymore.

"So — what's your story?" I asked, wanting some answers before they nodded off.

"We got kidnapped," said the girl, her dark eyes reflecting the flames.

Well, okay, I hadn't seen that coming. "Kidnapped?"

The boy nodded tiredly. "In south Jersey. From two different places — we're not related."

"We just ended up in the same place," said the girl, yawning.

"And where was that?" I asked.

"Here," said the boy. "We escaped a couple times. Even made it to the police station."

"But both times our kidnappers were already there, like, filing missing-kid notices. They just found us again, real easy." The girl sighed heavily and lay down on the ground, curling into a bony clump. We weren't going to get any good answers out of them tonight.

"So, who were your kidnappers?" Fang tried.

"They were, like, doctors," the boy said sleepily, lying down too. "In white coats."

He closed his eyes, and within seconds both he and the girl were asleep.

Which left the rest of us wide-awake, frozen in terror, staring at them as if they carried the plague.

108

Fang took the first watch, so I hunkered down close to the fire and tried to relax. Which was about as likely as Florida freezing over. Angel snuggled up to me on one side, and Total curled up next to her.

"So, what are you picking up from them?" I whispered to her, rubbing her back.

"Weird images," she whispered back. "Not like regular kids, like the ones at school. Like, flashes of grown-ups and darkness and water."

"Which I guess makes sense if they were kidnapped and experimented on by whitecoats," I said softly. I raised myself up on one elbow and caught Fang's eye. Using sign language, I reminded him to keep an eye on the strange kids. He used sign language to say "No freaking *duh.*" I shot him the bird. He grinned.

"Do you think they're mutants?" I asked Angel, lying down again. "They look pretty human."

She shrugged, frowning. "They're not Erasers. But they're not like regular kids either. I don't know, Max."

"Okay." Maybe we would figure it out tomorrow. "Try to get some sleep. Total's already snoring."

Angel smiled happily and pulled him closer to her. She just loved that dog so much.

I had third watch, from 4:00 to 7:00 a.m. or whenever everyone else woke up. I never minded night watches. All of our sleep patterns were permanently screwed, so it wasn't like I needed my forty minutes of REM all together. I woke instantly as soon as Iggy touched my arm. And why was the blind guy on *watch,* you might ask? Because a cockroach couldn't come within fifty feet of us without his knowing it. Iggy on watch meant I could relax, or at least relax as much as I ever did. Which, okay, is not that much.

At five I put more wood on our small fire. The slight smoke seemed to be keeping mosquitoes at bay — I had expected them in Florida, even in November. I left the firelight and walked the perimeter in the darkness of the woods. Everything was cool.

At daybreak I was sitting against a pine tree, which seemed even more popular here than in the mountains of Colorado. I was watching and being. The thing about watch is, it isn't the time to work through problems or write sappy poetry. As soon as you do, you're not paying attention to your surroundings. You basically have to sit and just be, be totally alert to everything around you. It's really kind of Zen, man.

Anyway. I was leaning back, being all Zen, when I saw one of the strange kids stir and sit up. Instantly I closed my eyes to the barest slits and let my breathing become deeper and more even, as if I were sleeping. Tricky Max, that's me.

The girl sat up and looked around at all of us: the Gasman sprawled out, one arm thrown across his backpack, Fang lying neatly on his side, Nudge and Angel curled up around Total, so that they made a heart shape around him.

Ever so quietly, the girl shook the boy's shoulder, and he woke up, startling out of sleep, already tense and on guard, the way kids are when waking up often = bad news. He glanced around also. I looked so asleep I almost *was* asleep. But I saw the two of them slip off into the woods so silently that not even Iggy twitched.

I waited several moments, as they made sure they weren't being followed, and then, just as soundlessly as they, I got up and began tracking them.

I moved stealthily from tree to tree, and though they glanced back a couple times, they didn't see me. About three hundred yards from camp, they crouched down. The girl took something from the dirty pocket of her ragged jeans. It looked like a pen — except she started speaking into it. A transmitter.

It took only a second for me to reach them with huge, bounding leaps. They stared up at me, stunned and afraid. I crashed down and knocked the pen from the girl's hand. Then I grabbed her shirt and hauled her to her feet.

"Ordering a pizza?" I snarled.

109

It's funny how different people are. If I'd been this kid and someone was snarling "Ordering a pizza?" at me, without even thinking, I would have snarled back, "Yeah. You want pepperoni?"

But not her. She stared up at me in horror and then immediately burst into great heaving sobs, her hands over her face. Next to her, the boy dropped to his knees and also started crying, without even trying to hide it.

"I'm sorry! I'm sorry!" the girl gasped out, and I lowered her to the ground by her shirt.

Crossing my arms over my chest, I scowled down at her. "Sorry for what? Be specific."

The girl pointed to the transmitter blinking on the ground. "I didn't want to!" she sobbed. "They made us! They made us do it!"

I picked up the transmitter and threw it out into the swampy area. It landed with a small splash and sank out of sight. "Who made you?" I demanded, knowing that the clock was now ticking.

For several moments the kids only sobbed. I nudged the girl with the toe of one sneaker. "Out with it!" I said. Yeah, I know: bully Max. It wasn't that I didn't feel sorry for these kids. I did. It was just that I valued our lives more than theirs. I know some people would be all, Oh, every life is precious, everyone is equally valuable. And maybe that's true, in Pixieland. But this was the real world, my flock and I were prey, and these kids had ratted us out. That was the bottom line, and in my life, you'd be surprised how often the bottom line is the only one that matters.

"*They* did," the girl said, still crying. By this time the noise had woken the others, and they were making their way through the trees to us.

I knelt down to the girl's level and took hold of one wrist. "Tell. Me. Who." I squeezed her wrist slightly, and her eyes widened.

"*They* did," she repeated, starting to hiccup. "The guys who — the people who kidnapped us. They've had us for months. They took me in August."

"Me too," said the boy, raising his face. Tears had made streaks through the dirt on his cheeks, and he looked stripy, like a zebra. "Those guys — sent us to find you. They didn't feed us for two days, so we'd try hard. And we did. And you gave us food." He started crying again.

"They said if we didn't find you, they would never come get us. We'd be lost in the swamp until something killed us." The girl was shuddering now, calmer, though tears still dripped off her chin. "I'm sorry. I had to." Her face crumpled again.

I understood. They were trying to survive, just like us.

They'd chosen themselves over us, which was exactly what I would have done.

I turned to Fang. "Get our stuff. We're gone."

The flock hurried off to dismantle our rough camp. I put my fingers under the girl's chin and raised it so she'd have to look at me. "I understand," I said levelly. "The transmitter will bring them here to find you. But we'll be gone, and you won't be able to tell them much. Now I'm going to ask you one more time: I need a name, a place, a logo, something. It's the difference between them picking you up alive and them finding your bodies. Get it?"

Her eyes widened again. After a moment, she barely nodded. She shot a glance at the boy, and he gave her a nod. "Itex," she whispered, then sank down on the damp ground. "The company was a really big one called Itex. I don't know anything else."

I stood quickly. No doubt people were on their way to the transmitter's coordinates. We had to get the heck out of here. The two kids, filthy and exhausted, lay on the ground like bodies at Pompeii. I reached into my pocket and dropped some protein bars and hard candy on the ground by their heads. They stared up at me, but I was already gone, flashing through the woods. I met up with the flock and then we were airborne, on the run.

Again.

110

An hour later we were almost a hundred miles away. I had no idea what would happen to those kids.

"So, Itex," I said to Fang.

"I told you it was like a deer," Angel said.

"That's *ibex,*" said Nudge. "And they're more goatlike than deerlike."

"Whatever," said Angel.

"It's not ringing a bell," said Fang.

"They have long horns and live mostly in mountains," Nudge explained.

"No, I mean Itex," Fang said. "They said it was a big company, but I've never heard of it. Which doesn't mean anything."

"Yeah, I guess your education has a few gaps in it," I said. Except for the past two months, none of us had been to regular school, ever. Thank God for television.

"Can we look it up somewhere?" Iggy asked. "Like at a library? Are we close to a town?"

I looked down at the incredibly flat land below us. I

saw the tiny buildings of a small town, about fifteen minutes away. "Yeah. Good plan. Twelve points west, everybody."

So it turned out that Itex owned, like, half the world. It wasn't just a company. It was a huge multinational, multifaceted conglomerate that had its fingers in virtually every type of business there was, including food, medicine, real estate, computer technology, manufacturing, and even book publishing — so heads up, whoever's reading this.

The more info we found on the Web, the more I started remembering the Itex logo. Now that I recognized it, I realized I'd seen it on a million things in my life, going all the way back to the School where we were created. It had been on test tubes, pill vials, lab equipment — you name it.

I logged off the computer and stood up. "Let's get out of here."

I'd seen enough.

111

"No."

"Please, Max," Nudge begged.

We were airborne, heading south. On the Web we'd found an address for Itex headquarters. It was roughly between Miami and Everglades National Park.

"No way. It's too risky. The whole place is fenced in. There's a million people there. We'll be in crowds."

"Fang?" Nudge wheedled.

Fang shrugged, as much as he could shrug while flying. He held up his hands as if to say, Talk to the boss. I'm just the hired help.

That wiener.

"Pleeeease, Max?" The Gasman added his voice.

I stared ahead stoically, refusing to look down at the tall water tower wearing mouse ears. Of course, we had to pass *right over* Orlando.

"Max?" Nudge said.

I didn't respond. I knew what she was trying to do.

"Oh, come on!" said Total, from Iggy's arms. "We're not going to the Magic Kingdom? How lame is that?"

I glared at him. It didn't faze him.

"A couple rides?" Angel asked wistfully. "Splash Mountain?"

"Maaax?" Nudge said again.

I made the supreme mistake of looking at Nudge. Shoot! I winced and looked away but not quickly enough. She got me. She had given me Bambi eyes. Now I had no choice.

I gritted my teeth. "Fine. A couple rides, some cotton candy, and we're out of there."

Everyone cheered. Fang gave me a look that said, You sap.

"Who let whom have a freaking dog?" I responded.

He chuckled.

And we were on our way to the land of the Mouse.

112

"Disney World?" Ari felt like his head was about to explode. *"Disney World?"* His gravelly voice rose into a harsh shriek. "They're not on *vacation!* They're on the *run!* They're running for their *lives!* Death is following them like a bullet, and they're on the Big Thunder Mountain Railroad?"

He snapped his teeth shut so hard the impact jarred his skull.

This was the end.

He would show *them* what a freaking Small World it was. There was about to be a rain of destruction on Main Street, U.S.A.

113

Disney World. You've probably been. I'm assuming that most of America has been there, because you all seemed to be there the day that we went. All of you at the same time.

When the gates opened, we poured in with the rest of the crowd and found ourselves on Main Street, U.S.A. It was, well, adorable. I admit it freely. Old-fashioned storefronts, an ice-cream parlor, a trolley line in the middle of the street — all painted bright, cheerful colors. Everything was pristine, everything in perfect shape.

"I want to go in every shop," Nudge said, awed. "I want to see every single thing."

"Don't these people have jobs?" Fang muttered. "Why aren't these kids in school?"

I ignored him. If he had backed me up, we wouldn't be here.

"We need to pick the most important things," I said, as we headed toward Cinderella's Castle. "In case we can't stay too long."

"I vote for Pirates of the Caribbean," said Total. He

was wearing a small leather halter and a special vest that said "Guide Dog at Work. Do Not Pet. Thank You." We'd bought sunglasses for Iggy, so the two of them had quite the team costume.

"Ooh, Swiss Family Treehouse!" said the Gasman.

"Yeah!" Angel agreed.

Nudge stopped and stared up at the castle. "It's so . . . *beautiful.*"

"Yeah," I said, smiling at her. Inside, of course, I was wound tighter than a yo-yo. All these people — we were horribly exposed and yet contained within a crowded space, so I was twitching like a water drop on a hot skillet.

Avoiding the worst of the crowds, we headed for Adventureland.

"Yes! Pirates of the Caribbean!" Total said. If he could have made a fist, he would have punched it.

Being in a dark, enclosed, watery place with a bunch of strangers sounded like a nightmare to me, but as usual I was in the sensible minority. We got in line, and actually, it didn't take too long to get onto a boat. I was trying hard to keep it together for the younger kids, but my heart was pounding and sweat broke out on my forehead. I glanced at Fang and saw that he was just as twitchy as I was. Because we were the only two who had any freaking *sense.*

Please, I begged silently, *please do not let my last moments on earth be me crammed into a tiny boat in the dark, surrounded by mechanical singing pirates.*

Yes, that would *be cruel,* my Voice said snidely.

I ignored it.

114

"I want my own treehouse like that," Gazzy said around a mouthful of cotton candy. "I mean, for all of us. Wouldn't that be so cool?"

"So, so cool," Angel agreed, ice cream dripping down her wrist. "Can we do the Swiss Family Treehouse again?"

I handed her a napkin. "Maybe after lunch." Biting off a piece of my ice-cream sandwich, I did another 360 sweep. No Erasers. I couldn't say for sure we were the only mutants here because, you know, Disney World. But so far no one had morphed right in front of us.

"We could make one," Iggy said. "Find a humongous tree and build our own treehouse."

"Yeah!" said Gazzy, pushing another wad of cotton candy into his mouth. "We could do it! I know we could."

I rubbed his shoulder. "Okay. I'll put that on our list of things to do. Try not to eat too much junk, huh, Gazzy? I don't want you hurling on Splash Mountain." He grinned at me, a lighthearted child's grin that tugged at my heart. Yeah, yeah, if only.

"This way to Frontierland," Fang said, pointing to a sign.

I scanned the crowd again, then looked down at my map. "First Frontierland, and then — looks like the only good thing in Liberty Square is the Haunted Mansion."

"I want to see Mickey's Country House," Angel said.

"That's in the Toontown Fair place," I told her. "We need to go through some other stuff first. But we'll go."

She shot me a beautiful, innocent smile, and I tried to put all thoughts of our country's government out of my head.

"You know what's creepy?" Nudge said, eating caramel popcorn. "A chipmunk that big." She pointed at an adult-sized costumed chipmunk who was waving and strolling around.

"Who is that?" Total asked. "Chip? Or Dale?"

"Don't know," I said. "As long as he doesn't turn into a huge, chipmunky Eraser, I'm good. Yo — look. There's Splash Mountain. Line doesn't seem too bad."

"Is your dog talking?"

I turned around. A sunburned child was looking at Total suspiciously.

I laughed. "Our *dog?* No. Why? Does *your* dog talk?" I gave her a patronizing smile.

"I thought he was talking," she muttered, still staring at Total.

I said to Gazzy, "Jason, have you been practicing your ventriloquism again?"

Gazzy shrugged with the perfect amount of bashfulness and nodded.

"Oh," said the girl, and looked away.

I narrowed my eyes at Total, who pulled his lips back over his teeth in an embarrassed, ingratiating grin.

Not amused, I glanced over at Fang. He smiled, lighting up our immediate area, and offered me some Cracker Jack.

115

He had them. Ari took a bite of his ice cream bar, feeling the thin chocolate crunch between his teeth.

He'd seen them go into Splash Mountain. Now he was sitting on a bench at the exit, waiting for them to come out. It had taken a long time to find them in this place. He couldn't fly here, and he couldn't unleash a huge crowd of Erasers to sweep the joint. Too much commotion.

But now he had them. They would be out any minute. He had radioed six backup teams, which were less than five minutes away. Ari smiled. The sun was shining, the weather was great, he was eating ice cream, and all his dreams were about to come true.

A small crowd of people momentarily passed between him and the ride's exit, and Ari moved so he could see around them. He knew that people were staring at him. He looked different. Even different from other Erasers. He wasn't as — seamless. He didn't look as human as the rest of them did when they weren't morphed. He kind of looked morphy all the time. He hadn't seen his plain real face in — a long time.

"I know who you are."

Ari almost jumped — he hadn't noticed the boy slide onto the bench next to him.

He frowned down at the small, open face. "What?" he growled. This was when the little boy would get scared and probably turn and run. It always happened.

The boy smiled. "I know who you are," he said, pointing at Ari happily.

Ari just snarled at him.

The boy wiggled with excitement. "You're Wolverine!"

Ari stared at him.

"You look awesome, dude," said the boy. "You're totally my favorite. You're the strongest one of all of them and the coolest too. I wish I was like you."

Ari almost gagged. No one had ever, ever said anything like that to him. His whole life, he'd been the dregs in everyone's coffee pot. When he was really little, he'd idolized the bird kids and they'd ignored him. He'd loved Max, and she'd barely known he was alive. It would have been great when they disappeared, except his father had disappeared too. Ari still tasted ashes when he remembered realizing that his own father had chosen them over him. Ari had been left behind, with strangers.

Then they'd started augmenting him. At first Ari had been glad — he would be an Eraser, be one of them. But he wasn't. He was too different, too patchworky. The others had all been made Erasers as infants, as embryos. When they were human they looked really human. When they were wolves they looked really wolfy. Not Ari. He was stuck in a partially morphed state, never all human and still less than wolf. He looked weird. Ugly. He didn't fit in anywhere.

"You're, like, a total celebrity," the boy chattered on. "I mean, who cares about SpongeBob SquarePants? I'm sitting here with Wolverine!"

Ari gave him a tentative smile. It didn't matter that the kid had mistaken him for somebody else. This kid thought he was cool. He wanted to be like Ari. He was impressed.

It felt so good. It felt amazing.

"Gosh, could I have your autograph?" the kid went on, starting to look for a piece of paper. "My mom wanted me to get Goofy's autograph. Like, I'm so sure. Goofy! But you — here, can you sign my shirt?"

He held out a black marker and pulled on his T-shirt to make it taut.

Ari hesitated.

The boy looked uncertain. "I mean — I'm sorry. I didn't mean to bug you. I know you're famous, and I'm just a little kid." His face fell.

"No, that's okay, kid. Hope your mom doesn't mind," Ari growled. He took the marker in one pawlike hand and signed "Wolverine" with a flourish.

The kid looked awed and thrilled. "Gosh, thanks, mister. I'll never wash this shirt again. You're the best. I can't wait till I get back to school and tell everyone I met Wolverine and he signed my shirt! This is the best day of my life!"

Ari's throat ached and his nose twitched. He swiped one hand across his eyes. "No prob. You better get on back to your folks."

"Okay. Thanks again! You rock!" The boy pumped a fist into the air and ran off.

Ari sat for a moment, dazed with emotion. Suddenly he straightened. The flock! Max! Where were they? His eyes raked the trickle of people passing through the exit. The bird kids were nowhere to be seen. Six minutes had gone by — they must have come out. He'd missed them!

For God's sake! That dumb little kid!

You need to stay focused, Ari, said his Voice. *Keep your eyes on the prize.*

Ari strode off to meet his backup teams, which were now in sight. Yeah, he knew he needed to stay focused. He was all business.

But inside, part of him still smiled and held on tight to that warm, wanted feeling.

116

"God, I'm soaked," I moaned, pulling my wet sweatshirt away from my skin. I shook my hair out of my eyes, sending drops flying.

"That was *so great,*" the Gasman said happily.

"Splash Mountain really lives up to its name," Nudge said, bouncing a little.

"I hated that ride." Total sounded grumpy. And he'd hardly gotten wet at all.

"Let's go again!" Gazzy said.

We were almost all the way through the exit when I saw him: Ari, sitting on a bench. A little kid was talking to him excitedly. I froze, and the others bumped into me.

"Turn around," I said under my breath. "Bandada — nayshapay."

"No — oh, no," Gazzy whispered. "I can't believe it. Not now."

But I was already pushing them back through the exiting crowd.

"Sorry, kids," the attendant said. "You have to exit out that way only."

"No, no," I said urgently. "We left our digital camera in the log! Mom will kill us! We just need to run back and check. . . ."

The attendant paused for a moment, and in that moment I forced us all past him. "Excuse us, excuse us, coming through!"

Then we were back inside the ride. A walkway, almost concealed by false boulders, ran along one wall. We zipped down it, hearing the attendant calling after us.

"Here!" Fang said, stopping suddenly. I'd almost passed the door completely — it was practically invisible. Quickly we shot through it and found ourselves in a long, dimly lit corridor. Child's play. In seconds we had raced to the end of it and out its exit. We found ourselves behind some large shrubs.

"Come on," I said grimly. "Over to that fake mountain and then an up-and-away."

Three minutes later we were airborne, fading into the setting sun, leaving Disney World far behind. Nudge had tears running down her cheeks, and Gazzy and Angel both looked bitterly disappointed.

"I —," the Gasman began.

"What?" I angled one wing slightly and pulled closer to him.

"I wish we could have gone into the Haunted Mansion," he said. "It's supposed to be awesome."

I sighed. "I know, guys." Everyone was flying steadily, but each face was a mask of disappointment and frustration. "There were a bunch of things I'd been hoping to do too." All involving seeing mouse ears in my rearview mirror. If I had one. "But you know we had to go." Flock, one. Ari, zip.

"I hate stupid Ari!" Gazzy said. He punched and kicked the air in front of him. "He always ruins everything! Why does he hate *us?* It's not our fault they turned him into an Eraser!"

"It's not that simple, sweetie," I said.

"His dad left him," said Iggy bitterly. "Just like all of ours. Then they Eraserfied him. He's a walking time bomb."

"How does he track us so easily?" Angel asked. When she'd seen Cinderella's Castle, her face had looked as though it were made of sunlight. She was still young enough to really get caught up in the magic of an enormous, all-powerful marketing juggernaut.

"I don't know, Ange," I said. That was the ten-thousand-dollar question, in fact.

Below, the landscape was a spongy green, with nothing but a carpet of treetops to look down on. The trees ended abruptly, and beyond them we could see huge refineries or some kind of water-treatment plants or something.

I heard a faint buzz only a split second before a bug-like helicopter popped up from behind the trees. It was pointed a bit away from us but almost immediately turned and headed in our direction, like a curious insect.

"Okay, guys, scatter and zoom," I instructed quickly. "Meet up in fifteen minutes, same heading." I angled my wings sharply and peeled off to one side. From a corner of my eye I saw the rest of the flock split up, zipping off in all directions.

The chopper hesitated. It had News 14 Florida painted

on the side. So maybe not an Eraser chopper, maybe just a news cam tracking traffic.

But they'd seen us. I arched my back, pointing downward, then dropped into a screamingly fast descent. I rocketed toward the ground at two hundred miles an hour, which meant in less than a minute I had to angle out of it and swoop up again so I didn't squish like a mosquito on the windshield of the world.

Who said poetry was dead?

When I finally looked back, the chopper was nowhere in sight. A few minutes later, I saw various-sized dark specks coming at me. My flock.

Fang arrived first.

"We need to get out of the air," I told him.

117

"Black Ranger to Feather One," Total said softly. "Coast is clear. Come in, Feather One."

"Total, I'm right *here,*" I whispered. "We don't even have walkie-talkies."

"No, but we should," Total whispered back. "*I* should have one, and it could —"

I put my hand over his mouth, looking at the mountains of rusted metal, ancient appliances, and empty car husks that stretched for acres around us. I signaled over my shoulder, and Fang, Gazzy, and Nudge scampered past me and crouched next to a bunch of doorless refrigerators.

There had been only one guard, who looked as if he couldn't guard his way out of a paper bag. We'd left him in front of his oil-drum fire clear on the other side of this enormous junkyard–chop shop. Or at least I assumed it was a chop shop, given the suspicious number of relatively late-model cars that were tucked away in an airport hangar–sized building.

Which was where we were heading.

"Okay, now, the last time we were in a car . . . ," Fang whispered in my ear.

"That was different," I said impatiently. "Anyway, we're not going to steal a van."

"What are we going to steal this time?" Iggy whispered. "Can I have a turn driving?"

"Oh, ha ha," I said drily, and he smothered a snicker.

"That one," I whispered, pointing to a low, sleek, sporty number.

Which turned out to have no engine.

In fact, every one of these stupid cars had some huge problem with it: no steering wheel, or no wheels, or no dashboard, or no seats. An hour later I was ready to smack something in frustration.

"What now?" Fang asked in a low voice, crouching next to me. "Public transportation?"

I gave him a sour look.

"Max?" Nudge's voice was uncharacteristically quiet. She brushed some long curls out of her face. "I've been thinking."

Oh, here we go, I thought tiredly.

"If we take the seats out of the Camry, and the wheels off the Bug, and the battery out of the Caddy, and then we get the steering wheel from the Accord, and we drop that engine back into the Echo and hook up a new air filter, we could just take the Echo and be good to go." Her big brown eyes looked at me anxiously. "Don'tcha think?"

"Whoa," said Total, sitting down.

"Uh," I said.

"There's its air filter right on that table," she added helpfully.

"Since when do you know all this?" I asked, flabbergasted.

"I like cars. I always used to read Jeb's annual car issue from *Consumer Reports.* Remember?"

"Huh. Well, I guess that sounds like a plan, then," I said. "Everyone clear on what to do?"

Even the loser guard would have heard an engine starting, so we had to push the Frankenstein car out through the junkyard gate and a couple blocks away before we could even see if any of this worked.

When we were far enough away, Fang slid behind the steering wheel, and I applied my talent to hot-wiring the car.

The engine actually fired! True, it sounded rough, and the car backfired several times like rifle shots, but we were running, baby.

"Everybody in!" I said.

Which was when we discovered the final problem.

Little Echos aren't designed to hold six, count them six, larger-than-average-sized children.

And their wings.

And a dog.

"This is like a clown car," Total grumbled from my lap in the front seat.

"Why does the dog get to sit in your lap?" Gazzy asked plaintively, as we rattled and banged down the dark streets. "How about a kid?"

"Oh. 'The dog.' Very nice," said Total.

"Because you're not allowed to have people on your lap in the front seats," I explained. "It's not safe. If a cop saw us, we'd be stopped for sure. You want Total back *there?*"

Everyone in the back screamed no at the same time.

"Let's just deal, people," I said. "Only for a little while. We're going to stop as soon as we find a place to sleep."

" 'The dog,' " Total muttered, still mad.

"Shh," I told him.

"Are you saying you're *not* a dog?" the Gasman asked. He was tired. We were all tired and hungry and cranky.

"Okay, you two," I said sternly. "Enough! Everyone quiet, okay? We're looking for a place to sleep. Just chill."

Fang glanced back in the rearview mirror. "Does anyone want to sing 'Ninety-nine Bottles of Beer on the Wall'?"

We all screamed no at the same time.

118

That night we hid the car in some overgrown brush on an abandoned farm and slept in the trees, swaying gently in the pleasant breeze. We weren't attacked or ratted on, so it was an up night for us.

In the morning we got back into our little car—emphasis on the *little*.

"There aren't enough seat belts," Gazzy complained from the backseat. The four of them looked like sardines back there.

"And God knows we live our lives totally paranoid about safety measures," I said, looking at a map.

"I'm just saying," said Gazzy. "Yow! Fang!"

Even Fang had winced at that last gear-grinding. I bit my lip so I wouldn't smirk and gave Fang a wide-eyed innocent look. Yes, I *swallowed down* all the snide comments I could make about his driving, unlike Fang, who had gone ahead and made snide comments when I drove. That's because I'm a better person, frankly. I am a freaking *princess* when it comes to other people's feelings.

"Yo, dogbreath," I said to Total. "Get your paws off the Everglades."

Total moved slightly so I could see the map, Fang ground the gears again, and we lurched on toward our destination: Itex headquarters.

Assuming Angel's intel was good, it was time for us to learn just what the heck I was supposed to do to stop this company from destroying the world. I was tired of dodging it. I was tired of asking about it. I was ready to *know.*

119

Here's something that might not occur to you: If a state trooper sees a weird, patchwork Toyota Echo hurtling down I-95, and it looks like half of a small country is immigrating to the States in this one little car, you might get stopped.

Just FYI.

In general, the six of us preferred to avoid law enforcement agents of any kind. Especially since we never knew whether they were the real thing or if they would suddenly turn into Erasers, as just another challenge in this twisted lab test of a life we led.

"Should we bail?" Fang asked, looking at the flashing lights in the rearview mirror.

"Probably." I rubbed my forehead, trying to muster energy for whatever might be coming. I turned back to the others. "We'll stop, and as soon as it looks freaky, up and away, okay?"

I got solemn nods from everyone.

"I'm with Iggy," Total said, leaping into the backseat.

Fang clumsily pulled onto the shoulder, kicking up dust and gravel. We shared a glance as a woman in a state trooper uniform got out of her cruiser and walked toward us. We unlocked the car doors and poised for takeoff.

The trooper leaned down into Fang's window, her broad-brimmed hat shadowing her face.

"Good morning, sir," she said, sounding unfriendly. "Do you know how fast you were traveling?"

Fang looked at the speedometer, which hadn't moved since we'd pushed the car out into the darkness last night. "No," he said truthfully.

"I tagged you at seventy miles an hour," she said, pulling out a clipboard.

I let out an impressed whistle. "Excellent! I never thought it'd be that fast!"

Fang shot me a look and I put my hand over my mouth.

"Can I see your license, your registration, and your proof of insurance?" the trooper asked, all business.

We were toast. We'd have to split, which meant we would lose our little jigsaw car, she would see our wings, and she'd probably notify the web of authorities who would make our lives miserable. Miserabler.

"Hi," said Angel from the backseat.

The trooper peered at her through the window. It was then that she seemed to notice how many of us there were, how we were all kids. She looked back at Fang, and this time she realized that he probably wasn't old enough to have a license at all.

"Are you from here? Florida is really flat, huh?" Angel said, getting the trooper's attention for a moment.

"Can you step out of the car, please, sir?" the trooper asked Fang.

"It sure is warm here, for fall," Angel went on. "You could practically go swimming."

Once again the trooper glanced at Angel, but this time something blunted her impulse to turn away. I didn't dare look back at Angel. Once again I was confronted with the whole Angel-doing-something-bad-for-good-reasons thing, and I didn't know what to do.

I decided to let her do it, then lecture her later. A win-win situation.

"We're kind of in a hurry," Angel said pleasantly.

"You're in a hurry," the trooper said. Her eyes were slightly vacant.

"Maybe you could just let us go," Angel went on. "And sort of forget you ever saw us."

"I could just let you go," the trooper repeated. It was incredibly creepy.

"You never saw us or our car," Angel said. "There's a problem somewhere else, and you need to get there now."

The trooper looked back at her cruiser. "I have to go," she said. "There's a problem."

"All right," said Angel. "Thanks."

And we were on our way. Riding in a stolen car with a six-year-old who could control people's minds. Not really the definition of comfortable.

We'd gone a couple miles when Angel spoke again. "I don't know, guys," she said. "I really think maybe I should be the leader."

"I'll be second-in-command," Total offered.

"Oh yeah, you'd be so focused on the job." Gazzy sneered. "Until a *rabbit* ran across your path."

"Hey!" said Total, glaring at him.

"Guys," I said tiredly. "Listen, Ange, it's sweet of you to offer, but I've got the whole leader thing down, okay? You don't have to worry about it."

"Well, I guess," Angel said, frowning. She didn't sound 100 percent convinced.

What was going on with her?

120

I believe I've mentioned how freaking slow driving is, compared with flying. In the air there are no stoplights, and there's surprisingly little traffic of other flying mutants. On the other hand, we were relatively hidden in a car.

"Well," said Fang, looking at the huge gates in front of us.

"Yep," I said.

After more than three hours of cautiously slow but still kidney-jarring travel and a pit stop for lunch, we had arrived at Itex headquarters. Through our sheer instinct and heightened powers of deduction, we had zeroed in on the place that might hold some answers for us.

Heightened powers of deduction meaning being able to read all the signs on the highway saying "Itex — Exit 398."

Now we examined the tall iron gates, the professional landscaping.

"No barbed wire," Fang muttered.

"No armed guards," said Nudge. "That little guardhouse is cute, though."

It seemed unusual, which set off blinking red lights in my brain. Was this where the world would get saved? Where my destiny would finally be played out?

Just then a smiling uniformed guard stepped out of the guardhouse. He had no gun or other weapon that we could see.

"Are you all here for the tour?" he asked pleasantly.

"Um, yes," said Fang, his hands tight on the steering wheel.

"I'm sorry — the last one was at four," the guard said. "But come back tomorrow — the tours are every hour on the hour, and they leave from the main lobby." He pointed through the gates to one of the larger buildings.

"Um, okay," said Fang, putting Jigsaw into reverse. "Thanks."

We pulled away but kept the guard in our sight as long as we could. We didn't see him speak to anyone or use his walkie-talkie or anything. It was weird. Once again I felt a heavy sense of unnamed dread settling on my shoulders. I wasn't stupid. Those kids had been sent to us, to give us a message. To get us to Itex. Sooner or later we would find out what was planned for us here, and odds were that it would be nothing good.

My Voice had been quiet for a while, and I almost — almost — wanted it to speak up again, just to drop some clues about what we were doing here.

But there was no way I'd ask it.

121

"Okay, Iggy, your turn," I said, pressing a small bottle of shampoo into his hand. "And just because you can't see is no excuse to not get all the grime off."

Iggy took the shampoo, and Gazzy directed him toward the bathroom door.

My hair was still wet, dampening my T-shirt at the shoulders. We were ensconced in the lack of luxury of the Twilight Inn, which was the kind of place that had shady deals going on in all the rooms. We hadn't had baths since we'd left Anne's, and the Twilight Inn had the bonus of its own pay laundry room. I'd just gotten back with the last load of warm, dry, clean clothes, which I dumped on one of the double beds.

I felt almost human.

That was a joke — get it?

Nudge, Gazzy, Angel, and Total were on the other bed, watching TV. The kids all had their wings out, letting them dry. I sat down and shoved some laundry at Fang.

"So, Itex," he said, starting to fold and pack.

"Yep. Guess who made the laundry detergent? Guess what gas station we stopped at? Guess who made the soda you're drinking?" Now that I was looking for it, I saw the Itex logo everywhere. It was unbelievable — the company seemed to touch every aspect of our lives. But we'd never thought about it before, never noticed it.

Wordlessly Fang held up a pair of Gazzy's jeans. The back label said Itex.

"This is bad," I said, keeping my voice down.

"You idiot!" Total shouted at the TV. "It's the red one! The red one!"

"They're everywhere, all right," I said. "What's worse is, the more I think about it, the more I remember them being everywhere our whole lives. I remember Angel drinking Itex formula from an Itex bottle, and wearing Itex diapers. It's like they've been taking over the world without anyone noticing it."

"Someone noticed it," Fang said slowly, folding a shirt of Iggy's. "Someone at the School noticed it at least fourteen years ago. And built you to try to stop them."

There was my destiny again, slapping me in the face. "Built *us*."

"Mostly you. I'm pretty sure the rest of us are redundant." Fang sounded matter-of-fact, but the idea bothered me.

"You're not redundant to *me,*" I said, stuffing a pair of shorts into a backpack.

Fang gave me one of his rare, quick smiles.

We turned the lights out early. I lay awake for a long time on the floor, thinking about Itex, the company that might blow up the world. My mission was to *save* the world. So I had to deal with Itex somehow, do something, find out something, stop them from doing something.

As a destiny, it was pretty fuzzy. It was like being told to climb Everest without a map and with no supplies. Plus be responsible for five other people. I felt overwhelmed and weirdly alone, though I was surrounded by my flock. I fell asleep hoping that maybe tomorrow I would be able to come up with something.

As it turned out, my "tomorrow" started in the pitch-darkness, with my hands and feet bound, and a strip of duct tape over my mouth.

122

Break free! My brain went from sleep to extreme, annihilating panic in an instant. I arched my back with all my strength, bucking myself off the floor. At the same time I tried yanking my hands and feet apart as hard as I could, only to find they wouldn't budge. *Think, Max, think! You can get out of this! They can't get you this easily!*

My scream was muffled by the duct tape. I heaved myself around, trying to knock into someone or break something to make some noise. I couldn't believe the others were sleeping through this — usually the slightest sound woke any of us. *Maybe there's something wrong with them.*

Two big, dark figures leaned over me, trying to gather me up, but I struggled against them with all my might. I managed to knee one in the stomach, but it didn't do much. Then the other one simply sat on me, knocking every bit of breath out of my body. Wild-eyed, I sucked in air through my nose, already feeling like I was suffocating.

It had been a long time since I'd been so completely helpless, and it made me crazy. All thought fled my brain — I went into frenzied animal instinct, struggling for my life, willing to kill my captors, to do anything to stay alive.

I was hyperventilating, screaming silently, gouging ridges in my ankles and wrists where they were bound with plastic ties. And still I was helpless.

Still unable to stop the black hood from coming over my head, unable to not breathe the sickly sweet smell, unable to stop myself from letting go, releasing into a deep, cold blackness where there was no pain, no fear, only nothingness.

Oh yeah, and one other bad thing. *Really bad,* I think. I saw that other Max in the room when they kidnapped me.

And I think she stayed there with the flock.

123

After the Erasers had taken the inferior Max away from the motel, I quickly lay down in her spot and pulled the blanket over me. I closed my eyes, positive I wouldn't sleep a wink.

I was so hyped up — it was all finally happening. No way would I sleep. . . . Out with the old Max, in with the new and improved Max. All according to plan.

"Wagh!" I woke up flailing, dreaming that I was being sponged by aliens.

My hand hit something furry and warm, and I felt the furriness jump away. Then I remembered: They had a dog. It must have been licking me. So gross.

I blinked slowly and looked around. The skeezy motel room looked even worse in the daylight than it had in the middle of the night.

"Max?" I looked up to see the little blond boy — Gasman, what a name — leaning over me.

"Uh, what?" I said.

"I'm hungry."

Showtime. Now I would see how well I could play Maximum Ride. "Right," I said, getting up. I was sore and stiff from sleeping on the floor. Now that I could see everyone close up, it was hard for me not to stare. They really were different from Erasers, from Ari. I didn't know how they could stand themselves.

"So, breakfast," I said, trying to remember the drill. "Does the, uh, dog need to go out?"

"We already went out," said the littlest kid. Angel. She cocked her head to one side, looking at me, and I gave her a big smile. Little weirdo. I had no idea why Max stayed with these losers. She would do so much better on her own. Every one of them was a ball and chain, holding her down. She should have dumped them a long time ago. But that was one of her weaknesses: She needed an audience, a pep squad. Someone to hold her hand and tell her how fabulous she was.

Anyway. There was a tiny kitchenette in one corner of the room. I went over and put a frying pan on one of the hot plates. "Okay, how about some eggs?" I said, looking inside the minifridge.

"You're going to cook?"

I turned around to see Fang, the older, dark-haired boy, looking at me.

"Aren't you hungry?"

"Not *that* hungry," Gasman muttered.

I didn't get it. The other older boy, the fair one, stood up.

"I'll do it. Gaz, you pour juice. Nudge, get out the paper plates."

"But you're blind," I said. He couldn't cook. Or was this some kind of joke?

"You're kidding! I am?" the guy — Iggy — said sarcastically. He brushed past me and turned on the hot plate. "Who wants scrambled?"

"Me," said Nudge, raising her hand. She dug out some paper plates and put them on the dinky Formica table.

Huh. Maybe because I was the leader, I didn't do stuff like cook. Well, I had to look busy, in charge.

"Nudge? Come over here and I'll fix your hair." I rummaged in a backpack for a brush. "We could do, like, ponytails or something, get it out of your eyes."

Nudge — another dumb name — looked at me. "You want to fix my hair?"

"Yeah." God, what did Max do all day? She didn't cook, she didn't fix people's hair. Did she just sit on her butt barking orders all the time? "Oh, and hey — you — off the bed." I snapped my fingers at the dog, who just looked at me.

"Why can't he sit on the bed?" Angel asked.

"Because I said so," I said, starting to brush Nudge's hair.

There was silence, and I looked up to see the other four mutant kids looking at me. Well, not the blind one, though his face was turned toward me, which was creepy.

"What?" I asked.

124

The last thing I remembered was being kidnapped from the motel room. No, the very last thing I remembered was seeing that other Max in the room. What happened? Had she replaced me? Why?

At the moment, I didn't know if I was awake or asleep, alive or dead. I blinked again and again, but there was complete and utter blackness: no shadows, no blurry forms, no pinprick of light. All of us except Iggy can see extremely well in the dark, so not being able to see anything at all made my blood run cold.

Was I blind now, like Iggy? Had they experimented on my *eyes?*

Where was I? I remembered being bound and gagged. I remembered passing out. Now I was here, but where "here" was I had no clue.

Where was the flock? None of them had woken up when I'd been taken. Had they been drugged? Something worse? Were they okay? I tried to sit up, but it was as if I was suspended somehow — I couldn't put my feet down, couldn't push off anything. But I felt wetness. I could touch my face. My hair was wet. I reached out with my hands and felt nothing. There was water or something all around me, but it wasn't like ordinary water — I couldn't sink.

I swallowed and blinked again, feeling myself start to panic. Where was my flock? Where was *I?* What was going on? *Was I dead?* If I was dead, I was going to be incredibly pissed because there was no way I could deal with this limitless nothingness for an *hour,* much less eternity. No one had said death would be so intensely boring.

My heart was beating fast, my breaths were quick and shallow, my skin was tingling because blood was rushing to my muscles and main organs: fight or flight. Which reminded me. I stretched out my wings and *couldn't feel a thing.* Wildly I reached back with one hand. My heavy wing muscles, the thick ridges where they joined my shoulders, were there. I still had wings. I just couldn't feel them.

Was I anesthetized? Was I having an operation? I tried as hard as I could to move, thrashing around in the blackness, but again felt nothing.

Very bad news.

Where the heck was I?

Try to calm down. Calm down. Get it together. If you're dead, you're dead, and there's nothing you can do about it. If you're not dead, you need to get it together so you can escape, rescue the others, open a can of whup-ass on whoever put you here. . . .

I was completely alone. I couldn't remember the last time I'd been completely alone. If I were in a hammock on a beach, sipping a drink with a little umbrella in it, and I knew the flock was safe and okay and everything was fine, I would be ecstatic. Being alone, off-duty, able to relax — it would be a dream come true.

Instead I was alone with darkness, with fear, with uncertainty. So where was I?

You might not want to know.

The Voice. I wasn't completely alone after all. The Voice was still with me.

"Do you know where I am?" I spoke out loud, my voice dropping away into dull nothingness.

Yes.

"So tell me!"

Are you sure you want to know?

"Oh no, I enjoy being in a state of complete ignorance!" I snapped. "This is why I don't want you around anymore! Now tell me, you jerk!"

You're in an isolation tank. A sensory-deprivation chamber. I don't know where, exactly.

"Oh, my God. You were right — I didn't want to know."

An isolation tank. Nothing but me, my totally screwed-up consciousness, and the Voice. Well, I could probably stand this for say, oh, ten minutes before I went stark-raving *nuts.*

Knowing the whitecoats, they probably planned to keep me in here a year or two, so they could take notes, see what happened to me.

I needed to die, right now.

125

But I'm Maximum Ride. So it wouldn't be that easy, would it?

Of course not. My life would never contain a convenient, pain-saving plan when it could stretch a problem out into an endless agony of uncertainty and torture.

I don't know how long I was in the tank. It could have been ten minutes. It felt like ten years. A lifetime. Maybe I slept. I know I hallucinated. Again and again I "woke up" to find myself back with the flock, back in our house in Colorado or in the subway tunnels of NYC or in the Twilight Inn. I saw Ella Martinez and her mom again, smiling and waving at me.

I think I cried for a while.

Basically every thought I'd ever had in my entire life, I had all over again, one after another in rapid-fire succession. Every memory, every color, every taste, every sensation of any kind replayed itself in my fevered brain, endless loops of thought and memory and dream and hope, over and over, until I couldn't tell what had been real and what had been wishful thinking and what had been a movie I'd seen or a book I'd read. I didn't know if I was really Max, or if I really had wings, or if I really had a family of bird kids like me. Nothing was real except being in this tank. And maybe not even that.

I sang for a while, I think. I talked. Finally my voice went. Weirdly, I was never hungry or thirsty. Nothing hurt; nothing felt good.

So when the tank was finally cracked open and light streamed in, it seemed like the worst, most painful thing that had ever happened to me.

126

I screamed, but the sound of my own voice was intensely loud, piercing my eardrums, so I shut up immediately. I squeezed my eyes shut against the blinding light and curled into a ball as much as I could. Big hands grabbed me and pulled me up, and just their touch, after so much nothingness, freaked out my senses.

They put me on a bed and covered me with a blanket. The feeling of anything touching me was torture. I huddled there trying not to move for a long, long time.

Finally I realized that I wasn't in so much pain anymore. I tried opening one eye a slit. It was too bright, but I didn't feel like my retina was searing.

"Max?" The hushed whisper woke every nerve all over again, sending unbearably painful chills down my spine. I tensed, my eyes closed. I no longer knew how to run, how to flee, how to fight.

I *wanted* to be back in the tank, the blessed darkness and silence and nothingness.

"Max, how are you doing?"

Jim Dandy, I thought hysterically. *Peachy. Never better.*

"Max, do you need anything?"

That was such a ludicrous question that I felt myself smile.

"I need to ask you some questions," the voice whispered. "I need to know where the flock is heading. I need to know what happened in Virginia."

That got me. A couple of synapses actually connected in my brain. I pulled the blanket down just a little and opened my eyes a slit. "You know what happened in Virginia," I said. My voice was thin and rusty, made of nails. "You were there, Jeb."

"Only at the end, sweetheart," Jeb said, his voice very quiet. He was kneeling on the floor next to the cot I was on. "I don't know what happened before then, how everything fell apart. I don't know where the flock is headed now or what your plan is."

Now I felt maybe 10 percent like myself. "Jeb, I'm afraid you're going to have to learn to live with not knowing." I chuckled a tiny bit. It sounded like a cat choking.

"That's my Max," Jeb said affectionately. "Tough till the end. Even after everything, you're still in better shape than anyone else would be. But I have to tell you, you need to get on board with this saving-the-world project."

"I'll try to pencil it in," I croaked. Now I felt enough like myself to be irritated.

Jeb leaned closer to me. I opened my eyes and looked him straight in the face, that familiar face that had represented everything good in my life, at one time. And now represented everything bad.

"Max, please," he whispered. "Please just play along.

They want to terminate you. They think you're a lost cause."

This was news.

"Who?"

"Itex. They're keeping you here while they try out their latest, greatest invention. They wanted you to lead with your head, not your heart, Max. I tried to teach you that, but maybe I failed. They're trying to take all of the heart out of you by keeping you here. But you care about things, and about *people,* Max. Like me. Please, don't make everything that's happened up till now meaningless. Don't give them cause to take you out, start over with someone else. Show them they're wrong about you. Show them you've got what it takes."

"I'll show them I've got what it takes to rip your spleen out through your nose," I said weakly.

"Batchelder!" I suddenly heard a deep voice from behind me. "You're not authorized to be in here."

Then my light was blocked again, the blanket was pulled off, and big hands picked me up and dropped me back into the horrible tank.

127

I led the five mutant freaks through the shadows toward Itex.

"In here." I held aside some bushes and motioned them through. It was dark, *finally.* I'd thought spending days watching a bunch of Erasers play Texas hold 'em was boring, but that didn't compare to today.

I didn't know how the original Max stood it. I'd lost count of how many times today I'd wanted to scream at them to shut up and get away from me. That Nudge *never* quit yapping, and Angel and Gasman had gotten into disputes like whether the sky was blue and what day this was. I hadn't found any chinks in Fang's armor, but it was just a matter of time. Angel frankly creeped me out — she was a loose cannon. Maybe she was kind of unstable. I would have to tell them that when I got back. Gasman seemed like a gullible idiot, and Iggy was dead weight, as far as I could tell. Except that he could cook, for some reason. Plus, they all talked to the dog like it was a person, asking it if it wanted this or that. I mean, it was a freaking dog.

But finally it was time. We'd gone on the tour of Itex today, and I'd made a big deal about noticing its weak points. Now we were "breaking in." I was trying to be careful, look like I was on guard.

I have to say, I was doing great. They didn't suspect a thing. All my training, the lessons, the practice — it was paying off. It was gratifying, how obvious it was that I was the new and improved version. In fact, it was weird how willing these freaks were to follow me around, do what I said. I'd told 'em we were going to break into Itex, and they were all on board. Even the dumb *dog.* When we were leaving the hotel, I'd tried to shut it inside the room, but Nudge had held the door open for it to trot out.

"The dog's coming on a raid?" I'd asked, my eyebrows raised.

"Of course he's coming," Nudge had said, looking surprised. "He always comes."

O-kaaay, I'd thought. *I'm starting to put my finger on why you guys are slated for termination.*

But whatever. They followed orders, anyway. I led them up a grassy hill, looking around — *like someone was going to catch us, right?* There was a huge HVAC box next to the main building, and we quickly unscrewed the cover. I jammed a stick in the enormous fan, and then we all hurried through. I yanked the stick out, the fan started spinning again, and we were in.

"That was a good idea," said Fang. Which was about five more words than he'd said all day.

I shrugged. I knew Max was totally full of herself, but

that didn't mean *I* had to be. We started moving through the air vent system.

I was trying to remember to seem nervous, to look around, to act like I was considering which way to go. Sometimes I stopped everyone and put my finger to my lips, as if someone were coming. It was hysterical.

We got to the main branch of the HVAC system, and I pretended to hesitate before I led them all into the vent that went to the basement. Just a few more minutes, another couple hundred yards, and my job would be over.

And so would they.

128

Being back in the isolation tank after seeing Jeb was a huge relief — for about two milliseconds. Then I started thinking about what he had said. I remembered that I had a flock depending on me. I remembered that I was Invincible Max and that the whitecoats making me run through their maze were a bunch of losers.

Which left the question: how to get out of here?

I still couldn't sit up, couldn't feel anything. I was spacing out and hallucinating again — it was way hard to concentrate, to remember what I was doing instead of floating off into la-la land.

Think, Max.

Then I remembered I had a Voice in my head. *Voice, you got any ideas?*

What is it they want from you? the Voice said, shocking me. It had never, ever responded to a direct question before. At least that I could remember, right then.

Uh . . . what did they want from me? *Just for me to be*

here. To be able to do things to me, make me jump through their hoops, be their lab rat.

What would happen if you took that away from them?

I thought. *They would be very upset?*

I smiled. But how could I take that away from them? I'd pretty much established that I couldn't break out of this sardine can.

Think about it.

Now that I really thought about it, realizing how limited my options truly were kind of freaked me out. Here was a situation where all my speed, my physical strength, my cunning — none of it would do me any good.

It was mind-blowing.

If I hadn't been so totally spaced, I would have panicked.

As it was, I felt oddly removed from the problem. Freaked, but removed at the same time. I was losing myself. Losing my mind.

Losing myself . . . losing me. They would be upset if they lost me. Because I wouldn't be around to jump through their hoops. But since I couldn't physically move, getting lost seemed pretty unworkable.

Except.

There *was* another way for them to lose me: if I died.

Which would sort of defeat my own purpose, as well as theirs. But — could I just make them think I was dead?

I bet there were monitors of some sort in here. When you put a rat in a maze, you hung around to observe the results. They'd probably been recording my crazed ranting and sobbing all along.

Now. How to be dead?

I lay back in the buoyant liquid. It supported me

totally — I didn't have to try to keep my head up or anything. My breathing slowed, in and out, one, two, three, four. I relaxed every single muscle. Then I just . . . went inside myself. It was like I was a machine and I was slowly flicking switches off. I just *willed* all my systems to slow down more and more.

In the yawning silence, my heart beat slower, then slower. My eyes closed. Everything was still and silent. Maybe I would lie in this watery tomb forever.

There was no time, no thought, no motion.

I hoped I wasn't actually dead.

That would make finding our parents and saving the world *really* hard.

129

I see no need to go into a lot of boring detail, but we found our way to the Itex computer room. So far, the plan was working beautifully.

I shooed everyone away to the darkest corner of the room, and they actually listened to me. Then I turned one computer on, and it booted up silently. I had been told Nudge was good with computers, so I motioned her over.

"See what you can find out about Itex," I whispered. "Be quick — I don't know how much time we have."

We had exactly six minutes, forty-seven seconds, according to my watch.

"Okay," Nudge whispered back. She slid onto the stool and instantly went to the "List Programs" menu. From there she got to a C prompt, and then she typed in a bunch of gibberish.

I sighed to myself, waiting for her to get stuck, and then I'd have to take over. They'd taught me everything I needed to make sure I could get us where we had to go.

"Oh, here," Nudge whispered, and I watched in surprise as page after page of information, all labeled "Restricted Access Only" filled the screen. Hmm. Maybe this mutant was smarter than she looked. Maybe somehow, something had come out right, with her.

"Okay, start reading," I said, looking over her shoulder. Time was running out for the freaks.

130

I, Maximum Ride, was dead, and nobody seemed to have noticed.

Maybe I really *was* dead. I was starting to not really care one way or another.

Finally, finally my captors figured out that instead of an interesting, captive lab rat, they now had a much less interactive dead body on their hands.

Deep in my trance, I had only a split second to brace myself as they ripped open the top of the tank, letting in retina-searing, blinding light. Staying limp was the hardest thing I had ever done.

Voices said, "What happened? Who was monitoring her? They're gonna have our butts!"

Once again hands grabbed me and hauled me out of there. Once again it was the most horrible, painful thing I could imagine. But this time I forced my eyes open, put my feet down, and *roared.*

My knees buckled under me, but I flung my wings out, shaking as much moisture as possible off them. I had a brief glimpse of astonished, then angry faces, and, with another raspy, croaky roar, not nearly as intimidating as I'd hoped, I leaped up shakily.

I saw a blurred image of a window and ran at it, hardly able to keep on my rubbery legs. When I was close, I threw myself at the glass as hands grabbed at my wet clothes and wings.

Please don't let this glass have chicken wire embedded in it, I remembered to pray at the last second. I guess it didn't, because I crashed right through it, which made every cell in my body feel as if it had been crushed by a truck. Screaming in pain, I felt damp air hit my cheeks and then I started to fall.

I tried to move my wings, tried to remember that familiar feeling of catching wind beneath them: light, beautiful sails of muscle and feather and bone. But I felt only numbness, a deadened sensation, as if I'd been dipped in novocaine.

Work, dang it, work! I thought, and had an image of myself crumpling into a broken heap on the ground, maybe five stories below.

It was dark out: less painful for my eyes. I opened them to see the ground rushing up at me way too fast. Once again I flung my wings out, desperate for them to catch me, to snatch me back up into the air.

And they did — just as my bare feet banged against the grass. Then I was lurching unsteadily upward, trying to remember how to fly, how to move my muscles, how to unhinge my shoulder blades to give me more freedom. I lifted up past the broken window, which had several angry faces crowded in it.

One face wasn't angry. Jeb's. He held his hand out the window, giving me a thumbs-up.

"See you soon, sweetheart!" he called.

I soared upward, the wind blowing my wet hair back.

What was with him?

131

"Geez, there's so much stuff here," Gasman whispered, reading over Nudge's shoulder.

Yeah-huh, no kidding, I thought. I hadn't expected nearly this amount of info on Itex. I wondered if they'd had any idea that this kid would be so successful at hacking in.

Nudge was scrolling through pages fast. I kept an eye on my watch, ready to hurry everyone on to part two of tonight's little charade.

"I wonder," Nudge said, suddenly stopping her typing and sitting very still. "I wonder if Jeb has been here. I feel something." *Cripes,* I thought. *This is getting creepy.*

"Why would Jeb have been here?" I snapped. "He has nothing to do with Itex."

"Max, I can feel his vibe. He was here. Maybe there is something on him, on us, in the Itex files." Her fingers started flying.

"What are you doing?" I whispered. "No ad-libbing — stick to the program."

Irritated, I quickly checked out the others. Gasman and Iggy were beneath a counter, and Gasman was looking up at something. Fang was standing guard by the door.

Angel and her unwanted flea-magnet were sitting very still, close to Fang. Angel's eyes were closed, I noticed with irritation. Nice time to take a nap. Just then her eyes popped open and she looked straight at me. I gave her a reassuring smile and turned back to Nudge.

"Oh, gosh," Nudge whispered as the screen suddenly filled again. "Look, look!"

Frowning, I watched as pages of documents tiled before us. On the top was a photograph of a baby. It was wearing a white hospital bracelet that said, "I'm a Girl! My name is Monique." The *Monique* part was handwritten.

"That's me, me as a baby," Nudge said excitedly.

I had no idea why she thought this, but whatever. She started scrolling through the pages and hit a huge patch of, like, blueprints or mechanical drawings, schematics, design plans. I looked closer and frowned. These were plans of how to recombine the baby's DNA, graft avian DNA into her stem cells.

"Max, Max, look at this," Nudge whispered, pointing. There, at the bottom of a long medical form, was the signature of Jeb Batchelder. "Oh, my gosh. Max — can you believe this? Fang?"

Fang came over silently and read over her shoulder. His eyes narrowed. I didn't understand — how could Jeb Batchelder be here in Itex's files? We were supposed to be finding out stuff about how evil Itex was — not about the scientists at the School.

Nudge clicked on a link, and a small media-player window popped up. It was labeled "Parents, two days post."

A fuzzy video clip of a black couple started playing. The woman was crying, and the man had a pained, frozen expression on his face, as if he'd just seen a horrible accident. The woman was saying, "My baby! Who would take my baby? Her name was Monique! If anyone knows where my baby is, please, *please* bring her back. She's my world!" The woman broke down sobbing and couldn't go on.

This wasn't the stuff we were *supposed* to be seeing. We were *supposed* to be looking at file after file about how Itex was polluting the planet, destroying natural resources, using child labor, and so on. Despite myself, I was intrigued by what Nudge was finding.

"That doesn't make sense," I said, after the video played. "We saw the medical consent form a few screens back."

Nudge sniffled and clicked back to the form. At the bottom were signatures of Monique's parents, authorizing someone named Roland ter Borcht to "treat" their baby.

But, now that we looked at them, the parent signatures looked exactly like Jeb Batchelder's.

I didn't know what to think. None of this agreed with what they had told me. What was real? Crying silently, Nudge continued to scroll through the file. Another photograph of the woman filled the screen. She looked older and incredibly sad. Stamped across the photo in red ink was the word "Terminated."

Suddenly Iggy pulled his head out from under the counter. He was holding some wires in one hand. "Someone's coming," he said.

132

Freedom is still freedom, even if you're soaked, practically nuts, and having trouble getting your muscles to cooperate.

First stop: the Twilight Inn. I checked it out carefully, but it seemed clear. The Echo was still in the parking lot. No one was in the room, however, though all of our stuff was still there. Was the flock out looking for me?

I wolfed down some food, then packed all of our stuff as fast as I could. I grabbed everything and took off, running twenty feet in the parking lot and leaping into the air, wings wide and gathering wind.

I kept up a constant surveillance, watching for flying Erasers, but saw nothing. The backpacks weighed me down too much — I needed to ditch them and have my hands free.

I hid our stuff at the top of a pine tree. Next stop: back to where I'd just busted out from. The more I felt like myself, the more myself felt like a murderous, enraged maniac. I tore through the night sky, rage rolling off me like steam. My whole life, the whitecoats had done countless heinous, inhuman, unforgivable things to me, to all of us. They had kidnapped Angel. But now they'd really crossed the line.

They had put me in a *freaking tank!*

I was amazed I was still coherent at all, could fly at all. I stayed out of sight, under the tree canopy, zipping through and among and between the pine trees.

When I shot out of the woods, I did a fast, fast circle around the whole compound, seven huge buildings. I backtracked my path, looking for a telltale broken window. And I found it. I'd just needed the confirmation that I'd really been held here, that this company was behind it. That Jeb was associated with Itex.

Now to find the flock.

Racing back to the woods, I screamed to a halt at the dark edge of the trees. I dropped lightly to the ground, shaking out my wings. I felt okay. Like I'd had the flu but was better now. My hands clenched and unclenched at my sides. I was *eager* for Erasers to show up. I was ready to rip something apart.

I pulled in my wings and sneaked through the shadows toward the main building.

I kept low to the ground, my eyes on the lighted windows of the building. Something hanging brushed my head, and I swiped at it absently. My hand touched something smooth and cool — and alive.

Stifling a gasp, I yanked my hand back, only to feel the something drop down on me with a thud. A snake!

I almost shrieked, but let out a horrified squeak instead.

133

Then there were snakes everywhere. Six- and seven-foot black snakes were dropping down on me, climbing my legs, winding around me, flicking me with their tongues. I was flinging them off me, doing a freaked-out dance, whirling, trying to shake them off. But they just kept coming.

I was about to completely lose it. If there was one thing I hated worse than small dark spaces, it was lousy *snakes!* "Oh God, oh God, oh God," I panted, ripping snakes off me. I felt hysteria rising and knew I was gonna blow.

Hunching down, I gathered my muscles and sprang straight up into the air. I whooshed my wings out as hard as I could, shaking and shuddering as I felt snakes slithering all over them. Oh God, *help, help, help!* In the air I shifted gears and went into hypersonic mode. The snakes began to peel away from me, dropping off and falling into the darkness below. I was trembling so hard I could barely fly, and I finally kicked off the last of them.

Snakes! Horrible snakes! Where had they come from? I hated, hated, *hated* snakes.

You're afraid of them, said my Voice, as cool and unruffled as always.

No freaking duh! I screamed inside my head.

Fear is your weakness. You must conquer all your weaknesses.

I was so horrified and furious that I thought I was gonna barf. Had that been another test? Had it all been in my imagination? My stomach was roiling, and adrenaline sang in my blood. My head was going to explode.

The flock. Have to get the flock.

Good, Max. Keep your eyes on the prize.

"Screw you, Voice." I put my shoulders back, set my jaw, and did a 180, back to Itex.

Excellent, Max. Sometimes you amaze me.

134

How did this blind guy Iggy know someone was coming? He was like a bat! Maybe he had some bat DNA —

Crash!

Ari burst through the computer room doors.

"Scatter!" Fang yelled, launching himself at canine boy. *What's* this *bonehead doing here?* I thought. I'd been expecting Itex's expert termination team, not any of those half-assed wolves. Where were they? I looked at the clock, then decided to watch the two male mutants tear each other up on the floor.

That is, until I heard Gasman shriek, "Spiders!" An enormous swarm of spiders poured under the doors, a black carpet of crawly legs moving toward him like lava.

Ari suddenly broke free from Fang to explore other mealtime options. "Here!" I said. I grabbed Angel's skinny arms and held her. She tried to push me toward the exit, but I braced my feet.

Grinning, Ari sprang forward and ripped a bite out of

Angel's forearm. She gave an earsplitting scream, and I winced.

"Nooo!" Fang bellowed across the room, but a cage dropped down out of nowhere and covered him.

"Rats! Rats!" Nudge wailed, scrambling onto a counter. She jumped from counter to counter, heading toward the door, but wherever she went, a river of squeaking pink-tailed rats scurried after her. Several ran up her jeans, and finally she just stood there shrieking, covering her face with her hands.

By now all of them were screaming at the top of their lungs. It was total craziness. Each person here, except me, was living out his worst nightmare, facing his biggest fear — even the dog. It was under a counter, staring horror-stricken at a bowl of generic dog food.

I was still holding Angel, who was struggling much harder than I thought she would. She kicked at both me and Ari, even though the huge gouge on her arm was running blood over my hands.

I couldn't help smiling — she was a tough little mutant.

Out of the corner of my eye I saw Fang staring at me in disbelief, hurling himself against the bars of his cage.

"Guys, guys!" Fang shouted. His deeper voice cut through the high-pitched wailing. "This can't be real! It isn't real!"

You wish, *freak,* I thought.

135

Get this: I could follow their scent. I didn't know if this was a newly enhanced skill or if they were just riper than usual, but I could actually follow where the flock had gone.

They'd gotten in through the air vents, and I tracked them, even reversing course a couple times, as they must have done. Finally I knew that they were near, and by concentrating, I picked up on whispered conversation. I found a ceiling vent that looked down into a computer room in the basement, kind of similar to the computer room at the Institute. As if there were an interior decorator who specialized in working with mad scientists.

I saw Fang! He was standing guard at the door. Angel was keeping Total quiet. I changed my angle and looked farther into the room. Nudge was at a computer, reading something. Her cheeks were streaked with tears, which made my heart tighten. Then — I saw her.

The other me.

"Max, Max, look at this," Nudge said, turning to her, and my blood ran cold.

I mean, she looked exactly like me, and as I watched, she flipped her hair back impatiently, the way I always did.

Fresh rage ignited in my chest, making it hard for me to breathe. They had actually made a *backup Max* and substituted her for me.

This was, like, a *seventeen* on a diabolical scale of one to ten.

I was going to kill the other Max. And what about my flock? How could they not know? How could she be that perfect a copy? But I swear, it was like watching a hologram of me, a video of me, interacting with Nudge.

I glanced around again — and saw Angel looking directly at me through the vent.

I pulled back immediately, not wanting her to give me away. Then I had a horrible thought: What if Angel thought *I* was the impostor? What if the fake Max had them snowed?

Oh God, I had to stop this now.

Grimly I started to undo the clips that held the ceiling vent in place. Then, below me, I spotted my favorite combat partner barreling toward the computer room. Ari. I would have to take care of him for good this time.

At the same time, I would have to take care of my ultimate enemy: me.

136

In the middle of the chaos and screaming, a crashing sound made our heads whip around. Unbelievably, the old Max, Maximum Ride, dropped through the ceiling vent into the room. Where had she come from? She was supposed to have been taken care of!

But here she was, and she looked *sooo mad.*

"My invite must have gotten lost in the mail," she said venomously. "But I don't mind crashing this party."

In that instant, the rats, the spiders, and the cage disappeared. While everyone else blinked, looking around — giving new meaning to the word *dumb* — I cursed under my breath. A fine time for the big guys' latest super-top-secret holographic virtual-reality system to crash. This — along with the untimely arrival of my charming predecessor — was going to make my job a little more difficult.

"Max?" Ari asked, staring at the other Max.

"Max!" Nudge shouted.

"Yes," we both answered.

The other Max looked at me, and her eyes narrowed. "They say imitation is the sincerest form of flattery," she said snidely. "So I guess you're really sucking up."

"Who are *you?*" I gasped, my eyes wide. "You're an impostor!"

"No, she isn't." The little creepy one, Angel, turned to look at me. Her arm was still bleeding where Ari had bitten it. "You are."

I swallowed my anger. Who did she think she was, her and her stupid dog? I gave a concerned smile. "But Angel," I said, sincerity dripping from my voice, "how can you say that? You know who I am."

"I think I'm Angel," she said. "And my dog isn't stupid. You're the stupid one, to think that you could fool us. I can read minds, you *idiot.*"

137

My stomach dropped faster than a falling elevator. No one had told me that.

"Yeah, you *idiot,*" said the dog.

I gaped at him. Had he just talked? Was this a trick?

Maximum Ride was checking out the mutants, one by one. They hugged her, and I glared at her. I couldn't *believe* she had shown up, ruining *everything.*

"Okay, let's solve your personality crisis," the other Max growled, turning to me. Her face was white, and her hands were clenched in fists.

"I was about to say the same thing," I growled back, getting ready to fight. "Keep your hands off my flock!"

"Oh good, you two have met each other."

We both whirled to see several scientists in white lab coats standing inside the doorway.

"Max, are you all right?" Jeb Batchelder asked.

I started to say yeah, but then saw he wasn't looking at me. It was the *other* Max he was concerned about, the *other* one he cared about. I was expendable.

Fury rose in me. I was exactly like Max, I *was* Max, I was *better* than she was in every way. But to everybody here, I was chopped liver. Nothing. Nobody.

But then I heard one of the other scientists step forward and say in a deep voice, "Take out the old version. She's no good. She's got an expiration date." He was looking at me to do the honors.

Without thinking, I launched myself at the other Max, right over a countertop, headfirst.

The other Max was braced, but I had insane jealousy and rage on my side. I managed to slam into her, knocking her against a wall. Instantly she regained her balance and squared off against me.

"You don't want to do this," she said in a low voice. "You don't want a piece of me."

"Wrong!" I said snidely.

"Uh, Max?" said Gasman. "There's something you should —"

"Shut up!" I snapped at him, and threw myself at Maximum Ride again. The scientists and Jeb eased out of the way as we got deadlocks on each other and rolled across the counters. She managed to pull a fist back and punch me in the head, making me cry out.

I kneed her in the stomach and heard a satisfying *oof!*

We were evenly matched — too evenly matched. We attacked in a flurry, with fists flying and roundhouse kicks and bruising connections. But then we retreated, circling each other warily.

"There can be only one Max," Jeb said softly.

"Yeah, the real one," I heard Ari say.

The scientist with a deep voice folded his arms across

his chest. "Let's see if what you say about her is true, Batchelder."

I yelled and lunged for Max again, knocking her down. She held me by my hair and head-butted me so hard I saw stars, but I didn't let go. I whaled into her side with my fist, once, twice, three times. The third time, I swore I heard a rib crack. It felt sooo good.

"Which one survives is up to you," Jeb said. "May the strongest Max win."

138

"Shut up, jerk!" Maximum Ride barked at him, just as I was about to say the exact same thing. She and I jumped up, looked at each other. It was like looking in a mirror. So weird.

But she had to go. There was one Max too many. With another roar I sprang forward, snapping out a side kick that sent her to the ground again. I dropped down onto her, sitting on her stomach, and punched her right in the nose. She winced, her head whipped to the side, and then blood spurted out her nose.

"You think you're so great," I hissed. She struggled underneath me, but I clamped her arms at her sides with my knees and reached for her throat.

This was going to end only one way: with me on top. I was built to survive. This was my destiny — to be able to outdo anything weaker that came before me. That was all I cared about. Max was weak because she cared about everything else — her stupid flock, their stupid parents, the way Jeb had betrayed her, everything other than what she should care about.

I chuckled aloud, thinking how pathetic she was. I was ready to squash her.

But suddenly she arched her back, snarling, throwing me off hard. On her feet again, she kicked my chin, cracking my head back with so much force I almost blacked out. Then she was straddling me, like I had done to her a moment ago. She grabbed my throat with both hands and started squeezing. With blood running from her nose, she looked murderous, unstoppable. One of her eyes was swollen shut, but she still had a choke hold on me. I grabbed her arms, trying to pull them away, but couldn't budge her.

"Max?" I heard Gasman say again. We both ignored him. "Kind of important . . ."

Oh, my God, I thought, struggling, vaguely surprised. *She's going to win.* It had never, ever occurred to me that she could. In every scenario I'd ever run through, every training exercise, I had always won. But amazingly, I was getting tunnel vision, and my world was going dark. I tried to buck her off with all my strength, but she was stronger than I was.

"There can be only one Max," I dimly heard Jeb say. It came from a distance, floating over my head.

This . . . is . . . it, I thought hazily. *This . . . is . . . the . . . end.*

Suddenly the pressure around my neck released.

With a huge, sucking rush, air poured into my lungs. Light filled my eyes, and I was gasping, wheezing, gulping in air.

The old Max got off me. I coughed, my hand to my throat. I was struggling just to sit up.

"I'm stronger," she yelled to the scientists. "Stronger than you. Because I'm not going to kill this girl for you. I won't sink to your pathetic level."

139

"Max," said Jeb, sounding surprised. "There can't be two Maxes."

I looked down at the fake Max, who was sucking in air like a fish on the ground. I'd seen her pupils go to pinpoints, knew just how close I'd come to finishing her. But this rat was leaping out of the maze right now.

"Then you shouldn't have *made* two of us," I said coldly. "Now it's your problem."

"You don't understand," one of the scientists said. "Only one of you can fulfill your mission, your destiny."

He sounded idiotic and pompous. Keeping my eyes on the fake Max, I circled back to where the flock was gathered, getting ready for fight or flight.

"You know," I told the whitecoat, "it sounds like you guys didn't really think this all the way through. You plugged us into an equation and predicted outcomes. Well, I got news for you, nimrod." I looked up at the group of scientists, at Jeb, at Ari. I was still totally hyped up on adrenaline, my nose was still bleeding, and I felt like kicking more butt. "In this equation of yours, we're *variables.* We're going to *vary.*" I was practically spitting my words at them. "What you sick jerks don't seem to get is that I'm an *actual person.*" I pointed to the other Max, who was on her hands and knees, trying to get up. "She's real too. She's a person. All of us are! And I'm done jumping through your hoops. You can tell yourselves that you're doing all this to save the world, but really you're just a bunch of psycho puppet-masters who probably didn't date enough in high school."

I stalked around, really worked up. Sweat ran down my forehead and stung my cheek where it was split.

Out of nowhere, an alarm sounded. Next we heard shouting and thundering footsteps.

Jeb and the other whitecoats looked at one another. I couldn't piece everything together right now. Were they part of Itex or not?

"Max?" said the Gasman again.

"We've got to get out of here," I said urgently, looking for a possible escape route. Then I remembered: We were *underground.* Oh, jeez. Now things were going to get sticky.

Jeb and the other whitecoats edged closer to the Erasers. The fake Max looked lost, uncertain whose side to be on. I almost felt sorry for her.

"Max, really —"

"What?" I snapped, wheeling to look at Gazzy. "We're up the creek, if you haven't noticed! What's so *important?*"

His big blue eyes, so like Angel's, looked at me earnestly. *"Duck."*

140

Within a millisecond, I had dropped to the floor. I rolled under a counter and covered my head with my hands. When some eight-year-olds said "duck," you might be facing a stream from a water pistol. When Gazzy said "duck," you prepared for all hell to break loose, and really freaking *fast,* man.

BOOM!!!

My eardrums practically ruptured from the force of the blast. Instantly my mouth was covered with dust, carpet fibers, and something wet I didn't want to identify. I got knocked about four feet, still curled in a ball, and then something collapsed on me, knocking my breath out. Aftershocks and a much smaller *boom* made me curl tighter, but as soon as the explosions seemed to be over I straightened my back, grunting with the effort of pushing away debris.

"Report!" I yelled, inhaling dust and coughing hysterically. Big chunks of desk or ceiling fell off me. If I didn't have some broken bones, it would be a miracle. I felt like I'd been hit by a tractor trailer, maybe a couple of them.

Clumsily, still coughing, I scrambled to my feet. "*Report!*" I yelled again frantically.

141

The room was full of billowing dust and fibers wafting everywhere. Red emergency lights were on, casting the whole scene in a horrible, bloody glare.

No one had answered me yet. I yelled even louder: *"Report!"*

I began to pick my way through the rubble. A sweeping glance told me that several whitecoats had been standing in the wrong place at the wrong time — they were lying crumpled and unconscious on the floor. I couldn't see Ari anywhere, but I did see a couple pairs of feet sticking out from beneath piles of debris. No feet I recognized.

Across the room Jeb was slowly getting up — gray with dust, blood running down his chin.

"Here!" said Angel, and I felt the first spark of relief.

"Here," croaked Nudge, and started coughing. I saw her crawl out from beneath a shattered desk.

"Here." Total's voice came from behind an overturned chair. I kicked it out of the way and saw that Total had turned completely gray, except for his eyes. "And I'm not happy about it, let me tell you," he added grumpily.

"Here," came Fang's quiet, calm voice, as he picked himself out of a Fang-shaped hole in the opposite wall. Ooh, I bet that hurt.

"That was so *awesome!*" Gazzy yelled, leaping to his feet. Bits of broken countertop and wall fell off him.

"I give it a solid ten," said Iggy, rolling out from under what used to be a desk. "Just for sonic blast alone."

It had been eerily quiet for a minute after the blast, but now voices started up in the hallway outside. Again we began hearing shouted orders, the clanking of weapons, running feet. Though the feet sounded less steady. I heard groaning from beneath rubble.

A quick survey showed me my flock was whole and ready to move. It also showed . . .

. . . a huge hole in the basement wall, big enough to drive a truck through, leading right outside into the night.

"Oh, excellent," Nudge said.

I grinned, feeling close to tears. Once again, the flock had come through. Our lives were one gnarly sitch after another. Again and again they tried to defeat us, and again and again we showed them what we were made of. I was so proud, and so mad, and now that I thought about it, really sore all over.

"You got that right," I said, already hurrying toward the hole. When I was next to Gazzy, I held up my hand. "Way to *be,*" I said, slapping him a high five.

"Max?" Angel said. She looked like she'd been dipped in gray flour.

"Yeah, sweetie?"

"Are we leaving now?"

"Oh, yeah," I said. "We're gonna —"

"Blow this joint!" the flock yelled with me.

"Total!" I clapped and held out my arms. The small dog ran and leaped into them. He stuck out his tongue to lick me happily, saw my face, and thought better of it.

Then the six — seven — of us raced for the hole and did an up-and-away that looked like poetry.

EPILOGUE

142

Needless to say, there was a tearful reunion, stories exchanged, hurts examined and gotten mad about all over again.

We grabbed our stuff and flew south until sunrise. Then we dropped down into the Everglades and found a patch of dryish land to sleep on. We felt exhausted and wrung out and yet deeply happy to be together again. To have won again.

Iggy, the younger kids, and Total crashed immediately. They curled up together like puppies, filthy and ragged, and I was so happy to have them all in one piece that tears leaked out of my eyes and ran down my bruised cheeks.

Fang sat next to me, and we split one of our last warm Cokes.

"Breakfast of champions," he said, raising the can in the air.

"Did you see what happened to the other Max?" I asked him.

"No, actually I didn't," he said. "But maybe she escaped."

I drank the warm soda, feeling it run down my parched throat. *Never* would be too soon to see the other Max again. But I couldn't make myself destroy her. Killing the fake Max would be like killing the Eraser Max who looked back at me from the mirror sometimes. Besides — it would just be *wrong.*

I was exhausted, beyond exhausted, but the last time I'd gone to sleep, I'd woken up with my mouth duct-taped shut and then gotten put in an isolation tank. So I didn't want to close my eyes anytime soon.

The tank. I shuddered just thinking about it.

"Was it bad?" Fang asked quietly, not looking at me.

"Yep," I said, not looking at him, and took another swig of Coke.

The sun was higher, the air heavy and warm and growing warmer. It was December. We'd been on the run for what felt like forever. I didn't know how much longer I could do it. I was ragged out, and between the tank and the Voice, I felt like I was losing my mind. I still wasn't sure how the Erasers were tracking us. I remembered Angel campaigning to be leader and didn't know what to think.

"Did you know that wasn't me, the other Max?" I asked.

"Yeah."

"When?"

"Right away."

"How?" I persisted. "We look *identical.* She even had identical scars and scratches. She was wearing my clothes. How could you tell us apart?"

He turned to me and grinned, making my world brighter. "She offered to cook breakfast."

A second later we were laughing so hard it brought tears to my eyes all over again. Fang and I leaned against each other and laughed and laughed, unable to speak, for the longest time.

There's one last chance to save the world in

MAXIMUM RIDE:
SAVING THE WORLD
AND OTHER EXTREME SPORTS

the closing chapter of
James Patterson's thrilling trilogy.

And saving the world is what Max, Fang, Iggy, Nudge, Gasman, and Angel have waited for their entire lives. But the flock now faces extermination by a new kind of enemy. Spectacularly frightening. Horrifyingly perfect. The glorious grand prize of a century of advanced science. This time it's inevitable: they'll get caught.

So they might as well have some fun.

Soar with Max and the flock in
their fiercest, fastest ride yet!

Coming Spring 2007!